LAIR OF THE DRAGON

Alonin halted outside the castle's huge estate. He knew he should wait, but he had entered a realm where reason had no power. He had come to face the dragon; he had come to kill or be killed. He felt the cold reality of his sword. In a defiant gesture, he swung the blade and cried: "Thudredid! I am Alonin, heir to Gristan, Lord of Caladon. I bid you come, dragon, to face me!"

"Abide, then," came a cold, inhuman voice, undeniably menacing. "Abide."

A faint red light shone from one of the towers. Then a huge, dark shape pressed out from the tower top. It sprang from the tower, and huge, night-black wings stroked the air. Slowly the dragon rose, swung about, and began to drop. Suddenly Alonin realized that the monstrous creature was plunging straight at him.

With a ragged cry, he lifted his sword to meet it.

By Craig Mills
Published by Ballantine Books:

THE BANE OF LORD CALADON
THE DREAMER IN DISCORD

THE BANE OF LORD CALADON

CRAIG MILLS

A Del Rey Book

BALLANTINE BOOKS • NEW YORK

A Del Rey Book
Published by Ballantine Books

ISBN 0-345-28972-2

Library of Congress Catalog Card Number: 81-68655

Manufactured in the United States of America

First Edition: April 1982
Fourth Printing: July 1988

Cover art by Michael Herring

For Dorrie
For Dorrie
For Dorrie

1

ALONIN was born on a bleak and rainy day in a small thatched house that stood not more than a mile from the castle of his ancestors.

His father, Gristan Lord Caladon, sat outside the bedroom in a battered old chair that smelled strongly of damp straw, impatiently awaiting the birth. Glumly, he watched the rain drip through the thatched roof as he thought bitterly of the imagined comforts of his fine castle on the hill, which neither he nor any of his family had set foot in since the time of his great-grandfather, Agwid.

Gristan fell to rubbing industriously with an oily rag the blade of the ancient greatsword that lay across his lap. As he worked, he muttered to himself, "Dragon, dragon, I will kill you. Perhaps today is the day. Perhaps I will face you today. If only it is a son. I hope that it is a son. Then I will face you for what is mine. And I will kill you, O Thudredid, O dragon!"

When the clamorous squall of a baby's crying burst forth from the bedroom, Gristan's hand tightened on the hilt of his sword, and his lips moved in silent prayer. He lifted himself stiffly out of the creaking chair, sheathing his sword. He stood in the gloom outside the bedroom for what seemed like a long time, waiting.

Finally, the door opened and the old midwife appeared. She was dressed drably in rough garments of mossy green. Her coarse skin hung loose about her jaw, and her cheeks were covered with swirling wrinkles that looked like the thumbprints of a giant. Standing outlined against the bright light streaming from the bedroom, she unleashed a crooked smile at Gristan.

"Well, what is it, old woman—boy or girl?" Gristan snapped gruffly.

"A boy. You have a fine young heir, *Lord Caladon*." She twisted the last two words ironically. Buried deep within her eyes, malice sparked darkly.

But Gristan did not notice. He pressed past the midwife into the bedroom. The room was small and low, and was dominated by the big feather bed in which his wife, Aleyna, lay.

She was pretty and pale. Her thin face was drawn taut with fatigue. The fine, smooth skin of her forehead glistened with perspiration. Against her bare breast she cradled a newborn infant. Her eyes were closed, and there was a faint, tired smile on her lips.

As Gristan came through the doorway, Aleyna opened her eyes, which were the deep green of the limitless sea, and smiled up at him.

"Husband," she started to say.

But then, looking up at Gristan, who loomed huge and somehow frightening against the dark frame of the door, she paused uncertainly, and the smile dropped from her lips.

"Gristan, what is it?" she asked. "You look so—strange."

The Lord of Caladon did not answer, did not, in fact, even appear to hear her. He strode up to the bed and knelt down by her side. Grasping the tiny hand of his son, he said in a low, intense voice, "A son, an heir—at last." His shadowed eyes dwelt hungrily on the boy for a long moment.

"Gristan," Aleyna repeated sharply.

He looked up at her distractedly. His hard, bearded face was flushed; his eyes were feverish, glassy.

"What are you going to do, Gristan?"

"I am going to do what I have waited to do for all these many years. I am going to kill that dragon."

"And what if it kills you?"

"It won't."

"How can you be sure?" she asked. "It killed your father, it killed your grandfather, it killed your great-grandfather. What is to say that it won't do the same to you?"

"It won't!" he insisted angrily. He stalked over to a long teakwood chest, pulled out a dented iron breastplate, and began clumsily to strap it on.

"What about our son? Do you want to leave him father-less on the very day of his birth?"

"What about our son?" Gristan returned fiercely. "Do you think that I would wish him this life—living like a peasant, in poverty—while the castle of his ancestors and riches await just up the hill?"

"We can go to Yggrs," Aleyna said, a shrill edge of des-peration building in her voice. "My father would be happy to have us. He would grant us land and—"

"No! I will not throw myself upon the charity of another man, not even if it is your father. By all the gods at once, I am a Lord of Caladon! I must do this thing. You cannot stop me; I will not be stopped!"

Aleyna closed her eyes on her tears. She drew a long, shuddering breath and held it for a long time before releas-ing it.

"Go, then," she said finally in a faint, dead voice. "Fol-low your fate, my lord. I wish you luck."

Gristan stood at the foot of the bed, the breastplate now in place over his worn and balding doublet. He seemed suddenly childlike and vulnerable.

"I'm sorry, but I have to try. I have sworn to do this thing and I have to try."

"I know," she said sorrowfully.

Gristan went to his wife's side and kissed her. "I shouldn't be long," he said quietly. With a brown and trem-bling hand he softly stroked the cheek of his son.

"His name is Alonin," Aleyna said. "Take that with you—his name is Alonin."

"Alonin," he repeated. "Alonin."

Wordlessly, he rose and went from the room, the pom-mel of his sword scraping dully against his breastplate.

"We'll not see him again," the old midwife said. "He goes to meet his ancestors."

"Be *silent*, old woman!" Aleyna cried with sudden des-perate fury. "Be silent!"

Gristan rode his proud black stallion up the broad cob-bled road that led to Castle Caladon. The day's light was failing fast; already the overcast sky had turned as dark as coal, with only a faint spectral glow in the west to mark the sun's final passage. The rain had stopped a few minutes before, but the great shadowy boughs that overhung the road like twisted, ghostly claws dripped warm, fat drops down on Gristan. The air was still and thick with the smell of moist, humus-rich soil.

Someone was chopping wood nearby; the sound of it cracked hollowly through the densely wooded hills. It was a sad, lonely sound, and it made Gristan feel lost, forsaken. Silently he raged against himself for this sign of his weakness.

This is the day I have waited for all my life, he reminded himself sternly. *I shouldn't feel this way. I should be happy.*

But despite all of his admonitions to himself, the melancholy feeling lingered, filling him with dark, shadowy doubts.

Savagely, Gristan spurred his horse to a faster pace, drowning the forlorn sound in a clatter of hooves. The woods flashed by him, and soon he was riding through a small, weathered-looking village. A few of the villagers stopped their business to stand by and watch him pass. Sullenly, almost defiantly, they stared after him, burning him with their fierce resentment. Gristan looked neither right nor left, but kept his eyes focused straight ahead, unwilling to meet their silent accusations.

He could not fault the villagers for their hostility toward him, not really. After all, it was his great-grandfather who had brought the doom down upon Caladon, albeit unwillingly. In the eyes of his people, Gristan had inherited, along with the lordship of Caladon, the blame for inciting the ire of the dragon and for the consequent destruction wreaked by it. Although in actuality Gristan had lost much more than had the people of Caladon, this mattered little to them, for they saw the losses of the Lords of Caladon as deserved and just, a consequence of their folly, while they considered themselves blameless, hence unjustly punished. So it was that they held more animosity for Gristan, their due lord, than for the dragon under whose shadow they slunk so fearfully.

But now at last, Gristan was riding out to do battle with the dragon, as each heir of Caladon had done since Agwid, and he was convinced, as he had to be, that he would succeed where they had failed.

Success. The concept was tantalizing. Gristan tried to hold the image of it steady in his mind, a glorious torch against the darkness, a bright image of the way the world would be once he rid the land of the dragon. Gradually the vision grew in power, pushing aside his previous doubts.

Turning a bend in the road, Gristan came at last within sight of Castle Caladon. Against the dark sky, it was a gaunt gray shadow, somber and forbidding. Its tall towers were half obscured by the pale, shifting mists that swirled about them to form vague, fleeting shapes and ghostly images. Its sheer, lichen-mottled walls rose up precipitously from a barren hillock on which nothing had grown for more than a century, and which was ringed by the long-dead ruins of Caladon Town.

Gristan halted for a moment to observe the castle, *his* castle. Looking at it, he was filled with an odd mingling of awe, terror, and anticipation. Never before had he seen it look so grim and forbidding, so hostile and unloving.

Gristan drew a deep breath for courage, flicked his reins, and rode slowly up the bare, rocky slope. On all sides of him the black ruins of Caladon Town spread out—an awesome testament to the dragon's power. The sight of such raw, unthinkable desolation did much to blunt Gristan's confidence. It was hard for him to grasp the dark, decaying ruins for what they actually were, a place where once men had lived, worked, loved, raised children, and carried out their daily business in peace. Now they were but a dusty maze of fallen stones and jagged, blackened timbers that jutted out from the rubble like so many broken ribs.

As Gristan rode on, nearing the massive, iron-bound gates of the castle, his face grew inflexible and white. Never before had he seen the blighted town so closely; always before he had been forced to survey it from a respectful distance, under the protection of far wooded ridges. Only now, with the continuance of his line ensured by the birth of his son, could he dare to approach the castle openly.

Gristan felt a terrible anger building up within him— anger for that which he saw around him and still greater anger for the many years of enforced helplessness he had been made to endure. Deep inside him, the imperative for revenge rang as clear and strong as through a great crystal bell.

Gristan drew his mount to a halt in front of the castle gates. Drawing his sword from its scabbard, he swung it aloft. Then, with all of his pain and hatred boiling up within him, aching for escape, he cried, "Thudredid!"

He waited for a moment. Only the wind stirred, crying mournfully through empty halls.

He called out again. "Thudredid! Dragon! I, Gristan Lord Caladon, call you. I summon you by the name of Agwid and all the dead that came after him!"

Again there was no response. Suddenly Gristan became afraid. What if the dragon did not come forth? What then? Gristan had a sobering moment of despair. The thought that the dragon might remain safely hidden in the castle rather than face him had never occurred to him before.

But then he became aware of a low rustling sound coming from one of the towers: a scraping noise like metal rubbing on stone. Looking up, Gristan saw that the mists about one of the towers glowed a dull, ominous red.

"Thudredid?" he called.

Scrape, scrape, rustle . . .

Gristan saw a huge, dark shape appear and then disappear in the curling fog and he knew that Thudredid had indeed come forth. He leaned back in his creaking saddle and peered up warily, trying to pierce the swirling grayness.

And then, suddenly, the dragon plunged out of the fog, hurtling down toward Gristan with eye-blurring speed. Startled, the Lord of Caladon brought up his sword in a desperate attempt to meet with the rapidly oncoming dragon. But his horse, neighing with terror, reared up unexpectedly, wrenching him violently from the saddle. Gristan watched the ground coming up at him for one vivid but curiously emotionless moment before he struck, and darkness was driven painfully into his skull.

Gristan awoke to a terrible, sickening pounding in his head. He lay very still for a moment, fighting to keep himself from sliding back into unconsciousness. When his hold on the world seemed firmer, he reached out with his right hand and felt cautiously for his lost sword. Finding it, he closed his hand firmly about it, drew a deep breath, and pushed himself up. The world seemed to tilt and wobble beneath him, and the scarlet mist that filled his head thickened and threatened to swallow him up. But somehow he managed to hold to his feet, and gradually reality began to reassert itself more firmly. Gristan began to search the skies for the dragon.

He found it perched calmly above the castle gates, regarding him implacably through its great golden eyes. With its powerful, leathery wings folded back tightly to its body, it did not look as large as Gristan had previously thought— although this, he knew, did not reduce the peril it represented at all.

Its scaly hide was green, but so dark a shade as to be almost black, and even in the dim light it glistened moistly, as if it gave off a light of its own. There was something indistinct about its form, as if there were many shadows shifting uneasily about it.

"Well, Man," the dragon said in a voice that was both like and unlike the hissing made by many jets of escaping steam, "why have you interrupted my slumber? Have you come to bring me my due?"

"Do you not know, dragon? Do you not indeed? Know then that I am Gristan, son of Erdue, Lord of Caladon!"

"I know very well who you are," the dragon said tartly. "That does not answer my question. As you appear to be very simpleminded indeed, I shall repeat myself. *Why have you come?*"

"I have come to face you in battle, to fight you for this castle, to slay you, and thus revenge my ancestors whom you have most foully slaughtered."

"You are a most foolish man. You cannot hope to succeed."

"That remains to be seen."

"You are most sadly wrong. The outcome of our meeting is ordained, inalterable. Do you not think that I could have caused your life to be ended by now, had I wished it? Just look about you and see the destruction that I have wrought upon this land of yours—and reflect that I did accomplish all that you see in but a single day. Now, think. Do you really believe that you can hope to best me?"

The dragon's glowing yellow eyes spun hypnotically. Hearing the certainty in its voice, Gristan felt a chill go through him. He felt strangely dizzy, disoriented. Could it be that Thudredid was speaking the truth? Did he truly have no chance against it? It seemed for that bleak instant that this was indeed the case. His death seemed painfully close to him; he could almost see it. It took a great effort on his part to put down the rising desire to turn and flee back to his wife and newborn son. A black heaviness oozed into his soul.

The dragon arched its long neck and blew a dense cloud of acrid, foul-smelling smoke from its nostrils. "You can still save yourself," it said. "Run, Man, run fast and far. And do not return until you bring me my due."

That broke the spell. Gristan shook his head and felt the despair that had come to fill him begin to dissipate.

The dragon tried to bewitch me! he realized, hope sparking again in his heart. *It must fear me, then, to go to such lengths to dissuade me from my cause.*

Fixing the dragon with a stubborn gaze, Gristan let a grim smile come to his lips. "Do you think that you can rid yourself of me so easily, dragon?" he asked quietly. "You have wronged me, you have wronged my family, and I have sworn to be revenged. Your words and your magic cannot deter me."

"Wronged you? How have I wronged you? I have simply followed the path that your own great-grandfather began. No doubt it has led to a pass that you find unpleasant, but that is not my concern, for I did not choose the path."

"Nor did I, Thudredid."

"Agreed. But Agwid did, as well you know. We are, both of us, caught up in a web of his making. And we can only muddle through it until the end. Unless . . ."

"Unless?"

"Unless we break from the pattern completely. Your choice, Mortal."

Gristan chewed on his lower lip for a moment. "I do not know what you are trying to accomplish with your words, dragon, but I am not afraid to fight you. I am not a coward."

Thudredid blinked twice. "I never suggested that you were a coward. It matters little to me. Why do men feel that they must be continually rattling their swords in order to prove their worth? Coward or hero, it is all the same to me."

"It is *not* all the same to me. To me, it matters. Come then, we are wasting time. Will you come down from your perch to fight with me? Or must I climb up there after you?"

"Mortal—"

"Enough! I am tired of this chatter. As far as I am concerned, it solves nothing. Nothing! Will you come down to face me?"

The dragon glared down balefully at Gristan. It lifted its dark wings and stretched them out to their full spread. A strange, hot wind arose, sweeping down from the castle.

"As you will, so be it," the dragon said.

Slowly, his eyes swam back into focus.

Gristan was lying motionless on his back, staring up at the bright patch of stars that winked out from behind the dark clouds. There was the acrid smell of burning grass in the air. Gristan struggled to draw a breath, and was pierced through by a sharp jolt of pain. His ribs were broken, he suddenly knew.

Tears formed in Gristan's irritated eyes and rolled down his face. He wanted to rub them away, but lacked the strength to lift his arms so far.

He was dying. He knew that with a complete surety that he had never felt about anything before. He could feel his life leaking slowly away. Dying—he was dying.

Remarkably, the thought held little terror for him. He felt calm, almost serene. It was all over now, the uncertainty, the striving. The pain, too, would soon be over.

If only his eyes weren't so clouded . . .

He had been a fool; he could admit that now. He had never had a chance against the dragon. Never. Like fury embodied, it had descended upon him, its fiery breath burning him, blinding him, its claws raking his body like hot daggers, tearing with equal ease through both clothes and flesh.

Gristan had tried valiantly to defend himself. His blade cut a bright, deadly path above his head. But it was all in vain. The dragon moved too swiftly for him. Suspended by its powerful wings, it hung over him just out of sword's reach, dropping down briefly to attack, then withdrawing again to safety. Then dropping, withdrawing, dropping . . .

Gristan's breathing grew labored, and his muscles twitched sympathetically as he relived the battle in his mind. He coughed bloodily, wishing immediately that he hadn't—the pain was almost unbearable.

Time passed, and gradually Gristan felt himself sinking into oblivion. A crawling drowsiness filled him. The sky above seemed to darken and run like molasses.

Then, unexpectedly, two faces came into his field of vision, two soft white smudges against the velvet blackness. *Who . . . ?* he wondered. *Villagers?* He felt vaguely that he should be able to recognize them but, as hard as he tried, he could not bring the faces into focus.

Gristan tried to speak, to say some final something to mark his passing from the world, but when he opened his lips all that came out was a soft, bubbling hiss. All of the muscles of his body suddenly tensed into tight, agonized knots, then abruptly relaxed. His contorted features eased, his head slumped to one side, and then he was still.

The two men squatted next to Gristan and stared down intently at him.

"Is he dead?"

"Aye."

"He was a brave man, a brave man."

The other man shrugged indifferently. "They all are. Come, let's get the body out of here. I don't want to be here if the dragon should decide to come back to check on its work."

"All right. Fetch his sword. The widow might want it."

Carefully, they wrapped the body in a coarse brown blanket, placing the sword on top of it. Slowly they lifted up their grisly burden and began to trudge down the hill, down to where the rest of the villagers waited with their flickering torches. Gravel crackled and popped beneath their boots. Other than that, there was no sound.

And so it was that at the age of one day, Alonin became the twelfth Lord of Caladon.

2

TIME passed; some twenty years went by . . .

When Alonin left Lanfarran Castle for the wide common that encircled it, he saw that the sun was beginning to sink low in the sky. Filtered through a thin haze of wood smoke, sunlight fell bright upon the steeply sloping roofs of the surrounding city, but left the overhung streets and the faces of the buildings in delicately hued shadow. Alonin paused at the edge of the common, just outside the castle walls, and gazed for a time at the sprawling town. In the fragile light, it was a beautiful sight and it was made even more so by the realization that soon he would have to leave it.

Alonin sighed, letting his eyes drift down to take in the common.

The common was a wide band of undeveloped space lying between the castle and the city. Originally it had been intended as a part of the castle's defenses, and had long been kept scrupulously clear of sight-obstructing vegetation—but after centuries of peace in Yggrs, this martial beginning was all but forgotten. Over the years, a variety of trees had been allowed to grow up and flourish, until they at last came to form a carefully sculpted wood—and gradually the area had become a park, a place where carnivals would sometimes be held, where people would spend their summer afternoons, and where children would play. This is where Alonin came when he wished particularly to be alone, when he was troubled or weary of spirit, or when he had difficult thoughts to consider, decisions to make. And when he came away from here, he usually brought with him the answers he required or the peace he sought.

Yet he knew that there were times when there were no

happy solutions to be found, when all possible actions could only be purchased at heavy cost, and he knew that, for him, this was one of those times.

Alonin bestirred himself and set off down a winding stone path, overshadowed by a line of tall sycamores. Gradually he lengthened his stride, swinging his arms with stiff, brusque movements, attempting to burn off his anxiety with a burst of frenetic activity. He saw no one else in the common. He was alone—a tall, slender young man, dressed in garments dark and severe. The features of his sharply angular face were compressed by a slight but noticeable tension, and there was a bleakness in his eyes of dark amber. He strode up and down the narrow paths of the common for nearly an hour, unable even to think about that which he had come to decide.

Finally, his energy spent, he settled on a large, lichen-speckled rock, feeling its coolness on the backs of his thighs. Through the wavering boughs of the trees, he could still see the rooftops of the city. Clasping his hands together, he rested his forehead against them.

He knew what he had to do, and that was the problem. It was not so much that he was afraid to take the required action, to put aside the comfort and security he had enjoyed as heir to King Clemmth, his grandfather. Rather, he simply did not want to go to the old king with his plans; he did not want to be the author of any pain to a man who had raised him from a small child, a man who in all that time had shown him naught but patience and kindness. It was a kind of moral cowardice that afflicted him, he knew, and he hated himself for it. Yet still he delayed.

When Alonin looked up again, he saw that the shadows had deepened. The sun had fallen behind the ornate spire of the joint temple of Cernon and Dinas, creating a blazing nimbus about the high tower. Alonin chuckled softly; it seemed a peculiarly deft touch.

The temperature was rapidly following the plunging sun, and Alonin, who had forgotten to bring a cloak, was starting to feel the chill. He rose slowly from the rock. It was time to go back, he knew. He could tarry no longer.

Alonin turned and started back up the hill, where stood Lanfarran Castle, all armored in its abrasive brown stone walls. Reaching the west gate of the castle, he passed beneath its heavy, ornately carved arch into the courtyard.

The sun had just dipped below the castle wall, and the courtyard was bathed in pale shadow. Above, ruddy light caught the tops of the buildings and reflected in a brilliant cascade of spectral colors from the loftiest windows. The air was thick with the familiar, homely smells of hay, of horses, and of baking bread. Alonin hurried across the courtyard, weaving his way among milling servants and mail-clad men-at-arms.

Directly in the center of the courtyard stood the Hall of Judgment, a large, imposing structure, faced with mottled green marble, and topped by a slender golden spire. It was old, Alonin knew, nearly as old as was the Kingdom of Yggrs itself.

Hurriedly, Alonin ascended the steps to the building, taking them two at a time. He went in through the main entrance, passing between two red-liveried guards, and proceeded down a long, somber corridor.

There was another guard stationed outside the elaborately carved doors of the throne room, garbed like the others in red, and in one hand grasping a long wicked-looking halberd.

"Good afternoon, Lord," the guard said as Alonin approached.

"Good afternoon, Hanly."

"Do you require an audience with the king?"

"If he is not otherwise occupied."

"One moment, Lord. I shall see," Hanly said, easing himself through a narrow opening between the doors.

Alonin waited, humming absently to himself. A minute later, Hanly reappeared, beckoning to him to enter. He did, and the doors snapped shut behind him.

Mustering as much dignity as he could, Alonin walked deliberately down the center of the vast, shadowy hall. On either side of him, finely sculpted stone walls rose to a high vaulted ceiling. There were no furnishings anywhere to be seen, save for two massive wrought-iron candelabra and the low carven throne on which the king sat. To Alonin, the hall seemed permeated by a feeling of heaviness, of gloom; it never failed to make him feel small, insignificant, alone.

He had often suspected that it had been designed to create that effect.

As Alonin crept forward, his grandfather rose majestically from the throne and stood at the edge of the broad stone dais, waiting.

Alonin found King Clemmth a formidable figure. Though old, his aura of peronal power was as yet undimmed; he remained as he always had, for as long as Alonin could remember. His stance was straight and proud, his chin held high and his back unbowed. His eyes were green and searching, and his face, though lined and marked by the slow passage of many years, was firm and hard. The hem of his sweeping crimson robe was edged with gold. A black cloak was draped over one shoulder, held in place by an intricate gold brooch.

Alonin came to the center of the hall and bowed low before his grandfather. "Sire," he said in a low, respectful voice.

"Enough of that!" the king said, his deep voice booming through the silent hall. "There are none here to be impressed by this formality. Come," he said, stretching out his arms to his grandson.

The two men closed on each other and clasped hands warmly. The king still had a firm, powerful grip. Firmer, Alonin suspected, than his own.

"How do you, grandson? How goes the levy?"

"Finished," Alonin said with a sigh of relief. "Today I assessed the last of the landholdings of the great barons."

"Heard you any complaints?"

"No more than usual. As always, they all curse and cry poverty, telling me lengthy sagas of drought, of sudden disastrous storms, of plague and pestilence, and of suchlike misfortunes as should rightly herald the end of the world. I, of course, listened to all of this with most sympathetic aspect, heeding none of it."

"Typical, typical," Clemmth said with a chuckle. "So it has ever been. I cannot tell you how many times I have been forced to sit through these same tales of woe. How I would dread the coming of autumn because of them! It makes me glad that you are now grown old enough to assume this unpleasant duty." The king clapped Alonin affectionately on the shoulder, then drew back slightly as his keen emerald eyes rose to study his grandson's face.

"Yet I perceive that you have not come to discuss this matter. Am I correct?"

"Grandfather, you are. It is a personal affair that I have to speak with you about, if you can spare me the time."

Clemmth continued to contemplate Alonin for a moment. The young lord's eyes fell to the floor, rather than face that powerful gaze. Finally, the king gave out an almost inaudible grunt. He turned to the door and called out, "Hanly!"

The doors to the hall groaned open, admitting a pale stream of gray light and the guard's sturdy brown face. "Your Highness?"

"That will be all, Hanly. You may lock up now. My grandson and I will retire to my apartments through my private entrance."

"Yes, Highness."

The guard withdrew from sight. A moment later, Alonin heard the sound of a key being turned in the lock.

"Come," the king said, as he pulled aside a red velvet drape behind the throne.

Alonin followed his grandfather behind the plush wall hanging and into a narrow corridor of rough, naked stone. The air was still, close, musty, smelling of dust. The fine, airborne particles made Alonin's nose itch and burn maddeningly.

Wordlessly, they went slowly down the gloomy passage, following it as it turned sharply to the right, then to the left. As they came around this last corner, the passage came to an abrupt end. A solid wall ran directly across their path.

Clemmth reached out, and his fingers sought out a tiny niche in the wall. He pushed inward at an odd angle. There was a faint *click*, and a small portion of the wall sprang suddenly toward them, exposing the shadowy outlines of a room beyond.

Stooping slightly to avoid striking their heads on the low entrance, the two men stepped into the king's apartments. Clemmth turned and closed their way behind them.

"Would you build a fire, grandson? It's a bit cold in here."

Alonin nodded, dropping to his knees on the cold, hard flagstone floor before the fireplace. Bending forward, he blew life into the few dull red coals that lingered yet beneath the powdery gray ashes. He carefully sprinkled a handful of tinder on the coals and waited for it to take. Then, one piece at a time, he began to add larger lengths of wood to the rapidly growing fire. Soon, flames were crackling vigorously, sending out a constant wall of warmth.

Sitting in a high-backed wooden chair, the king extended his hands, palms outward, toward the flickering flames. "Ah, that feels good! You know, each year, as I grow older, the world seems to grow a little colder."

The king stretched out his legs, settling back into his chair with a sigh. "Now, grandson, what is this matter you wish to discuss?"

Alonin rose from his place by the fire, dusted his hands against each other, and stood there awkwardly. "I do not know where to begin."

"Sit, grandson. Be comfortable."

Sinking into a thickly cushioned chair beside his grandfather, Alonin stared silently into the blazing fire, his thoughts vague and far away. He tensed his jaw, and drew a long, deep breath.

"I feel the time has come for me to go, grandfather," he said in a faint voice.

"Go? Go where?"

"To the land of my fathers. To Caladon."

There was a long, uncomfortable silence. Alonin felt his grandfather's eyes upon him, intense and searching, filled with an old and tender sadness. When the old king finally spoke, his voice came softly, weary with defeat. "Caladon. So it has come at last. I had half succeeded in convincing myself that it wouldn't. I had hoped."

"Grandfather . . . I am sorry. But you know that I must go, and you know why."

The king rose ponderously and strode from the fireside, his hands clasped behind his broad back. "No," he said, "I cannot ever really know the why of this thing; it is something between you and your shadow. I cannot understand it, but I will strive to accept your decision."

"But it is not such a difficult thing to understand!"

"No? Not for you, perhaps."

"Thudredid must be destroyed!" Alonin said, eyes blazing, face held tight against the passion flooding him. His right hand clenched and pounded the arm of his chair. "It must!"

With solemn expression, Clemmth regarded his grandson for a moment. "I had not known that your hate was so great. I had sought to shield you from this, the fault of your fathers. It would seem that I failed."

"Why should I not hate? You know my reasons as well as any. That monster killed my father! It robs me of my birthright!"

"I cannot think how to answer you, except to say that another death—yours or Thudredid's—will not bring back your father. And Caladon you do not need. You are my grandson, heir to my throne. When I am gone, all Yggrs will be yours to rule."

"And how long will I rule if I do not face Thudredid? Already it is whispered in the realm that I am afraid. You know as well as I do that kingship cannot long bear even the suspicion of cowardice. If I do not face this thing, the land will soon be filled with countless ambitious lordlings anxious to try my mettle with steel. Yggrs will be swallowed up by chaos. Your wise rule will go for nothing. Would you have this?"

"Let fools say what they will. You know that you are no coward—is that not enough? And as for what may come when I am dead . . . I am not worried. You have the capacity for strength in you. It would not be long before your enemies discovered this and forbore strife."

"Grandfather, your confidence in me is heartening. Believe me, I would stay here in Yggrs with you forever, if I could. But I cannot. How can I remain here in safety and comfort, knowing that the blood of my ancestors remains unavenged, and still keep my good opinion of myself? No, I will never be able to rest easy with myself until I have done what must be done."

Clemmth did not respond at once. He seemed to sag. He rubbed his eyes wearily. For the first time that Alonin could remember, the king appeared his age, tired, worldworn, burdened. Finally he said, "So be it, then. I shall not try to dissuade you further; I can see it would avail me naught, for you are as stubborn as was your father. If you must go, then go.

"But be ruled by me in one thing, grandson: do not let your end be as Gristan's was. If you must go against this dragon, bring your wits with you. Remember that four successive Lords of Caladon tried to conquer Thudredid by strength of arms alone, and all of them failed. I would not have you follow them in this. Bide your time, watch, wait. When the proper opportunity comes, seize it!"

Alonin smiled. He felt a chuckle rise in his throat. "Don't worry, grandfather. I have given this matter some thought—I have had years to consider it. I will make sure that I can succeed against Thudredid before I strike. What, did you think you had raised yourself a fool?"

Clemmth fixed Alonin with a level gaze. "I don't know," he said. "I did not think Gristan was one when he came to Lanfarran many years ago. Yet he fell. I fear that the strange compulsion of your forefathers may prove too strong for you to resist. There is a dark fate that clouds the souls of the heirs of Caladon, which drives them against reason."

"Be assured, then. This time it shall be Thudredid that falls, and not I. Of this I shall be certain before I move against it."

"Yet what is certain when one deals with dragons?"

"Nothing," Alonin agreed. "The point is well taken, and I am mindful of it."

"Then I can ask nothing more. When do you leave?"

"Soon. I have finished with the levy, and within several days' time I shall have discharged the rest of my duties."

"If you need anything to see you through your journey, you have only to ask. You know that, don't you?"

"Yes, grandfather. Thank you."

"Do you see that chest? The one against the wall there?"

"Yes."

"Open it. There are some things in it that belong to you."

Wrinkling his brow in puzzlement, Alonin glanced at his grandfather, then went to the chest and knelt down before it. The chest was old and plainly fashioned. Its length was unusual, almost six feet, though Alonin had never given it much thought before. It had always been there, in the same corner of the room, for as long as he could remember—to him, it was a permanent feature, a thing not to be wondered at, but to be taken for granted.

Alonin pulled up gently on the lid of the chest. It was balky and would not budge. He pulled harder, and it came loose in his hands with a sudden jerk. Propping the lid up against the wall, he leaned forward and peered inside. Eyes widening, he reached in and gently lifted out a long, heavy sword.

"It was your father's," Clemmth said. "Now it is yours. You will need a stout blade where you are going."

Alonin studied the ancient weapon with wondering eyes.

Its blade was wider, thicker, heavier than was normal for modern blades. Although primarily a cutting weapon, its graceful point and splendid balance would allow it to be used efficiently to deliver a quick thrust in need. It was designed so that it could be wielded by either one hand or two. The grip was fashioned of a black substance, perhaps ebony. The pommel was a walnut-sized sphere of crystal ringed by a thick band of gold. Finely engraved runes graced the hard blue steel of the blade. In the right hands, Alonin knew, it could be a devastating weapon.

"I never knew that you had this," he murmured.

"There is something else," the king said.

Alonin looked up briefly at his grandfather, then down again into the dark, cedar-scented depths of the chest. He reached in and closed his hand about something. Slowly he brought out his hand and opened it, staring down into his palm.

"The signet of Caladon!" he exclaimed.

"Yes—for now you are truly the Lord of Caladon."

Alonin felt tears forming in his eyes. With an effort, he choked them back, feeling a dull ache in his sockets.

He worked the weighty gold ring onto his finger, and then sat back for a long time, staring at it.

After a time, he closed the lid to the chest, placing the sword down gingerly on top of it. Rising then, Alonin went to where his grandfather stood.

The old king was grasping the back of a chair with stiff white fingers. His face was solemn, and his eyes glistened moistly in the firelight.

Alonin said in a hushed, wavering voice, "Grandfather, I can't . . . I don't know how . . . to say—" He broke off, embarrassed by his sudden inability to make sense of his thoughts.

"Don't. There is no need. I know. By the gods I know!"

Clemmth reached out to Alonin, encircling the younger man firmly in his arms. Alonin returned the rough embrace, his tears flowing now, a metallic taste in his mouth. And it seemed for one fleeting moment that they were not two apart, but one, united all too briefly by the sudden terrible violence of their emotion.

3

THREE days later, on a morning cold and cloudless, Alonin bade farewell to his grandfather and rode forth from Lanfarran Castle. The sun had not yet risen above the hilltops, and the world, quivering on the edge of dawn, was lit with a soft and delicate glow. The sky shone a startling shade of blue, deep and intense.

Alonin guided his horse—a sturdy chestnut gelding called Gendas—down the gently curving length of the Avenue of the Kings, that great way which led from the castle gates through the city and into the rolling farmlands beyond, until it at last joined with the Northern Highway in the remote Kilthur province. Alonin rode first through the circular common surrounding the castle, then passed under a wide ornamental arch and into the city.

The city of Lanfarran fell into two distinct sections, upper and lower. First came Upper Lanfarran. Perched proudly on Castle Hill, and cut off from the rest of the city by the old city walls, it held itself staunchly aloof from Lower Lanfarran like a rich old matriarch forced to stand beside a tattered and disreputable beggar woman. Here were built the palaces of the wealthy, temples, broad boulevards lined with heroic statuary, fancy shops, and stately parks.

Winding down through the various levels of the city, Alonin passed by wide streets of richly ornate manses, a section of more modest townhouses, several blocks of three- and four-tiered apartment buildings, side streets crowded with brightly painted shops and sidewalk taverns. Finally, he came within sight of West Gate. Opposite the gate, its gilded façade resplendent in the ruddy light of dawn, stood the joint temple of Dinas, the three-fold goddess, and of her horned consort, Cernon. Alonin found the avenue out-

21

side the temple thronged with black-garbed devotees. They parted slowly before him, and he passed beneath the grand arches of West Gate, and so into Lower Lanfarran.

Consisting of tiny shops and markets, unassuming houses and apartments, and rows of conical brick storehouses, Lower Lanfarran was both younger and less magnificent than the upper city. Extending from the base of Castle Hill, it meandered helter-skelter into the fertile farmlands beyond, existing at points side by side with orchards, pasturelands, and old farmhouses.

With the rise of a new day, the city was now starting to come alive, and the Avenue of the Kings, which had narrowed to half its previous width since entering the lower city, was quickly becoming crowded with traffic: cumbersome horse-drawn wagons, handcarts, endlessly milling pedestrians. Alonin had to fight to restrain his impatience at the slow pace the crowd forced him to keep. He smiled and nodded politely to those hailing him from the press, all the while filled with a gnawing irritation at the delay.

He found himself greatly relieved when at last the avenue passed through the outskirts of town and only apple orchards and fragrant meadows surrounded him. He reined in Gendas and twisted about in his saddle for a last look at Lanfarran. City and castle were but dark outlines against a blazing yellow sky. Alonin allowed himself a brief moment of nostalgia for all he was leaving behind him, for his childhood. Then, with bleak aspect, he turned away and set off once more toward Caladon and an uncertain future.

It was a hard three-day ride from Lanfarran to Caladon, he knew—across the wide and fertile Yggrs valley, over the barren Corune Hills, to the densely wooded basin that marked the beginning of Caladon. The hours dragged long and uneventful as he rode his solitary and melancholy road north, to a home he had never seen, his heart full of bright hopes and calamitous doubts.

The end of the first day found him shivering at the base of the Corune Hills, where he decided to establish his camp for the night. A cold, wintry wind blew fiercely from over the hills, weaving icy fingers through his hair and making the flesh of his thin, impassive face feel as hard and insensitive as polished marble. Staring up at the dead brown hills, Alonin was filled with a sudden oppressive dread. In the drear twilight, the hills seemed like sinister entities warning him away. Alonin stood watching them for a long time, while darkness drew its veil across the world, trying to rid himself of this fancy, to master his dread—for he knew that the hills were no more than hills, and that it was his own fear that spoke through them.

The next morning he ascended into the hills. A golden sea of wild grass surrounded him, stretching for as far as he could see, undulating like flaxen waves. Occasionally, there were a few small groves of stunted oaks clustered among the folds and gullies between the hills, but there was nothing else.

Alonin found himself growing quickly bored with the unchanging terrain, and he wished himself already in Caladon. Yet what would he do there? He did not know. His ultimate objective was clear, of course, but he could not think how he would accomplish it. He was proceeding in the hope that his path would become clear to him once he reached his destination. Yes, he would know what to do when the time came, he was sure of that.

The dragon Thudredid he would destroy, for this was his fate, a fate he had felt the pressure of even before he was old enough to comprehend fully how much the dragon had cheated and damaged him. His father would at last rest avenged and unburdened in his grave, and Caladon would be freed. This was how it had to be.

Alonin followed the dusty road through the bleak hills for the rest of the day. On the next day—the third since leaving Lanfarran—he noticed that the road bent downward more often than it did upward, and he guessed that he had almost come to the end of the Corune Hills.

But it was not until the bright blush of sunset was in the sky that Alonin came over a low, windswept crest and gained his first sight of the vast Caladon forest, cupped within a huge, rolling valley. The sun was sinking into a cushion of bloody clouds; its radiance fell on the long, slender river that twisted along the edge of the forest, making it seem a ribbon of crimson.

That would be the river Evigge, thought Alonin. It was the last obstacle between him and Caladon, he knew.

Alonin sat almost immobile in his saddle for a long time,

drinking in the somber, tragic splendor of the land. He sank into a well of melancholy; there was a desolation in him that was both painful and—in a strange but very real way—beautiful. Grasping the reins in his trembling hands, he urged Gendas down the sharp slope. Caught by the wind, his long black cloak billowed and cracked behind him.

He reached the river and rode along it until he came to the arching stone bridge spanning it. The bridge was very old, he could tell, its curving balustrade was carved in an archaic style, all ornate curves and whorls. Drab green moss mottled it. In places it was badly worn and chipped.

Alonin decided to make camp where he was. For some reason he did not want to ride into Caladon under shroud of darkness; when he came at last into his lost homeland, he wanted the sun shining on his back, dispelling all shadows.

Alonin built his fire and ate his meal by the side of the river Evigge. He could hear the water rushing quietly over the rocks beside and below him. He knew that he should sleep; he was tired from the long ride. But he was too full of anticipation and dread to sleep. His mind was full of brave and dire thoughts as he lay there under the bright, bright stars.

Evigge spoke to him. Its conversation told of but one thing, and that was revenge.

The sun rose slowly on a new day. Smothered behind a layer of overcast, it was a wan silver disc in the sky. There was a strong wind, roaring moodily through the treetops. Alonin, still stiff and aching from the damp chill that had clung to the riverbank while he slept, saddled his horse and broke camp.

He crossed over the bridge, ears full of the hushed murmurings of the river below him. His horse's hooves beat a sharp rhythm on the ancient cobblestones. Reaching the other side of the bridge, Alonin reined in Gendas. He sat there for a long moment, straight and still in the saddle, his senses straining outward. The rich smell of moist earth and the perfume of the pines came to him, curling on the wind.

He was here at last. For how long had he dreamed of

this? For ever, it seemed. His eyes blurred with tears; with an effort, he suppressed them, and rode on.

Huge, wild, and overpowering, the great forests of Caladon closed in on him. The wind raged above, a demon uncaged, roaring through the towering spires of the forest. The gnarled branches overhanging the road thrashed about violently, groaning with eerie menace. Through breaks in the forest roof, Alonin saw that the overcast sky had taken on an unhealthy yellow tinge. A great weight settled on his soul, as oppressive as was the moisture-heavy atmosphere. Try as he might, he could not shake the sudden feeling that he was lost, engulfed by something too huge for him to comprehend.

Fortunately the woods soon began to thin, and Alonin started to come across a number of small, impoverished-looking houses set back far from the road, hidden by deep shadow. A little while later, he came to a tiny village, which consisted of five or six long buildings constructed of bleached timbers with high thatched roofs. Over them, long branches wavered like grasping claws.

Two old men dressed in tattered leather and homespun sat in ancient chairs outside the first building Alonin came to. Without moving, they watched Alonin, the curiosity in their eyes almost obliterated by what seemed a habitual apathy. Alonin was painfully conscious of their faded old eyes on his back as he rode by them.

A small knot of children dashed out suddenly from between several of the buildings, uttering shrill laughs and cries as they ran. Despite the chill of the day, they were only half-clothed, and their slight bodies were streaked with dirt. Seeing Alonin, they halted at the side of the road, regarding him with big, solemn eyes.

Alonin was pained by guilt and shame as he looked upon their poverty; he was uncomfortably aware of the contrast between their nakedness and his good, warm clothes. He could not escape the fact that he was responsible for them, for they were of his people, his to protect and provide for—and he was ashamed, knowing that the Lords of Caladon, his fathers, had failed in their duty to their people for more than a hundred years. There could be no evading the guilt of this; it could only be expunged with Thudredid's blood.

In front of the last building in the row, there was set a tall post; from it there hung a faded sign, suspended by rusted chains, bearing the picture of a green crow. Caught by the gusty wind, the sign swung violently, chains creaking.

Alonin guessed that the sign marked the village inn. He halted in front of the weathered structure for a moment and thought. If he were looking for information, surely there could be no better place to search it out than the local inn, for as a rule such a place was the center of gossip for any community. Yes, he decided, it would be well to see what he could find out there before going further.

Dismounting, he secured his horse to a long rail, and then entered the inn. As he scanned the room briefly, he saw white-plastered walls, dark oiled beams, some scarred wooden tables and benches, and a long counter at the back of the room. The inn was obviously old, but was just as obviously well-loved and maintained by its owner.

Alonin saw no other patron in the inn; aside from himself, there was only one other present, whom Alonin took to be the innkeeper. He was a fat, florid little man in his middle years, wearing a loose white shirt, a pair of much worn and patched breeches, and a leather apron. Seeing Alonin enter, the man started eagerly toward him. The wide grin that spread itself on his big, jowly face seemed genuine, not simply the professional smile of the tavern keeper.

"Ah! Sir, sir!" he said. "Welcome to the Green Crow, the finest—nay, the only—inn in all of Caladon. How may I serve you this day?"

"Some beer," Alonin said. Then, realizing that he was hungry, "And food. I've not yet supped today."

"Alas! We are not used to receiving guests of your obvious quality, so our menu is unfortunately limited. We have some cheese, some nice smoked meats, and some bread that was fresh this morning, if you've a mind for simple fare."

"That will be fine. Anything."

"Very good, sir. If you care to have a seat, I'll bring you a tankard of our best."

Alonin unbuckled his sword belt and leaned the great blade against the table. He seated himself and watched while the innkeeper filled a tall wooden tankard and placed it on the table in front of him. The little man bustled out of the room, to return a minute later with a large platter of food.

While Alonin ate, he noticed that the innkeeper was hanging over his left shoulder, regarding him with a look of uncertain appraisal, as if wondering whether or not to approach him. "Will you join me?" Alonin said to him finally.

A look that seemed almost like gratitude came over the innkeeper's blunt features. "Thanks, young sir. I believe I will, if you don't mind." He seated himself across the table from Alonin, giving out a weary grunt as he eased his bulk down to the bench. Regarding the young lord with small, bright eyes, he licked his lips uneasily. It seemed to Alonin that there was a painful battle between delicacy and a deep need to speak going on within the other man, which he found most uncomfortable to watch. Alonin pushed back his empty plate and smiled encouragingly at the man.

Abruptly, the innkeeper said, "I do hope I'm not bothering you. If I am, just say so and I'll go away. No? Well, I guess I just like to talk. Some say too much. And as you can see—" He gestured at the empty room. "—yours are the only ears in the house. Being an innkeeper in Caladon can be a lonely business, yes indeed. Especially if you haven't any family. I never had any children, you see—and my wife, she died two years ago."

He drew a long, sad breath, then said effusively, "A fine woman, she was. The finest. I miss her still."

He gave Alonin an anxious look. "I'm not boring you, am I?"

"No . . . no. Go on."

"Good. I try not to make too much of a nuisance of myself with the customers. It's hard, though. I don't see too many people, and when I do . . . Well. You see, business is bad. Hah! It's been bad for as long as I can remember. It's the dragon, you know. It's because of the dragon. You've heard of Caladon's dragon?"

There was a note of urgency in the innkeeper's voice as he asked this that Alonin had not noticed before. "I've heard of it," he answered in a somewhat remote voice. He leaned forward suddenly and fixed the other man with a piercing look. "Have you seen it yourself? With your own eyes?"

"Oh, yes! Certainly. Several times. Only briefly, though—or from far away, for I am a very great coward and I had the good sense to hide myself whenever it passed near." The innkeeper's manner changed now, becoming less timid, more confident. There was a glow of what seemed like happiness in his eyes, and for a moment he seemed to forget about his patron. "I remember one time, though . . . nearly twenty years ago . . . the day Gristan, the old Lord of Caladon, died . . ."

Alonin felt a chill of excitement spread through him. "You saw it? Gristan's death?"

Disturbed from his reverie, the innkeeper gave him a perplexed look. "Eh? Well, yes and no, sir . . . yes and no. I remember it well, that day. Gristan came riding through the village . . . and he looked fine . . . proud and brave and . . . fine. Black, his horse was, and bigger than any I've seen before or since. The lord wore a breastplate that shone like gilt, and at his side there was his great sword. I knew as soon as I saw him what he was going to try—you could see it in his eyes, in the way he held his jaw. Well, sir, most everyone decided right then to go hide themselves. Me, I was younger then, and bolder; me and the blacksmith's son—Walthur by name—stayed to watch. We did not dare approach the castle too closely, yet we came close enough—for it was not long before we heard a fearsome crash. It was like thunder, it was! The earth shook, and the evening sky took fire, and against the brightness we saw two shadows: one, the smaller of the two, stood atop the hillock, swinging a weighty sword with mighty fury—this was Gristan, we knew. Above him hung a larger shadow on great huge wings, and this was Thudredid, and it was like something out of a nightmare. Talons extended, it was descending. All this we saw for only an instant, for then there came a flash of light too bright for our mortal eyes to bear, projecting from the dragon, and we were forced to look away. When at last we were able to look back, the fire was gone from the sky. All was deathly still . . . Yet it was a long time before we dared stir from our hiding place. Finally, though, we realized that the battle was over. So out we crept, half unwillingly, yet strangely drawn. We mounted Castle Hill, which stood in ominous silence—and there we found him, Gristan."

Unable to restrain himself further, Alonin broke in, "Was he still alive? Did he speak?" He was suddenly aware of the sharp thudding of his heart in his breast, a surge of anticipation.

The innkeeper replied in a low voice, an awed tone, "He was alive, yes; but he did not speak. Oh, sir! it was terrible! There was the stench of burnt flesh in the air, and Gristan's blood flowed from a hundred wounds. We leaned down over him, Walthur and I, and he looked up at us with eyes great with pain. And then, mercifully, he died. We bore him away for burial, poor brave fool that he was."

Alonin's anticipation abruptly turned into disappointment and black despair. So there had been nothing, no word, from his father. But what had he expected, really? That in his agony Gristan should have used his last breath to propel a message to his son of less than one day? Foolish, foolish! Yet this was just what Alonin had hoped for in his heart. A word. Something. Something that might throw a light, no matter how dim, on the dark path given him to follow.

But Thudredid had deprived him of his father's guidance, just as it had taken from him his birthright. And for that the dragon would be made to pay, he assured himself grimly.

His mouth twisted with repressed rage. In a hollow voice he asked, "Where lies Castle Caladon from here?"

"Not far, not far. Less than a mile away, up the road. But if you are thinking of going there to try and catch a glimpse of the dragon, I would say you'd be wasting your time. It seldom leaves its lair in the castle these days, and when it does, it's because it's hungry. If you catch my meaning, sir."

"I do," Alonin said. "And I will bear your warning in mind." He raised his tankard and drained off the last of his beer. It had gone flat, and it left him with a bitter taste in his mouth.

The innkeeper was now scrutinizing him closely, a thoughtful look on his broad face. "Pardon me for asking, but what brings you to poor Caladon, young sir? We are far from the main roads, and there is no employment to be had for a fighting man, such as yourself."

Mystified, Alonin stared uncomprehending at the other man for a moment. Then he understood, with his dusty traveling clothes and his greatsword, what else could he be taken for but a blank shield, a wandering mercenary? He smiled. "I have personal business."

"Eh? Personal, you say? Wait! I have it! Be you a local boy?"

"In a manner of speaking."

The innkeeper looked suddenly dubious. He tugged on his lower lip. "Strange, though, that I don't recognize you. I know most everyone in these parts."

"My family left Caladon many years ago; I was very young at the time."

"That would explain it, then. So many have deserted this place since the dragon came. I myself have been thinking of going elsewhere, ever since the wife died. But where would I go? I'm too old to pick up and start over again. Ah, I'll probably die here, like my father before me."

He gave Alonin a thoughtful look. "You know, now that I think of it, you do look familiar, in a way. Perhaps I knew your father. "Who—"

"—I must be on my way," Alonin cut in hastily. "I tarry too long." He pushed himself back from the table, rose, and dug in his pouch for a large silver coin, which he slapped down on the table. "Will this cover the cost of the meal?"

The innkeeper's eyes fixed happily on the coin. "Oh, aye, sir. That and more, that and more. Let me bring you your change." He made a tentative move toward the back counter.

"No, that's all right. Keep it," Alonin said, strapping on his sword. "Your conversation has been worth at least that to me."

"Well, if you insist, sir . . . if you insist," the innkeeper said, his hand leaping onto the coin. "Come back anytime. It is always a pleasure to serve a gentleman of your quality. Good-bye, sir."

"Good-bye," Alonin said, thrusting himself through the door. Outside it was raw and cold. The wind had increased while he had been inside the inn, the trees were thrashing about wildly, and whirling dust clouds swept along the road. Clutching his cloak to him with his left hand, Alonin boosted himself into the saddle. He set himself a modest pace as he rode from the village, his face thoughtful.

His conversation with the innkeeper had affected him oddly. Hearing of his father's defeat from one who had actually witnessed it was, in itself, enough to cause a bewildering surge of emotion to spin through his mind. But there was something even more affecting in the *manner* of the man who had told the tale; something that was a moment of unparalleled tragedy for Alonin was the innkeeper's moment of greatest glory. Did the man tell the same story to any stranger happening into the inn? Probably, Alonin thought. It made the young lord sad and outraged to think that the man had grown old and fat and cowardly telling all who would listen of his part in the terrible fall of Gristan—his one moment of worth, when he had risked the wrath of the dragon in order to witness the end of one greater than he. Alonin might have hated him for that, were he not so pathetic. As it was, Alonin could not help feeling sorry for the man. In a way, he had to admit, he even liked him.

After all, had not the innkeeper spent his entire life under the dire threat of the dragon? Might not anyone subjected to such a pressure be forced into a similar mold? No! Alonin denied this to himself. He knew that he himself could never be brought to such a base pass, despite the forces used against him. As if to affirm this, he spurred his horse to a faster pace.

Somewhere in the back of his mind he realized that things were happening too quickly for him to grasp fully, and that he should stop, consider, plan. Yet he could not restrain himself. He continued on, driven by his terrible compulsion, headlong and heedless toward the castle of his ancestors.

Many things crowded his mind as he rode that grim path: pity for the unfortunate inhabitants of Caladon, and his responsibility toward them; his own pride and rage. In many ways the impulses he felt were contradictory, yet all pointed to the same goal: that he should slay Thudredid.

The woods thinned; the ragged line of thatch-topped huts ceased. The road looped around a low, blunt hillock;

and, suddenly, there it was, harsh and gray under sickly, jaundiced skies—Castle Caladon.

Alonin pulled back on the reins, halting his mount. He gazed long and hard on this, his lost ancestral home, hated and beloved, dreaded and wished-for.

Shivering from more than the chill of the wind, he finally urged the gelding up the hill on which stood the crumbling castle. Gaunt ruins rose all about him, all that remained of old Caladon Town. Did the ghosts of those slain by Thudredid still linger in those ruins? And if so, did they yearn for vengeance? Suddenly, he had the image of scores of ghastly gray spirits crowding the side of the road, urging him on. An unsettling fancy!

Reaching the top of the hill, he pulled to a halt outside the castle's huge metal-bound gates. The wind howled dolefully through gutted towers, and flattened the few sere tussocks of grass that grew on that barren hill.

Here it was at last, the place where his father had met his death. The hurt that Alonin felt at this moment was so great that he feared that it would burst his heart, if he could not let it out. The muscles of his face were bunched and cramped, and his skin drained of blood. In a low but fervent voice, he said, "Father, can you hear me? I have come at last to avenge you. Do you hear, father?"

As if in answer, the wind keened higher. A strange, dark passion arose within Alonin, a terrible seething. His eyes traced the length of the castle towers. He knew, suddenly and with perfect clarity, that he had not come to spy out Thudredid, its habits and weaknesses, despite what he had previously thought and what he had told his grandfather; any illusion he might have had about this now fell away. He had come to face the dragon. He had come to kill.

It was as if something greater than himself had taken hold of him. He knew that he should wait, bide his time; but this he could not do, despite all logic. He had entered a realm where the ruling forces were archaic and dark, where reason had no power.

Alonin felt his sword tugging heavily at his side. A raindrop stung his cheek. He drew a long, deep breath. He was decided, then.

He put his hand to his sword hilt, felt the cold reality of it. Slowly he withdrew the blade, hearing it rasp softly against the dark leather of his scabbard. In a defiant gesture, he swung the blade up so that it pointed tip skyward. He cried out: *"Thudredid!"*

He waited. The wind blew fine flecks of grit into his wildly staring eyes. For what seemed a very long time there was no sign that the dragon had heeded his cry. But then . . . Did he hear a rustle of activity, the faintest of sounds, almost completely obscured by the roar of the wind coming from one of the towers?

"Thudredid!" he cried again.

There it was again, unmistakable now: an uneasy stirring, a metallic rasp that raised up the small hairs on the back of Alonin's neck. Without further warning, there came a voice, echoing from above him, disembodied. "Who calls me thus from my slumber?" it asked, soft as a breath, yet cold, inhuman, undeniably menacing.

Alonin did not respond immediately. He was suddenly afraid. *There is still time*, he told himself. *I can still turn back*. But he knew that he could not turn back; not now—no, nor ever. He tightened his grip on his sword and, in a clear, ringing voice, called fiercely, "It is Alonin, heir to Gristan, Lord of Caladon! I bid you come, dragon, to face me!"

"Abide, then," the voice said after a slight pause. "Abide."

Alonin slowly and uncertainly lowered his sword. The metallic stirrings from above grew louder, and Alonin saw that a faint red light shone from one of the towers. The young lord strained his eyes upward, tensely, until—

There! A huge, dark shape pressed out from the tower top. Suddenly, it sprang outward from the tower, and seemed for a moment to be falling; then, a pair of mighty wings—night-black and shaped like a bat's, though many times larger—extended themselves and stroked the air. Slowly and with infinite grace, the dragon rose, swung about, and began to drop.

Alonin, who had frozen into stillness at first sight of the dragon, suddenly realized that the monstrous creature was plunging straight at him. With a ragged cry, he lifted his sword to meet it.

The dragon hurtled toward him, and Alonin clenched his teeth together, summoning what courage he could. His mount reared, crying out in terror, flailing the air with its front hooves. Alonin pulled back on the reins, trying to restrain the frightened beast. The horse bucked, turned, and bucked again. "Whoa!" Alonin yelled. "Whoa! Easy, boy, easy!" From the corner of his eye, he saw the dragon descending at terrifying speed. "*Easy!*" he said again, cold desperation entering his heart.

Alonin fought the horse's fear, and his own. He glanced upward, and saw that Thudredid was almost upon him. *Gods! It's huge!* he thought, suddenly giddy. At that moment, the dragon's wings spread to their full length, and churned the air with a slow, powerful stroke. The wind from those great wings washed over Alonin, and the dragon suddenly veered away, soaring high above the castle. It wheeled about, descending quickly, and came down over the castle gates.

Alonin managed to get control of his horse. The big animal tossed its head nervously and snorted. Alonin stroked its damp mane, feeling it tremble. "Good boy," he said in a soft, soothing voice, "Good Gendas."

Alonin glanced up at the dragon, which was perched over the gates, its long talons gripping stone, glimmering like blued steel. Its barbed tail swished twice, then coiled sinuously about its ankles.

There was something strangely fluid about its form, Alonin decided, as if it were flowing in and out of reality; yet also there was some sort of magnetic force woven about it, which made it seem the very hub of all around it. All else in the world seemed but confused shadow, revolving about the inhuman substance of Thudredid.

It is like a dream, yet it is more real than I, Alonin said to himself, vaguely surprised at the thought.

Thudredid gazed down on him, eyes like great yellow moons. Alonin remembered to avoid looking directly into those eyes, for it was said that the eyes of a dragon had the power to drink a man's will. It was difficult, though—extremely difficult—to avoid them. For they were the center of the center, and Alonin felt himself drawn to them like a leaf caught in a whirlwind. And—as hard as this was to explain to himself—he had to admit that there was that part of him that wanted to look into the eyes of immortal Thudredid, to look and be chastened.

"Well, Man, what is your will with me that you venture thus to disturb my slumber? Have you come to bring me my due?" Thudredid asked in a weary but faintly scornful tone. Its voice was sibilant, yet as hard and clear as a diamond. It seemed to linger in Alonin's ears long after the dragon had finished its speech.

"I can not think what you consider your due from me," Alonin replied in a measured voice, "save it be your death. If that is what you mean, then I shall deliver it to you, and speedily." In his heart, Alonin was afraid, deeply afraid, but there was a wildness on him now, operating quite apart from reason and caution.

The dragon peered down sharply on him. "O Stripling, if what you say is true . . . if you truly do not know . . . then you are more ignorant than you have wit to comprehend."

Alonin narrowed his eyes at the huge shape poised above him. "Your words lack meaning, ancient Thudredid. Has age enfeebled you? Or—as I think it more likely—are you trying to confuse me? Is this the trickery you used to defeat my father, noble Gristan?"

"I did not need trickery to bring Gristan low," the dragon said, "nor would I need it against you. But the point is moot, for I do perceive that you have come to me too soon, Stripling. You lack an heir, and I may not contest with you."

"What is this? What lies speak you, dread monster?"

"No lies, but simple fact. Open your ears and hear the truth: you have come to me before your time, without son; without bringing me my due; and I am regrettably enforced from slaying you. Rejoice that this is so, for you may now depart with your life. Leave this place, I say, and do not return until you satisfy either one or both of these requirements, for until then you will have no satisfaction from me."

"No!" Alonin shouted. "I would not have it so! I came here to fight you and, by Cernon's horns, fight you I will!"

Thudredid blinked, its narrow face implacable and unreadable. "What you would or would not have is of no consequence. What is, is. Go, I say, for I will not do battle with you this day."

"But why?" Alonin cried into the wild wind. "I hear

your words but understand them not. What difference does it make that I have no son? What is it you feel I owe you?"

"Ask me not. I am no oracle, nor am I here to wait on your convenience. If you would know of these things, seek you Mernon the wise, he who dwells in the grove of the thirty oaks. Mayhap he can teach you wisdom—although this, I fear, may be an impossible task."

"No! *You* tell me! Otherwise, I must think you are afraid to face me. Is great Thudredid a coward?"

"You cannot provoke me so easily, Mortal; a name spoken by a fool has no power against me. I grow weary with this conversation, so I will repeat myself once and then no more: seek you Mernon if you would know the nature of the fate that binds you. I will say no more." The dragon lifted up its great wings. Steely muscles tensed and rippled beneath its shimmering hide. Alonin noticed that the undersides of those inky dark wings were streaked with deepest crimson.

"No, Thudredid, wait!" he cried. But it was too late. The huge dragon rose ponderously into the air, and from its nostrils there issued a gust of scalding steam, which struck Alonin full in the face, blinding him. His horse reared, mad with fear, and bolted down the hill, as fast and straight as a loosed arrow. Alonin tried to restrain the panicked beast, to no avail. The ruins of Caladon Town flashed by him, seen but dimly through his tear-filled eyes. He threw his great blade to the ground, so that he could better grasp the reins, which gave him his only chance of staying in the saddle. The horse plunged on, reaching the base of the hill, before he could at last gain control over it.

By the time that he was able to calm it completely, his vision was starting to clear. His eyes still burned, though, and the skin of his face felt as if it had been rubbed hard with coarse sand. The pain fanned the flames of his fury, and he turned Gendas about and headed back up the hill. Thudredid was gone, returned to its lair in the tower. Reaching the spot where he had thrown his sword, he stopped and scanned the now silent castle. "Thudredid!" he called, seething. "Thudredid, answer me!" There was no response, but then he had not really expected one.

He lingered there at the base of the castle for a long

time, helpless, his throat thick with rage, humiliation, and
bewilderment, unwilling to leave but uncertain as to what
he could do. He studied the walls and gates of the castle
with a keen professional eye, finally concluding regretfully
that he was powerless to penetrate them. While in a sadly
deteriorated condition, the fortress had been built well and
soundly; it would require mighty machines of war to
breach it, battering rams or siege towers. Alonin scowled.
The solid work of his own ancestors conspired to defeat
him.

Alonin got down from his mount and retrieved his
sword, which he returned to its sheath. What, then, to do
now? Alonin frowned, thoughtful. Suddenly he remembered
that Thudredid had told him to seek out one called Mernon. Alonin knew this Mernon—or, rather, he knew of
him, for Mernon was a wizard renowned throughout all the
world for his skill and wisdom. It might have seemed a
worthwhile idea to seek out Mernon—or at least one of
Mernon's attainment—had not his enemy suggested it to
him. Even so . . . It was obvious that he needed more information to defeat Thudredid; certainly there was more to
this affair than he had previously thought. Yes, all things
considered, it might be a good idea to seek out this Mernon. He could lose nothing by it, except perhaps time, and
he seemed to have plenty of that. But where? Wizards were
by nature secretive; they seldom made their whereabouts
generally known. According to Thudredid, Mernon dwelled
in the grove of the thirty oaks, but this description was so
vague as to be useless. Perhaps, Alonin surmised, that was
what the dragon had intended—to tantalize him with obscure clues and riddles, sending him on a long and fruitless
errand, while it lay secure in its stolen lair. This seemed to
make as much sense as anything. Alonin could not imagine
that the dragon would give him any information that was
of any real value, yet he did not think that a wizard of
Mernon's reputation would actually be in league with a
dragon.

But that left Alonin precisely where he had been before,
with no idea of what step to take next.

Balling up his fists in frustration, he scanned the surrounding area. The wind was lessening, he saw, and the

overcast was starting to break up. Sunlight fell streaming
through the broken patches in the cloud cover, in one spot
illuminating a portion of the road that had led him to Castle Caladon. It was the same road, he bitterly recalled, that
had led his father to his death, leaving behind a wife and a
newborn son . . .

Alonin gave a start, abruptly realizing that he knew what
he had to do next. He would trace back Gristan's final
road, back to the humble house in which he had been born.
The thought of this brought to him a flood of profound
emotion, a peculiar feeling, akin to homesickness, except
that it was for a home that he could not even remember.
Perhaps he would find there, in the place of his birth, the
inspiration he needed to go on. Yes.

He cast his eyes once more about that melancholy spot,
last of all peering up at the castle tower taken by Thudredid for its lair. "I'll be back, dragon," he called. "You have
not escaped me." So saying, he mounted his horse and rode
slowly from the castle of his ancestors.

Returning to the tiny village harboring the Green Crow,
he stopped only long enough to make sure of his direction
from the two old men he had seen there earlier. Then, riding on, he came to a fork in the road, and took the branch
he had not previously followed.

The road took on a pronounced upward slant. The woods
grew up thick and tangled beside it, tall pines and feathery
cedars for the most part, but also some few brooding old
oaks. From the occasional glimpses he got of the sky, he
saw that only a few tattered tendrils remained of the overcast. The sun was lowering, and the sky shone with autumn
gold.

He began thinking about where he should spend the
night. Perhaps, he thought, he would go back to the Green
Crow. A bed would be nice. And a fire . . .

Alonin rode on for what seemed a very long time—too
long, he was starting to feel. The house he was seeking was
supposed to be very near to the village, less than a mile
removed, in fact. It seemed to him that he had already
gone farther than that.

Reining back his horse, he scanned the woods. It was
possible that he had already passed the place he was look-

ing for. The forest was so dense here that a house set back even a few yards from the road would be nearly invisible. On the other hand, it might be just another hundred yards or so up the road. After a few moments of consideration, Alonin decided to go on for a little while more—then, if he still had not found his goal, he would double back.

He spurred his horse forward. Someone was chopping wood nearby, off in the woods somewhere ahead of him. It was a dolorous sound: dull, heavy, sad, echoing hollowly through the hills, muffled by the trees. It seemed to accentuate the loneliness of the woods and the terrible completeness of his isolation.

A few minutes later, Alonin drew roughly even with the sound of the heavy fall of the axe. He stopped and listened to it for a moment. It occurred to him that he might be able to get accurate directions from the woodcutter. From the sound, he seemed near enough, and there was a narrow trail cutting into the dark woods, which seemed to lead in the right direction. It might be a waste of time, of course— the woodcutter might not know where to find the house Alonin was looking for—but, then again, riding up and down the same stretch of road could also be considered a waste of time.

In the end, Alonin decided to leave the road and search out the woodcutter, if for nothing else than for the human contact. Turning aside, he set his horse onto the faint trail. The deep shadows of the woods accepted him.

The trail led steeply upward, twisting aimlessly among the trees. But it seemed always to lead toward the crack of the woodsman's axe—although it was hard to say for certain, as the hills tended to distort the sound, making it seem to shift position.

An eerie feeling began to settle on Alonin. There seemed something in the woods, in their stillness, that was, if not unnatural, then at least uncanny. He felt he had entered a secret realm where time had no meaning, where man and all of man's arts were as nothing. He searched the thickets crowding the trail for some objective foundation for his feeling, but could find none.

He told himself that he was just tired, that fatigue was making shadows in his mind. It had been a hard day, fruitless and baffling in the extreme. He decided that he would definitely spend the night at the Green Crow; this was not a day for camping out in the woods.

The road continued to rise. The forest thinned; oaks began to supplant the pines. The steady fall of the axe seemed very close now.

With the forest dwindling away, Alonin could see now that he had been ascending a low hill. He followed the trail almost to the top before it ended abruptly in a small, dusty grove of oak trees. At the far end of the grove, half hidden from view by the heavy boughs of the trees, there stood an old, rambling house. In front of the house, the woodcutter swung his great axe.

Alonin drew his horse to a halt beside the man with the axe. He said, "Pardon, sir, I do not wish to disturb you, but I am looking for a certain house, and I seem to have lost my way."

The woodcutter was an old man, short and gone a bit stout about the middle. Leaning his axe against the nearby length of wood, his fingers sought a fold in his drab robe of gray homespun. Finding a faded red cloth, he squinted up at Alonin and began mopping his ruddy face.

He was almost aggressively ugly. His hair was an explosion of silver-gray curls, which were in the process of receding from a basset hound forehead. His face was so full of sags and pouches that it appeared to be carved from warm putty. His eyes, though, were a bright, vivid blue, and as they studied Alonin they conveyed a keen sense of amusement.

"What house is it that you seek?" he asked.

Alonin paused for a moment before answering, for he was hesitant to name it. "The house where lived Gristan, the former Lord of Caladon, before his untimely death."

"A strange request! Strange indeed! Why seek you this place that has lain forgotten and abandoned these many years?"

"Because—" Alonin broke off. His voice dropped low. "I would prefer just to say that it is a personal matter."

"I see! I believe I know you, then. Are you not Gristan's son, the one called Alonin, who is now Lord Caladon?"

Startled, Alonin studied the man suspiciously. The old

man gazed back at him, eyes as bright and unconcerned as ever. "How is it that you know me?" Alonin demanded.

"You favor your father somewhat, and I see the same darkness upon you. And, truth to say, I have expected you."

"But how could you know that I would come here? It was merest chance. I was lost . . . I heard the sound of your axe . . ."

"Ah, well, how does a spider know that a fly will land in its web?" the old man answered. Alonin imagined that there was a threat in these words, and he put his hand to the hilt of his sword. The old man smiled evenly. "But perhaps that is a rather too sinister way of putting it, eh? Then let me amend myself thus: I willed that you come, and come you did."

A moment passed in silence. Alonin peered down at the old man, bewildered, with the foolish feeling that he had missed something. Suddenly, a thought leaped to him from nowhere. It was complete nonsense, of course. It had to be. But . . .

"Could it be that you are Mernon the wizard, he who sits on the Council of Attas, whose deeds are spoken of in legend?" he asked.

The old man executed a grandly theatrical bow. "You have hit aright, my lad. I am he. And this—" He gestured to the gray, wind-worn cottage behind him. "—is my abode."

For a long time Alonin could do nothing but gape doubtfully at the wizard. He had a difficult time reconciling his image of what a wizard should look like with the ugly, shabby little man standing before him. He had carried a very different picture of Mernon in his mind—old, yes; but tall, straight, unbent by years, with hair white as newfallen snow, marked by a nobility of bearing . . . This Mernon had hair that was as gray as greasy smoke, and there was not a hint of nobility about him.

"I was told to seek you," Alonin murmured faintly.

"Yes, yes, of course. You will have questions to ask, I imagine. Yes? Well, come with me into my house where we can at least be comfortable."

Mernon scooped up an arm load of firewood and padded

briskly to the house. When he reached the doorway, he turned back to Alonin, who, in his bafflement, had not moved.

"Come along, young man," the wizard said. "Come along."

4

"YOUR family's spectacular fall is well known
among the wise," the wizard said, sinking back into his
chair so that his face fell into deep shadow. "For many
years have I studied it, and with Thudredid itself have I
discussed it. So it may be that I know more about it than
even you yourself do."

"That is entirely possible," Alonin conceded quietly. "As
you must know, I am the last living member of my father's
line. My mother, too, is dead. Taken by sickness, they
say—but I know that it was grief at the loss of my father
that killed her. May Thudredid be doubly cursed for that!
And my grandfather has been reluctant to discuss the matter—understandably so, I suppose. So you see, whatever I
know I have been forced to piece together from legends,
stories, and whatever my mother's father has been able to
tell me. I really know very little."

"Yet, ignorant as you know yourself to be, you can still
demand revenge against Thudredid?"

"Yes!" Alonin said fiercely, his voice a harsh whisper.
"As little as my knowledge is, yet it is certainly enough to
give me just cause for vengeance. Need I enumerate the
wrongs done me?"

"No. I know them all, lad. They are the same that led
Gristan to his doom. But, tell me, do you know why it was
that Thudredid came to attack Caladon?"

"It has never occurred to me that dragons need reasons to
do anything."

"Dragons are sentient creatures, as men are. They too
have their motives, their reasons, although these may dif-
fer significantly from those of men."

"This is all very interesting, of course," Alonin said with

a weary sigh, "but I don't see how it affects my particular problem."

"You will, if you have patience." With that, Mernon rose abruptly from his chair, and for the first time Alonin thought that he could sense a great power within the man. Crossing to a big oaken cabinet, the wizard said, "But it is a long tale I have to tell, and I think that we could both do with something to drink before I begin." He opened the cabinet, and took out two wooden cups and large stiffened leather bottle.

As the wizard carefully poured out a portion of whatever was in the bottle into the cups, Alonin looked about the room. It was small and very cluttered, but there was a rustic simplicity about it that Alonin found comfortable. The furnishings were all substantial, rough-hewn, constructed of wood and leather, functional and unpretentious. Long shelves ran along all of the walls, each crowded with an amazing array of books, parchment scrolls, peculiar curios and devices. Bunches of drying herbs were hung from the bare rafters, and a pleasantly green aroma drifted down from them.

Recorking the bottle, Mernon restored it to its place in the cabinet. He said, "For untold ages men have hated and feared dragons, and for good reason, for they are creatures out of man's dark night, powerful and beyond understanding. And they are even more frightening when they are possessed of a terrible purpose, as Thudredid is, when they thirst for revenge."

These last words came as such an outrage to Alonin that he could not help jumping up from his chair and turning on Mernon. "Revenge! What are you saying? Against whom?" he sputtered, his spinning mind unable to keep up with the sudden fury of his emotions.

"Sit down," Mernon said firmly. "I will tell you all in due time."

Alonin started to protest again, but the wizard's compelling blue eyes locked with his own, and he found himself meekly sinking back down into his chair.

Mernon handed him a cup. He gingerly sniffed the contents, then took a sip, finding it a light, delicate wine. Meanwhile, the wizard took up his place across from the young man. Taking a long drink from his own cup, he regarded Alonin closely for a moment. His face was grave.

"Long ago," the wizard began at last, "Thudredid dwelt in the mountains far to the north of Caladon. It had lived there peacefully for many years, seldom venturing from its lair deep in the heart of the mountains. It had amassed a large and fabulous treasure there: precious gems, artfully worked metals, and many other things of worth. But there was one thing of more worth than all the rest of the treasure combined—a great gem, nearly as large as a man's fist, set in purest silver . . ."

Mernon now lifted up an arm and made an obscure but compelling gesture toward a gloomy corner of the room. Alonin watched in fascination as the shadows themselves seemed to gather together into a thick, amorphous blob, then shift, spread, and begin to take shape. The young lord saw the gem Mernon had described suddenly take form. Its setting was worked in a crude but vital style into the shape of two intertwined serpents; atop the setting, there were affixed two small silver loops, as if the gem were meant to be suspended from a chain, although the chain itself was absent. As for the stone, it was curiously irregular and lumpish for use as a jewel. Alonin first thought that the stone was black and opaque, but then a color bluer than any sapphire spread rapidly outward from the center of the gem, and a dreadful light burst from its heart, transfixing Alonin, as the wizard continued:

"It was called of old the Dylcaer, from the days when it was first brought across the ocean before the ruin and sinking of ancient Ictha and Acynia. It was woven with an old and powerful magic, but no one now knows what that was, save that it was no wholesome magic; for, in all its long history, the Dylcaer has ever been involved in terrible wars, dark times, and struggles of power. It is said that Antirides himself, known by some as the Dark Master of Heggoth, wielded it and derived much of his dreadful power from it in those days when he had his seat of power in the once-mighty land of Klu; and it is said that it was the Dylcaer that shaped Klu into what it is now—a vile and corrupted wasteland where nothing grows and only wicked things thrive. When dark Antirides at last fell, the gem was lost and passed from the sight of men, having somehow found its way into Thudredid's hoard."

Mernon paused, taking a drink from his cup. The image of the Dylcaer wavered, grew thin, and gradually faded from sight. Alonin impatiently gripped the arms of his chair with tense, white fingers. The wizard took note of this and smiled thinly.

He continued. "Your great-great grandfather—Agwid, I believe was his name—was still a young man when the legends of the dragon's hoard reached him. Eager for adventure and anxious to prove himself, he decided that he would attempt to steal the Dylcaer from Thudredid. He journeyed to the mountains of the north, and after a long and laborious search, he succeeded in locating the dragon's lair. There he waited until, as he knew it eventually must, the dragon flew forth one day in search of food. Agwid wasted no time, but took good advantage of Thudredid's absence. He stole into its dark lair, seized the Dylcaer, and then fled across the mountains with his prize. Somehow, he managed to reach home without serious incident, which was no mean feat, I can assure you, as he was undoubtedly being hunted by a very angry and determined dragon. Once safely ensconced in his castle, Agwid rejoiced, thinking that he had brought his adventure to a successful conclusion, that he had completely fooled the dragon."

Mernon stopped and licked his lips. Except for the pale flickering of a single candle and the ruddy glow of the embers in the fireplace, the room was completely dark. In the dim light, his coarse peasant's face managed to seem solemn and enigmatic.

"But?" Alonin prompted.

Mernon smiled grimly. "But as we both know now, it was not to be that easy. Dragons have their own magic, their own way of knowing things. The wind itself is their servant and it bears them news of many things; it brought Agwid's boasts at last to the ears of Thudredid. In great wrath, Thudredid flew south to Castle Caladon, and in one hour, so it is said, it razed the town that ringed the massive walls of the castle, threatening further devastation if its property were not returned. Overly proud, as young men often are, and already, I think, seduced by the power of the gem, Agwid unwisely refused. A terrible battle then ensued, and in the end Agwid was driven forth from his stronghold, amidst much destruction and death. Thudredid then took possession of Castle Caladon, saying, 'As you have taken a thing of value from me, so will I take a thing of value from you. If I am not to have my own, then neither you nor your children shall ever set foot in this castle again; and when you walk this land that once was yours it shall be in fear of me.' Such was the curse of Thudredid.

"What followed after that, of course, you well know," the wizard concluded.

Alonin sat in silence for a long time, trying to digest what he had just been told. His face was pale and troubled, and his fingers clenched his cup with unnatural pressure.

At last he spoke. "So you maintain that everything was Agwid's fault, that it was his theft of the Dylcaer which brought Thudredid down on Caladon."

"Yes. Believe it, lad. I have no reason to lie to you."

Alonin thought about that for a moment, then conceded a little reluctantly, "No, you don't."

He squeezed his eyes shut and drew his brows together, before looking up again and fixing the wizard with a piercing stare. "That explains what Thudredid feels is its due from me, but why should my lack of a son keep it from doing battle with me?"

"Ah, well, that is a simple matter. You must understand that Thudredid is as much bound by its curse as you are. It must remain in Castle Caladon, guarding it from the Lords of Caladon, slaying those who challenge it, until the Dylcaer is returned to it, or until the stars die and the world is no more. Yet it may not kill the last of the line, for that would forever end the possibility of the Dylcaer's eventual return. Any of the Lords of Caladon who wish to go against the dragon must first have an heir."

"So if I sired me a son, I would then be free to do battle with Thudredid. Is that the way of it?"

"Yes, you would," the wizard said. "But you would fail, and the curse would descend to your heir."

Alonin froze for an instant. "You sound as if that were a certainty."

"It is, if you do not first return the Dylcaer."

"Why?"

"Come walk with me," Mernon said, "and I will tell you."

Together they rose and made their way wordlessly out of the house.

It was a clear, windless night. The sky was black as polished jet, and the stars stood out with incredible brilliance. They shone and sparkled like a scattering of fine diamonds.

Alonin stared up, awed by the stars' cold fire. In the eastern sky, he located the constellation of the Armor Forger, one of the few constellations he could easily identify. He picked out the anvil, the hammer, the bowed head of the forger. Somehow performing this mental exercise relaxed him, eased the confused workings of his mind.

Focusing once again on his earthly surroundings, Alonin followed Mernon up a wide cut in the side of the hill. Dried leaves crackled under his boots. All about him, the shadowy outlines of great oaks were thrust up against the velvet sky like gnarled giants, frozen warriors. Alonin sensed that at another time he might have found them threatening and forbidding, but somehow in Mernon's company they lost all menace. He felt totally at one with them, as if he and the grove were in some mysterious and wonderful way connected.

"Dragons are of a different order than are men," Mernon said, after a time. "Older than men, they are ruled by an older order, one which was in existence before the dawn of time when chaos ruled the world. Certain peculiar laws bind them that do not ordinarily bind us. However, when Agwid stole the Dylcaer from Thudredid and received the dragon's curse, he and all of his line became subject to this ancient order."

"Which means?"

"It means, in essence, that certain potent primal forces have been called into play, forces that maintain Thudredid's right to Castle Caladon. No matter what you do, Thudredid may not be driven from there until the wrong done it by Agwid is redressed, until the Dylcaer is restored to it."

"Thudredid may not be defeated without the return of the Dylcaer?" Alonin asked doubtfully.

"Not by any of your line."

"But surely you must know some way to circumvent these forces—a charm, a spell, something?"

"No. I am helpless in this matter. Dragon magic is not my magic, and Thudredid's curse cannot be broken by me."

Alonin thought a moment. "If I sent another man, one not bound by the dragon's curse, what then?"

"As he would be your agent, the same laws would apply."

Alonin fell silent. The implications of Mernon's words were starting to become painfully clear to him.

"You are saying that my father, and his father, and his father, all died uselessly."

"I am afraid so, lad," Mernon said, his voice as soft and gentle as a breeze.

Throughout their conversation, the two men had been making their way slowly up the tree-grown slope; now they came to the top of the hill. Sadly, Alonin gazed down across the countryside below, which, swarthed by night's black cloak, was as vast, formless, and dark as the abyss of death. Alonin's face twisted with withheld grief.

In a voice that was unnaturally flat and trimmed of emotion, he asked, "This Dylcaer, why was it not taken by Thudredid when it slew Agwid?"

"Agwid sent it away for safety before his last encounter with the dragon, to his cousin, the then King of Thuria."

"Thuria. Is that where it is now?"

"No. It never reached there. The messenger was waylaid by outlaws, and the Dylcaer taken."

"Where then? Do you know?"

"It is my belief that it fell into the hands of Queen Urganni of the island empire of Agiza-Saligor, brought to her by one of her pirate lords. And there it remains to the best of my knowledge."

"Urganni. I have heard of her. She has an evil reputation."

"And it is well deserved, I can assure you," Mernon said grimly. "For years now her pirates have harried the southeastern coast, driven on by her dark scorceries. She has done much ill with her comparatively minor powers; if she were to discover the black potentials of the gem she holds, it would be disastrous."

"I cannot help but wonder how it is that you know so much about the Dylcaer," Alonin said.

"We of the Council of Attas are greatly interested in it.

We invested years in our efforts to locate it. It is potentially very dangerous, and we would see that danger removed."

"In what way is it dangerous?"

"If I could answer that with any certainty I would feel much more secure. I don't know—no one now alive does."

Alonin sat down on a large, flat stone, rubbing his brow in distraction. He sighed heavily. Everything had turned out to be so much more complicated than he had ever imagined. Suddenly reality seemed a thin and fragile veil.

In a voice weighted down by despondency, he said, "I don't know. There doesn't seem to be any use to going on. Perhaps it would be best for me just to go back to Yggrs and make what peace I can with myself, setting aside Caladon and my revenge."

"Perhaps it would be best," Mernon said sharply, "but that you cannot do. Have you not heard me at all? You are bound to Thudredid by the dragon's curse, and there is no escape from that. Sooner or later, willingly or unwillingly, your path must lead you to Castle Caladon, and there you will die, unless you can surrender up the Dylcaer."

"If I do recover the Dylcaer and return it to Thudredid, then will I be able to kill the accursed creature?"

"Perhaps. But even so, a dragon is a fearsome thing to face in combat. Returning the Dylcaer will in no way insure your triumph against it."

"But it will be possible?"

"It will be possible."

Alonin set his face into a grim mask. "Well, there is nothing for it, then. I seem to have little choice. I must go to Agiza-Saligor and attempt somehow to regain the gem. And then . . ." His voice trailed off abruptly as his eyes sought out the sky.

A shooting star had appeared in the sky, tracing a bright path across the heavens. Both men watched it thoughtfully, until it faded on the horizon.

An omen? Alonin wondered. And if an omen, was it for good or for ill.

Presently the wizard said, "I must warn you: you go into great danger—and not only from Urganni and her cutthroats, or the perils of the road, either, but from the Dylcaer itself. If you do manage to acquire it, be wary, be wary! It has the power to twist a man's soul, and it will attempt to subvert you to its own fell purposes if it can."

"You talk as if it were a living thing."

"It is, make no mistake! It does not have life as we know life, yet it possesses its own peculiar vitality, and an intelligence and a will to destruction.

"You will stay with me tonight, and I will weave a charm for you which may prove a defense against its baleful power."

"I understand none of this," Alonin said, shaking his head slowly, "so I can only thank you for whatever aid you are able to give me."

They took one long last look at the darkened landscape below; then, carefully, they began to pick their way down the rough slope toward the wizard's house.

5

STANDING beside his horse, Alonin said good-bye to Mernon. A fine gray mist hung over the hills that morning, making everything seem slightly indistinct, slightly unreal, as if the world were but newly formed and its outlines not yet fully settled.

The damp cold penetrated Alonin's clothing easily, for all its thickness, making him shiver. He was tired, very tired, and his mind was as murky as the fog. He had not slept well the night before; his dreams had been full of dark, threatening shapes and frightening occurrences. He had awakened that morning without memory of any of the details, but with a clear impression of evil.

Mernon stood beside him, his gray garb making him seem a fantastic creation of the curling mists. Alonin turned to the wizard and said, "Well, good-bye. For your help, you have my thanks, small thing though that is."

"Wait, lad," the old wizard said. "Before you go, I have something for you." He extended his hand to the young man, and Alonin saw that something shiny dangled by a heavy chain from Mernon's thick fingers. It was a medallion of some kind, he saw—a simple silver disc, engraved in a circular fashion with a fine lettering of a type with which Alonin was unfamiliar. As soon as his eyes touched the medallion, his attention was entirely taken up by it, for it had something of that quality objects sometimes have in dreams: a singular vividness, a sense of deep innate significance. It had a powerful magic attached to it, he was sure—but what sort of magic that might be he could not say.

"Take it," Mernon said. And Alonin reached out and took hold of the medallion, feeling its power enter him with

53

a faint throbbing force. "Put it on," came the wizard's voice.

Slightly dazed, Alonin looked up at the other man, then spread the chain and slipped it over his head. The medallion fell against the breast of his doublet.

"No," Mernon said softly. "Against your skin. You must wear it always against your skin."

Alonin opened his doublet and dropped the medallion down it, so that the cold metal disc came to rest against his bare breast. He had the sudden impression that the world had been altered in some subtle way, as if his senses had expanded into a strange area of which he had been previously unaware. But this sensation faded quickly, leaving only a legacy of dreamlike unreality.

"It is a powerful talisman you wear—invested with the full force of my magic," the wizard said. "It will help you to resist the soul-twisting power of the Dylcaer. And it will also enable you to detect and prevail against any other evil enchantments laid on you, which may or may not prove useful to you on your journey. Keep it always against your bare flesh, for it will have no potency otherwise.

"But keep in mind that great danger clings yet to the Dylcaer. If you manage to gain possession of it, do not handle it or look upon it any more than is absolutely necessary, for it may prove strong enough to overwhelm your talisman if you do."

"I understand; I will be careful," Alonin said. "Mernon, I would thank you, but I can think of no adequate means of doing this."

"Thanks are not required. Carry out your quest faithfully and I will consider myself sufficiently rewarded."

"Do you think I can? Have I any real chance of success, or am I just following a vain dream? You are a wise man, so it is said, and I respect the depth of your knowledge, so I would have you tell me truly what you think."

"I don't know, lad. It has not been given me to see any resolution to your quest. But I do know this: you have a powerful destiny on you. Whether this will lead you to success or failure, happiness or sorrow, only the gods can say."

"Well, then, I can only trust to my luck. Mayhap I will survive to tell you of my adventures."

"I hope so, lad."

"Well . . ." Alonin turned to his horse, fitted a foot to the stirrup, and boosted himself into the saddle. His mount shifted nervously beneath him. He eased it with a few gentle words and a soft stroke of its silken mane, and then looked down upon Mernon and said, simply, "Good-bye."

"Good-bye. Are you quite sure of your directions now?" Mernon asked with a crooked smile.

Alonin laughed. "I certainly hope so."

"Farewell!" the wizard cried, as Alonin turned his prancing horse about to go. "May Cernon and Dinas be with you and protect you!"

By the time Alonin reached the main road, the fog had begun to clear. Wisps of white mist still drifted like dwindling ghosts through the woods and along the road, but no longer did the fog hang like a thick, unbroken shroud upon the land.

Alonin turned onto the road, heading back in the direction of the village, where Mernon had assured him that he would find the house in which his father and mother had lived, in which he had been born. And, a very short time later, he did.

He was amazed that he could have missed it the day before—for there it was, plain for anyone to see. It was well back in the trees, certainly, but it was by no means hidden. It seemed incredible to him that he had ridden by it and not seen it.

There was only one explanation, as far as he could tell. He simply had not been meant to see it. An obscuring glamour had been placed there, so that he had passed it unknowingly . . . and so on to Mernon.

The house was a small, timber-built affair with a thatched roof that was now mostly all fallen in. Even compensating for the years of abandonment, it looked unspeakably poor and wretched; it was humbling for Alonin to look on it, knowing that it was the place of his birth. Certainly it was far removed from the magnificence of Lanfarran Castle, or even the somber ruined splendor of Castle Caladon. What a bitter thing it must have been for his father to be forced to live in such a state, knowing that he had been born for better.

Alonin got down from his horse and walked slowly toward the house. The stiff, spiney underbrush that had grown up thick and tangled about the walls of the house caught and pulled at his legs. He circled around the side of the ruined structure, seeing nothing of interest: just a few rotten boards lying in the weeds, some broken fragments of pottery, and the remnants of an old stone wall, now fallen down.

Coming up directly to the house, then, he peered in through a window, past a gauzy fabric of cobwebs. Inside, he saw the caved-in remains of the roof, dirt, and a broken-down armchair, its leather cover torn and peeling. There was nothing else.

Disappointed, he stepped back from the window. What was it that he had expected to find here? Whatever it was, he had not found it. There was nothing here for him.

Turning his back on the old house, Alonin went back to where his horse was restlessly pawing the forest carpet of matted pine needles with its right front hoof. Alonin swung himself up into the saddle and lightly touched the big animal's throat. "Come, Gendas. Shall we go home? Let's go home."

Immediately upon returning to Lanfarran Castle, Alonin presented himself before his grandfather in the monarch's private chambers. The old king was greatly relieved to see Alonin safely home. But when the young man told him of the perilous quest he must soon undertake, the king's face turned grim and ashen once more, and he heaved a great sigh.

"So it must be from danger to greater danger," he said. "The gods are indeed cruel to give me back my grandson only to take him away again. *Ach!* I wish now that I had kept the circumstances of your birth from you, so you would not feel the need for this desperate mission."

"It is well that you could not, grandfather," Alonin said gently. "It would not have changed the nature of my fate. Eventually I would still have had to follow the same path I follow now, but blindly, without understanding. At least this way I am prepared."

"I wish then that I could have stayed your mother from marrying your father," the king said in agitation, pacing off the length of the room with long strides. "I tried. She had many suitors, your mother, but she would have none but Gristan, the vagabond lord—" He stopped himself abruptly, turning to face his grandson. His features softened with remorse. "I am sorry, grandson; it is not fair of me to speak so in front of you. I . . . I don't know what I was thinking of. Your father was a good man, and he did love your mother."

The old king smiled wanly. "At least you know now that you come by your stubbornness honestly, from both father and mother."

"I understand your feelings, grandfather," Alonin said. "I only wish that I could spare them. But my course was determined for me before I was ever born, and I have no choice but to follow it."

"I know, grandson. But knowing doesn't make it any easier."

A moment of melancholy silence closed oppressively on the two men; but then, abruptly, the king roused himself with what seemed to Alonin a false display of energy. "But on to practical matters. Have you decided what route you will take on your journey?"

"No, not yet."

"Come, then. I have maps here. It is best to settle these thing early, rather than leaving them to the last minute . . ."

Alonin lingered in Lanfarran for more than a week, gathering the supplies he would need for his long journey, saying farewell to his few good friends, reviewing with his grandfather the route he would take, the dangers he was likely to meet on the way. Finally, he knew that he could not justify any further delay and he made plans to leave.

On the night before he was to go, he met to take one last private meal with his grandfather. The finest foods and wines were served for the occasion, including many of Alonin's favorite dishes, yet he could hardly bring himself to eat anything and he barely tasted what little he did eat. There was a tense knot in his stomach, and his hands were icy and pale, as if drained of blood. He found himself drinking too much. Tomorrow, he kept thinking, he would be leaving the only home he had never known, and from then on the future was an unknowable blank. He had not felt anywhere near this degree of trepidation when he had left for Caladon—but he had thought of that as the leaving of one home for another, and it was a trip of only a few days. There was no forseeable end to the journey he was now about to embark on; it would take him halfway across the Thaerdayne Continent, and then back again.

Throughout the meal, by some mysterious consensus, neither man mentioned Alonin's impending departure. Instead, they talked of trivial things: of the lack of rain that season; of the new king of Doria; of people whom they knew, both friend and enemy; of things they had done or wanted to do. It was not until the last plate was taken away that King Clemmth said to Alonin: "So. You leave tomorrow."

"Yes." Alonin fell silent for a moment, and his eyes acquired a clouded, vacant look, as if they were focused somewhere beyond the world. In a moody voice, he said, "Do you know what I would like? I would like to be making this trip without the dire purpose that drives me. I would like just to travel, setting my own pace, not knowing what I would find along the way, without goals. I would like to feel that freedom. Freedom to go where I would, do what I would, without encumbrances or obligations."

His gaze came back into the world, and he laughed, a little bitterly. "Freedom. Let us drink to freedom—what all men want and few men find."

The two men raised their goblets and drained them. When they were through, the king said, "I think you are wrong in one thing, though, grandson. I do not think that all men truly desire freedom. Some are terrified of it; they want someone to tell them what to do, what not to do, what is permissible—to place tolerable borders on their lives. Some even want to be told what to think, for it saves them the trouble of having to do it for themselves. There is a little of this mentality in most of us, I think. Partly it is simple laziness, but mainly it is because to be absolutely free is to leave yourself exposed to all the wild, sometimes contradictory mysteries of the world. Limits are needed to reduce the confusion.

"And as for that ideal state of freedom you seem to aspire to, grandson—well, that is very difficult to sustain in a civilized society. To stay totally without obligations and unencumbered requires either great strength or great selfishness. I am a king—and I am not free, though I am more free than many. There are things that I find I must do, even though I would rather not do them. I do them because it is expected of me, because I expect it of myself."

"In that you do expect it of yourself, then you are free," Alonin objected.

"That is open to question. Do I expect it of myself *for* myself, or to satisfy other people? I don't always know. It is all a matter of outlook. It is like trying to untangle a knotted skein of yarn: where do you start, how do you approach it? I confess that coming to any set answer is beyond me."

Alonin lifted up a slender gold flagon and refilled both their cups. The two men sat drinking thoughtfully for a while, then the king spoke again. "There is a question I have not yet asked you, grandson. How do you intend to acquire the Dylcaer, once you reach Agiza-Saligor? From what I have heard of Queen Urganni, it seems unlikely that she will just hand it over to you."

"I cannot answer that question, I'm afraid. I will try first to buy it from her, I suppose. If that doesn't work . . . Well, who knows? All I can do is wait until the time comes and trust that something will occur to me."

"You may be going a long way for nothing, then."

"No, grandfather. I will get the Dylcaer somehow. By subtlety, by theft, by force if need be! But I will get it, on that you can depend!"

It was still early when Alonin returned to his own quarters. He was planning to leave with the dawn, and he needed his sleep. He stripped off his heavy clothes and collapsed into bed. But sleep could not be induced to come. He was far too anxious and excited, and darkness was a screen upon which all of his hopes, dreams, and fears for the future were brightly limned. Feverish, Alonin rolled and thrashed in his tumbled bedclothes. Finally, after a long hour of this, he muttered a dark curse and sprang out of bed, sending his warm blankets sprawling to the floor.

He dressed quickly and went out into the dark castle courtyard, hoping that the fresh night air would induce drowsiness in him.

The courtyard was deserted and still. It was so quiet that

Alonin could hear the soft, measured tread of the guards patrolling the walls and the wind whistling eerily through the battlements.

His thumbs hooked in his broad belt, Alonin wandered across the courtyard, his boots making faint slithering sounds on the wet, gritty cobblestones. He came at last to a rough wooden staircase set against the East Wall and started to climb it. The staircase creaked and shifted slightly beneath him, giving him the disquieting impression that it could fall apart under him at any moment. This was just an illusion, he knew; it had been built to take the weight of a dozen such as he.

Coming to the top of the stairs, Alonin stepped off onto a narrow walkway at the top of the wall. He made his way cautiously along it, until he came to a place where the wall bulged out into a small battlement.

His hands upon chill stone, Alonin gazed down over the wall on the black roofs of the sleeping town below. The moon lacked but a few days until full, so the silent streets were lit with a pale gray radiance. Somewhere a dog was baying mournfully, its voice echoing through the deserted streets.

Beyond the city, the rich Yggrs farmlands tumbled away to where the far-distant hills stood over them like shadowy sentinels. This was the way that Alonin would be going, come the morning—past the hills, past Yggrs, into the great unknown wilderness beyond.

A faint whisper of fear went through him, and clawing doubts began to assail him. Why, why did he have to do this thing? To avenge a father he had never known? To gain a land he did not need?

There was *something*, a reason. It was something deep within him, something mysterious. He knew that it was there, even though it had no name, no certain form. He could feel it, touch on it, and almost—*almost*—give name to it. But as soon as he came close to defining it, it skirted away from him, leaving him with only empty air in his grasp.

Revenge, was that it? Only partially. Pride? Ambition? Responsibility? Yes, yes, and yes. But there was something else, and that was the mystery. He dimly realized that whatever it was, it was something he needed to fill a dark, empty place within him. And that was all he knew.

He stood there brooding on this, his fate, for a few minutes more, before a wave of drowsiness washed over him. He turned, went slowly down the staircase, and returned to his rooms. Undressing, he fell into bed and was almost instantly asleep.

The next morning, under a sky untroubled by clouds, he departed Lanfarran Castle, beginning the first of many days of journeying.

6

THE ancient monolith jutted from the midst of the rolling green downs like a gnarled stone finger questing for the sky. It spanned about three feet across at its widest point, tapering to a rounded point at the top, and it was a good foot taller than Alonin, who was himself a tall man. The stone from which it was cut was hard and glassy, a pale jade green in color, shimmering coolly in the late afternoon sun.

Alonin swung down from his mount and walked up the low, grassy mound from which the monolith grew. At the top of the mound he paused and stood facing the towering stone. The surface of the stone was marked with many rows of curious runes. The characters were unknown to Alonin, although they were much like those engraved upon the blade he wore at his side, and even more like those marking the talisman the wizard had given him.

Alonin extended a wondering hand to the monolith. It seemed for a moment that the air itself resisted him, as if the lifeless stone exuded some uncanny repelling force. But then his hand broke through the resistance and touched lightly upon the slick stone. He felt a faint pulsing energy pass between the stone and his fingers for a bare instant; then, abruptly, the sensation ceased. Alonin withdrew his hand. There were five glowing points where his fingers had touched the monolith. As he watched, marveling, the points grew dim and faded.

The monolith, he knew, was just one of the many that ringed the borders of Yggrs, dividing that country from all other lands. From where Alonin stood, if he looked far to his left, he could see another such stone at the farthest boundary of his sight. To his right, at exactly the same distance from him, there was yet another monolith, but it was masked from view by a narrow ridge of higher hills.

No one knew for certain when the stones had been erected, but it was said to have been some time during those dim, troubled days after the Western Lands, home to all of Alonin's race, were lost. It was said that for as long as the stones stood Yggrs would be impervious to attack, and that when they fell, so inexorably would the kingdom. History tended to support this contention; in seven hundred years no hostile force had been able to penetrate Yggrs. It had been nearly two centuries since anyone had tried.

At that moment, Alonin stood at the easternmost edge of the kingdom. If he were to step past the monolith, he would be passing beyond Yggrs, beyond the six Acynian Kingdoms themselves. The very thought of this filled him with a vast coldness and summoned a formless terror to nibble tauntingly at the borders of his consciousness.

Unwilling to let himself be possessed by the morbid thoughts he felt gathering in him, Alonin went down from the mound to where his horses were pulling at the lush grass. He busied himself for a while with caring for the animals, trying to still his thoughts in the process. Unfastening the cinch strap from the belly of the horse that he had been riding, he slid the heavy, silver-studded saddle from its back and onto the ground. Then he turned to the pack horse and began, piece by piece, to remove its load. When this was done, he brushed both animals thoroughly and tethered them to a bramble.

He felt better after that, his phantoms having shrunk to manageable proportions, so he sat down on the cool grass, facing Yggrs.

High on a commanding ridge, a cold gray keep glowered down upon the bare, rolling plain. Thick plumes of smoke issued from its chimneys, drifting ghostlike across the downs. Beyond the keep, the sun was sinking toward the western hills, partially obscured by thick stratifications of low-lying clouds. Bright crimson and gold, the clouds blazed with the sun's reflected glory.

Chewing thoughtfully on a blade of grass, Alonin regarded the molten sky until the sun sank below the hills and the sky was brushed with the deep purple of twilight; then he picked himself up from the ground and rummaged in his gear until he found his hand axe. He went down to the road, where earlier he had spotted a dead tree lying beside a shallow gully. A few minutes later, he returned with an armful of firewood, which he deposited on the grass next to the monolith.

Legend had it that those who spent the night beside one of these ancient border stones were often visited by prophetic dreams. Even while still in Lanfarran, Alonin had decided that he would try the legend. If anyone was in need of prophecy, he felt, it was he.

Alonin built a fire and made a modest meal for himself of bread, cheese, and some dried meat from his packs. After satisfying his hunger, he sat beside the fire, sipping at some steaming herbal tea from an earthenware cup.

Darkness drifted gradually upon the world, and a low wind began moaning across the downs like a disembodied spirit. The moon rose, bathing the land in its ghostly glow.

Drowsiness began to steal over Alonin. Wrapping himself in his warm, thick cloak, he stretched out beside the smokeless fire. After a time, he slept.

And then, in the troubled dimness of sleep, the dream was upon him . . .

He was lying in a dark, gloomy place, the borders of which were shadowy and ill-defined. Iron chains and manacles were hanging down all about him. His back was to a wall, and his hands and feet were tied with silken bonds, so that he could not move them. He was completely, terrifyingly helpless.

Suddenly, a thick, iron-studded door groaned open, flooding the chamber with blinding white light. His eyes watering, Alonin blinked dully at the opened door. He saw that a figure occupied the doorway, a vague dark silhouette against the streaming brightness. The figure drifted gracefully into the room, and the door clanged shut behind it with a thunderous echo. Alonin could see now that the figure was a woman—a woman almost supernatural in her beauty. Long hair tumbled down her shoulders like fine gold silk. Her lips were full and red. Her skin was unblemished white satin, and her eyes were the rich, deep blue of the early morning sky. The gown she wore was a shimmering silver-white, and it clung to her lithe figure with the sensuous ardency of a lover.

Alonin's entire being ached with the sight of her, and he was seized by a sudden terrible yearning. His heart seemed to stop in his breast.

The woman crossed the room, her gown rustling softly in the unnatural silence, and stood over Alonin. Her face was at first calm, serene, unreadable; then, as she began to lean over him, she smiled a queer smile. She laughed, and the echoes took her laughter and twisted it into something terrible and menacing.

Alonin noticed with a shock of surprise that there was a slender knife glinting in her small, pale hand. It came down at him with incredible exaggerated slowness, as if in some strange symbolic ritual. Panic swelled within Alonin. He did not know whether she meant to kill him or merely to cut his bonds, but he was suddenly terrified. He tried to speak, but the words were frozen in his constricted throat. The knife came ever closer. With a tremendous effort, he managed to cry out . . .

And then, abruptly, there was soft grass beneath him, a dwindling fire beside him, and the velvet downs all about him. Reality.

With a low groan, Alonin sat up, shuddering violently. He threw some more wood on the fire, then sat back, his arms stretched about his knees, and stared at the flickering tongues of flame as they devoured the fresh fuel.

The dream had unsettled him. He had the uneasy feeling that he should understand it, but he didn't; he was completely baffled by it. Neither the dragon nor the Dylcaer—which were what he most wanted to know about—had appeared in the dream, and that which had appeared was completely incomprehensible to him. Having no reference points on which to base a judgment, he could not interpret the dream. Was it merely symbolic, as dreams tended to be, or was what he saw actually going to happen to him at some indeterminate point along his journey? And if it were symbolic, what on earth did it symbolize? Alonin had no way of telling. He realized that all he could do was wait and trust that the dream would become clear to him at the proper moment.

Still, it troubled him. Unbidden, his mind kept returning to the dream, and a faint feeling of dread returned to him. Eventually he stretched out again, still staring into the red heart of the fire, still thinking on the dream, even as it became dim in his mind. He fell asleep like that. This time there were no dreams.

He awoke again in the cold light of morning. He sat up and stretched, looking blearily across the downs. A thick white mist lay upon the land, lent a glaring luminescence by the rising sun behind it. Brushing the silver-beaded dew from his cloak, Alonin got up stiffly and began making preparations to depart.

After breaking his fast on the remains of the last night's meal, he readied his horses and then led them down to the road. He swung up onto the back of his mount and, trailing the pack horse behind, rode slowly away from Yggrs. He did not look back, thinking it best that way.

By midmorning, the fog had burnt off and the day turned bright and clear, though cold. As Alonin rode, the character of the land began gradually to change. The downs flattened, and trees began to appear beside the road. At first, they were few and widely scattered but they became more and more common as he went on, until a vast wood stretched out on both sides of the road. Elm and oak predominated, loosing leaves of scarlet and gold to the whistling autumn wind, but there were also a few scattered conifers; pine, spruce, and fir, splitting the pale blue sky with their swaying, wind-blown tops.

The road was littered with dead, dry leaves, which shifted and danced with each changing breeze. Above, brightly plumed jays swooped from branch to branch, calling harshly to one another. Squirrels romped among the rustling leaves, or chattered angrily at Alonin from low-hanging branches.

A feeling of contentment came into Alonin's heart. For the first time in many days he felt good, really good. His fears and doubts were gone, forgotten. He felt liberated. He began to wonder why he had ever been apprehensive of this journey.

The world seemed suddenly fresh, new, beautiful. It was as if he had been given new eyes with which to see, eyes that were untainted, unjaded. It was a feeling that he knew to be too good to last, but he intended to enjoy it while he could.

So, as he rode, he began to sing a ballad that he remembered from his childhood. It was a soft, easy tune, and it made him glad just to sing it. He went on like that—carefree, singing at times—for several hours. Then, as the late afternoon shadows began to grow, he came around a bend in the road and suddenly saw a large, coal-black horse trotting along the road toward him. It wore both bridle and saddle, but bore no rider.

Alonin found that curious. He rode up to the horse and grabbed ahold of its hanging reins. There was a touch of madness in the animal's liquid eyes, so Alonin reached out and gingerly stroked its warm, damp mane. It tossed its head fitfully. "Easy, easy there," he said soothingly. "Where did you come from? Where is your master?"

Trailing the still-skittish horse by its reins, Alonin urged his own mount forward at a cautious pace. He scanned both sides of the road carefully as he went, expecting perhaps to find a thrown rider.

He had proceeded about thirty yards along the road when he heard the sounds of a disturbance emanating from the woods to his right. Pausing, Alonin cocked his head slightly and listened intently. He heard the loud, unmistakable clash of steel against steel and, beneath it, a low, piteous moaning. A shouted curse split through the woods.

Alonin slid down from his mount, tied all three horses to a low branch, and stealthily entered the woods. The sounds of strife grew steadily more immediate, until he reached the edge of a small clearing. Partially shielded behind a gnarled tree trunk, Alonin peered out, able to see clearly now what the matter was. It was much as he had thought.

His back to a tree, a young, red-haired man stood alone against three opponents. In his right hand he held a long slender blade, dripping red from the point. He wielded the weapon skillfully, cutting and thrusting with enough speed and energy to keep his foes at bay. The three facing him were less able, but they had the advantage of sheer weight of numbers. It was an advantage that they seemed reluctant to press; they fought cautiously, seemingly content with wearing their prey down. Alonin saw the probable reason for this judicious tactic nearby: another man, doubled over on the ground, propped up on his knees and one elbow, his free hand clutching his belly, blood leaking slowly from between his fingers.

For an ignominious moment, Alonin considered backing quietly away and leaving the men to their sport. But three against one! Alonin knew that the red-haired man would not have a chance unless he interceded. He had to do something.

Uncertain, Alonin bit at his lower lip. As a youth, he had been given the best fencing masters in all of Yggrs, and he had been an apt enough pupil—but this was different, this was battle in earnest, and in this he had no experience. He had to admit that he was afraid. He wished now that he had not refused the men his grandfather had offered to have accompany him.

But he knew what he had to do, and there was no sense in delay. He took in a sharp breath and drew his sword from its oiled leather sheath. With a muttered curse, he stepped into the clearing. The three ruffians remained unaware of his presence, but the red-haired man did glance over at him for an instant, fixing him with a brief inquiring look, before being forced to return his full attention to the fight. Alonin tightened his grip on his sword, and said in his most commanding voice, *"Cease this!"*

Startled, the three did break off their attack for a moment, looking around cautiously to where Alonin stood, while still keeping sight of the red-haired man. But then, seeing that he was but one man alone, they merely laughed.

"Take 'im, Jaegge," one of the three growled.

"Aye, take 'im," a second man enjoined. The two of them returned their attention to the red-haired man, while the third man advanced slowly on Alonin.

The man, Jaegge, was short and sallow in complexion. His shoulders were wide and brawny, and his bare arms were thickly knotted with hard muscle. His head was protected by a conical iron cap, stained with rust. There was a puckering V-shaped scar below his left cheekbone. One of his front teeth was missing, and the rest were stained and crooked. In his right hand he bore a brutally ugly sword, its short, wide blade notched and pitted from hard use.

He came at Alonin, grinning savagely. There was murder glistening in his small, dark eyes.

His sword held out in both hands before him, Alonin squared off to face his opponent.

The other man started to circle Alonin, threatening him ominously with short, quick thrusts of his blade, obviously trying to get the young lord to turn his back on the man's two cohorts. Alonin smiled thinly at the transparency of this tactic; he certainly knew better than to allow himself to be maneuvered into so dangerous a position.

Falling back a step, Alonin thrust out sharply with his blade to keep his adversary from getting around his side. Then, while his iron-helmed attacker was still off-balance from dodging the thrust, Alonin experimented with a quick cut to the man's right side. It was effectively beaten down, and the two of them squared off once more, glaring intently at each other from over their weapons.

His nerves thrilling with excitement and fear, Alonin considered his chances. He was confident that he was the better swordsman, but the other man had him in strength and sheer ferocity, so the outcome of their fight was by no means assured. Alonin's mind cast about for some stratagem that would put the advantage more definitely in his favor.

But before he could think of anything, his opponent leaped suddenly forward, swinging his sword up and around at Alonin's head.

Alonin knew what he had to do. He also launched himself forward, extending his sword out crosswise, and caught the other's blade before it come come down from the top of its arc. The two weapons grated against each other as Alonin bore down with all his might against his opponent's blade.

Caught with the inferior leverage, Jaegge was slowly bowed backward, grunting and trembling with effort. Giving a fierce animal cry, he dropped suddenly and lunged forward, driving his shoulder into Alonin's stomach.

His breath knocked from him, Alonin gasped and staggered back. The other man wrapped his arms about the young lord's middle and tried to bear him down onto the ground. Somehow, staggered though he was, Alonin managed to stay on his feet. With the pommel of his sword he struck his attacker a desperate blow to the center of the back. With a grunt of pain, the man let go of Alonin and hunched away.

The two men separated, fixing each other with unblinking stares. They shifted warily, their blades wavering slightly, as each sought for an entry.

Perspiration was rolling from Alonin's forehead, stinging his eyes. So far he had mainly responded to the other's challenges; now he wanted to take the offensive. He did not think that the red-haired man could last much longer without aid.

He tried a tricky attack he had once learned, which consisted of a beat to his opponent's blade, a feint to the belly, a lunge that veered to the shoulder. It worked perfectly, he found to his delight, leaving a deep bloody gash. Alonin felt a flood of exaltation.

This feeling, however, was short-lived. Bellowing like an injured bull, the man charged Alonin, whirling his blade savagely at the young lord's skull. It was a move inspired by pure blind rage, but it was no less frightful for that. Leaping quickly to the side, Alonin deftly avoided the blow.

Still snarling his anger, apparently enraged beyond caution, Jaegge stubbornly turned to Alonin's new position, and drew back to deliver another fierce cut. But Alonin was already bringing his blade around in a wide, deadly arc. He brought the edge of his blade down on his adversary's helm with a resounding crash. The helm flew off and clattered noisily to the ground several feet away. Nervelessly, the man collapsed, his head jutting from his body at an odd angle.

Drawn by the sound of the blow, the two who had been battling the red-haired man turned and saw their comrade slumped senseless on the ground. Uncertainty and fear filled their eyes. A minute before, they had been three against one; now the odds were even. Apparently, the altered circumstances were not to their liking. Swinging their blades threateningly from Alonin to the red-haired man and back again, they backed slowly away. When they reached the edge of the clearing, they turned and fled off into the woods.

The red-haired man staggered a few steps toward

Alonin, his breath coming in ragged gulps. Despite the cold, sweat ran in rivers down his ruddy face and into his curly red beard. He leaned down and caught hold of his knees.

"Thank . . . you . . . for coming . . . to my rescue," he gasped.

"What happened?" Alonin asked. "Who were those men?"

The man drew a few more deep breaths, each one becoming a little less labored than the one before, then straightened up again. He was slightly shorter than Alonin, and wider in build. His face was a broad, lightly freckled oval. His nose was large and flat; his lips were generous and quirked up at the corners. His garments were old and weather-stained, but well made. Sheathing his sword, he said, "They were thieves, outlaws. They were laboring under the mistaken notion that I had something worth stealing."

"I thought as much."

"It was my own damn fault, really. I was riding toward the town of Kestra, when I saw a man by the side of the road, making a great show of being hurt. Stupidly, I stopped to see if I could help, and the scoundrel reached up and pulled me from the saddle! The next thing I knew, the rest of the gang were coming out of the woods at me. I decided the best thing I could do was take to my feet and run. But, as you can probably guess, I didn't get far before they caught up with me. Serves me right for being so trusting.

"By the way, my name is Dalkin aer Aunne, late of the great city of Imre in Thuria. Dalkin, for short," he said with an amiable grin. "What may I call you?"

"Alonin," the young lord said, clasping hands with his new acquaintance. "Alonin of Caladon."

"Well met, Alonin."

Alonin noticed suddenly that Dalkin's left sleeve was slashed open and wet with fresh blood. "You're wounded!" he exclaimed.

"Um, yes, this," Dalkin said, gingerly probing the wound with the fingers of his right hand. "Cernon's horns, that hurts! Ah, well, I won't die of it."

Dalkin turned his attention to the man Alonin had

felled. Kneeling down, he gave the stricken man a quick examination. "Dead," he pronounced. "Neck's broken. That was some blow you gave him," he said with some admiration.

"I did not mean to kill him," Alonin said quietly. There was a sick, sour taste in his mouth. He had never slain a man before.

"Oh?" Dalkin said without the slightest emotion. He dug into the dead man's pouch and came out with two small copper tokens, which he slipped into his own pouch.

"Robbing the dead . . ." Alonin protested numbly.

"Why not? The dead need nothing from this world."

Dalkin moved on to the other man, who was now slumped limply with his face in the dirt. When Dalkin nudged him in the ribs with the toe of his boot, the man did not move. "This one's dead also. Or close enough to it." A search of the second outlaw's purse yielded up only a crudely cut quartz crystal; Dalkin discarded the worthless stone.

Alonin shivered, crossing his arms over his chest and clutching his shoulders. "I suppose that we had better bury them."

"Bury? Let the buzzards have them! Those two who escaped might have friends nearby. They might be back."

"I suppose that you're right," Alonin admitted reluctantly.

"Certainly I'm right. Which way are you headed?"

"Tonight, to Kestra."

"Splendid. So am I. Shall we ride together?"

Alonin scrutinized Dalkin sharply for a moment. He was not yet entirely sure how he felt about this strange red-haired man who seemed so callously indifferent to death.

Still, it didn't seem likely that he meant Alonin any harm. And recent events had made the young lord a little apprehensive of traveling alone.

"Why not?" he said finally.

7

"YOU'RE going all the way to the coast, you say?" Dalkin frowned into his second tankard of ale of the evening. "Hmm. Interesting." He looked up, fixing Alonin with a speculative gaze. "If you don't mind my saying so, I find that rather peculiar."

"How so?"

"No one travels between here and there at this time of year, especially not alone. It's a perilous route at the best of times, but now, with winter coming on, it's . . . Well, I'd say it shows either great courage or a complete disdain for your own life." He paused and, with a sly smile, added, "Or perhaps just simple ignorance."

"Which do you think?"

Dalkin laughed. "I'll give you the benefit of the doubt and say courage."

"I thank you for that, at least. But really, it is nothing all that unusual. I, ah, have pressing business in the city of Tulin that cannot be put off."

"Umm?" Dalkin rescued a partially burning twig from the hearth. Applying the glowing red end to the bowl of his pipe, he puffed vigorously. A dense wreath of blue smoke encircled his head. Discarding the burning twig, he sat back with a deeply satisfied sigh. "May I ask what this business is that it is so important?"

Alonin paused uncertainly. There was no reason why he should keep his quest a secret, but he was afraid that to a stranger his tale of dragons and magic gems might seem either an imaginative boast or the product of an unbalanced mind. This, coupled with his natural reticence, made him answer, "I would prefer not to go into that now, if you don't mind."

"Certainly, certainly. I don't mean to pry." Dalkin raised

his tankard and drained off its remaining contents in one
heroic gulp. He grimaced. "Damn," he said, "but the ale at
this inn is three cuts below adequate!"

"Would you care for another?"

Dalkin grinned. "Love it," he said.

Twisting around in his chair, Alonin motioned to the
innkeeper, a large, flabby man in a stained yellow shirt and
brown breeches. The man's face was pale and swollen, and
his head was perfectly hairless. His watery blue eyes were
rimmed with red, and his fleshy earlobes were webbed with
prominent red veins. At first, the innkeeper did not notice
him, but eventually Alonin managed to get his attention.

"Another tankard for my friend," Alonin said, inclining
his head slightly toward Dalkin. The innkeeper nodded
dumbly and went behind the counter to fill a fresh cup.

In the meantime, Alonin looked out across the small,
shabby inn. It was a gloomy place. The only illumination
was provided by the niggardly fire in the blackened stone
hearth and several small oil lamps which smoked and sputtered constantly from the cheap oil used in them. Only two
of the other tables were occupied, one by an old, sad-faced
drunk who muttered continuously and incomprehensibly to
himself, the other by a group of blustery middle-aged merchants who talked and laughed amongst themselves a little
too loudly. Apparently the majority of the townsfolk of
Kestra were of the same opinion as Dalkin on the quality
of the ale and went elsewhere. The inn probably survived
on the patronage of unwary travelers.

At last, the innkeeper came over with the fresh tankard
and slammed it down, sloshing some of the frothy ale on
the table.

"Not much of a crowd tonight, is there?" Alonin asked,
pressing a triangular copper coin into the man's hand.

"No, sir," the innkeeper said, wiping his wet hands on
his coarse breeches. "We don't get many in here this time
of year. It's not hardly worth staying open, if you know
what I mean. In the summer, it's different. This place is
full most every night." His eyes sparkled greedily for a moment before returning to their normal dullness.

"No," he said again wistfully, "we don't get many this
time of year." He trudged away heavily, taking the empty
tankard with him.

Dalkin stared down pensively at his ale, turning the old wooden tankard around and around on the scarred oak table. His pipe had gone out, but he kept it clamped between his teeth. After a few minutes he looked up at Alonin, removing the stem of the pipe from his lips. "Would you be interested in having company on this journey of yours?"

Surprised, Alonin took his time in answering. "Is that an offer?" he asked finally.

Dalkin regarded Alonin steadily. "Yes."

Alonin blinked back quizzically at his companion. "Only a few minutes ago you were telling me how difficult my way will be. Have you changed your mind so soon?"

"No. I am sure that you know as well as I do how hard it will be. I might point out, though, that two would have an easier time of it than one."

"But why would you possibly want to come?"

Dalkin shrugged. "I've never been to Tulin. Call it adventurousness."

"You must have a better reason than that."

"All right, to be honest, I do—though it might sound strange to you. I, ah, have fallen on hard times, you see. Aside from what I took from that outlaw, I haven't a copper. My horse, my sword, and the clothes I am wearing are just about all I have in the world. You, on the other hand, seem very well provisioned. If I go with you, at least I won't have to worry about where my next meal is coming from."

"That seems a dubious reason to risk you life."

"So maybe it is. Why should you worry about it? Call me a fool, but I am content enough to go with you."

"It just seems to me that you could find easier ways to come by your bread."

"No doubt, no doubt. But most of them I would find demeaning—and all of them would require that I stay in one place for a prolonged period of time. I prefer mobility. If this were another time of the year, I could find employment as an escort for a trade caravan, a line of work that I am well familiar with. But it will be months now before the caravans start coming through this region again."

"Well, your offer is more than generous."

"As I said, I am not motivated by generosity but by simple expediency."

Pensively rubbing the depression between his nose and forehead, Alonin slowly let out his breath. "You tempt me."

"You'll accept my services, then?"

"I don't know."

"You've seen me fight. You know that I could be useful to you."

"Well . . . I think that before you commit yourself, I had better tell you who I am and what my business is, after all. Then, if you still wish it, I will be glad for your company."

"Fair enough," Dalkin said. "But I warn you, I will not be easy to discourage."

Later that night, while he lay in a small drafty room on the inn's second storey, waiting for sleep to come, Alonin's thoughts turned to Dalkin. Was he right to allow the redhaired man to accompany him? Up until this time, it had never occurred to him to consider sharing the journey with anyone, mainly because it had not occurred to him that anyone would want to come. Yet Dalkin did, or so he said, and for no better reason than the prospect of a few free meals and a chance to go where he had never been before.

Dalkin. Alonin rolled the name around in his mind. What did he know about the man? Not much. Only that he had a strong sword arm, an easy tongue, a goodly thirst, and a face that was, somehow, both roguish and trustworthy.

And there was something else, something that Alonin sensed—and envied—in Dalkin. There was a great vitality in the man, a relish for life, an uncommon ability to throw himself fully into whatever presented itself to him at a given moment. Alonin knew this talent—for it was a talent—to be largely absent in himself. His own world was constructed mainly in the past and in the future: what was, before his father and mother died, and what would be when he completed the task before him. The present was only something to occupy the space between the one point and the other. Perhaps later, when what had to be done was done, there would be time for the present, for simple enjoyment. But not now.

In the darkness, Alonin tried to dredge up the memory

of his mother. It was hard; she had been taken so long ago. A glimpse of hair, a touch, a vague outline were all that he could conjure up and as he fought to enlarge his remembrance even these faded, leaving only an aching hollowness.

And as he slipped into troubled slumber, a secret painfilled chamber of his mind opened wide, filling the pulsating gray vagueness with but one thought: *I will kill you, kill you, O Thudredid . . .*

Alonin was awakened the next morning by the sunlight streaming in through the dusty windowpanes across from his bed. Stretching, he crawled out from between his tumbled blankets. The tiny bedroom was cold enough to cause his skin to stiffen and pull tight across his bare chest. Consequently, he dressed quickly, his icy fingers fumbling impatiently with the fastenings of his garments. He slung his cloak over his broad shoulders without bothering to secure it, and then, hefting up his gear, he went downstairs.

When he came down, Dalkin was already sitting on a low bench facing the fireplace, looking every bit as miserable as Alonin felt. His face was pale and puffy, and his eyes were red. His light brown cloak was wrapped about him like a blanket. The effect was somehow gratifying to Alonin.

Alonin sank down on the bench next to Dalkin, stretching his long legs out toward the warmth of the fire. The two grunted out their good-mornings, and then sat there wordlessly for several minutes. Finally, for no better reason than to break the silence, Alonin cleared his throat and asked, "Did you sleep well?"

Dalkin chuckled mirthlessly. "Slight chance of that. I think that they stuff their mattresses with sand here, with rocks and twigs thrown in for variety."

Another minute passed. Dalkin said, "By the way, I took the liberty of ordering breakfast for the both of us. It should be ready soon."

Alonin nodded dully. "Um."

As if on cue, a young serving girl bustled into the room from the kitchen. She was a stocky girl with long, dark hair and a forgettable face. She wore a ragged shift of an indeterminate yellow-brown color. Her posture was slightly stooped from the weight of the large tray she carried. Setting the tray down on one of the tables, the girl began skillfully laying out the platters, plates, and utensils. "Your breakfast, sirs," she said in a flat, uninteresting voice.

Alonin and Dalkin got up and seated themselves at the table, while the girl finished setting out their meal. Alonin gave her several small coins for her trouble, and she respectfully withdrew from the room, leaving the two men alone.

Meanwhile, apparently revived by the smell of the food, Dalkin attacked his breakfast, voraciously scooping egg and greasy sausage into his mouth with obvious enjoyment. Alonin, however, had difficulty facing food with any great relish at such an early hour; he toyed with it on his plate, eating little.

After a time, he asked, "Is it still your wish to accompany me?"

Dalkin swallowed a bite and smiled. "Of course."

Alonin found himself to be vastly relieved; he had been afraid that Dalkin's offer of the night before had been bravery inspired by ale, which would be dissipated by the cold light of day. And Alonin knew now that he did not want to go on alone. The carefree sense of well-being that had been with him briefly before coming upon Dalkin was gone now. The fear was back in full force, and the burden of his mission seemed too much to bear in loneliness.

After breakfast the two went out to their horses, which were already saddled and ready for their departure. Mounting, they rode through the still-sleeping town of Kestra. It was a tidy little town of sharply gabled houses and neat stone shops. In the still morning air it seemed an idyllic place to Alonin.

"A nice town," he murmured.

Dalkin gave him a blank look. "Nice enough," he said.

Alonin thought once again on how little he knew of his companion. But then he cleared his mind of questions. Time enough for discovery later, he thought.

A short distance out from Kestra, the two came to the crossroads. Turning onto the old East Road, they headed into Corwood Forest. Here, stout, ancient trees overhung the road with bare, wavering branches, casting weird shadows across their path. An elusive dusty odor hung in the air.

"From here on we must be ever on our guard," Dalkin

warned. "Corwood is a strange place, and anything can happen here."

Alonin had to agree. Corwood was one of the last places left on the Thaerdayne Continent that still remained entirely outside the reach of civilization. No king ruled there, and no order was there imposed. As a consequence, its depths concealed a variety of unsavory and unfriendly creatures, creatures that either rejected or were rejected by the greater humanity of the Acynian Kingdoms and the Icthan States. There were human misfits of all sorts: outlaws, mad witches, solitary sorcerers, and far-ranging bands of the Cydri—that barbaric, warlike race that held little love for Alonin's kind, since their dominance over Thaerdayne had been supplanted by the superior Acynians centuries before. In addition, there were the reputed inhuman and unnatural perils of Corwood—remnants, it was said, of those foul creatures raised by the Dark Master of Heggoth in the great wars of more than seven hundred years before. Many were those who entered Corwood and were never seen again. Alonin felt suddenly grateful to have so able a swordsman as Dalkin with him, for it did not seem likely that they would leave that great forest without encountering some difficulty.

They traveled deep into the wood that first day, camping by night at the side of a small, clear stream. On the second day of their journey the character of the land began to change. The land heaved upward, slowly gaining in altitude; towering evergreens gradually replaced the oak and elm; until, by the afternoon of the fifth day, the lordly conifers ruled the land uninterrupted.

The two men were now in Corwood proper, a vast forested tract that stretched to the harsh granite mountains of the east, still some thirty leagues distant. As Alonin and Dalkin rode deeper into the forest they kept an ever more careful watch on their surroundings, but, fortunately, they never saw anything more threatening than a lone deer frozen in the dusky shadows of the brooding woods.

One night, while they sat huddled next to the campfire, Alonin said thoughtfully, "You know, it's strange."

"What is?" Dalkin was sitting on a low, flat rock, carefully scraping out his pipe with the point of his dagger.

"I've only been away from Lanfarran for two weeks, and

yet already I feel as if my life there was just a vague
dream. It doesn't seem real. I feel as if I have been on the
road forever."

"I know what you mean," Dalkin said. Putting the stem
of the pipe in his mouth, he sucked thoughtfully on it. He
frowned in dissatisfaction, removed the pipe, and began
scraping at it once more. "However, when you have been
away for a while longer, believe me, it will start to seem
real again. Perhaps painfully so. When you are cold or
lonely, you will long for familiar things, familiar places.
You'll wake up some morning unable to remember where
you are, and then it will all seem very, very real."

Alonin thought that he caught a trace of melancholy in
Dalkin's voice. He glanced over at his companion for con-
firmation, but Dalkin's face, sunk in darkness, revealed
nothing. Abruptly Alonin asked, "Where do you come
from, Dalkin? What brings you to this place?"

There was no answer immediately forthcoming, so
Alonin asked, "Do you mind my asking? If you do, I'll
withdraw my question."

"No, of course I don't mind. I can appreciate your curiosity." After a short pause, he said, "All right, then. Here
is the brief comical history of Dalkin aer Aunne. Let's see,
I was born in the city of Imre, the third and youngest son
of a prominent merchant, a dealer in rare oils and spices.
My two brothers and I were never very fond of each other.
To be honest, we detested each other—I shan't bore you
with the reasons, but we did.

"Well, to make a long story short, when my father died,
my brothers naturally inherited everything—the business,
the family house, money, everything. I, being the youngest,
got nothing except a few of my father's cherished but es-
sentially worthless knickknacks.

"After what they considered a proper period of mourn-
ing—for they were eminently proper—my brothers came
to me and delivered my options; either I could stay at
home, despised and unwanted, working at whatever nasty
little jobs they could find for me, or I could leave home—
their home, now—to seek my fortune elsewhere. They
made it clear that they strongly preferred the second option. What could I do? There was no purpose to be served
by staying there—though I warrant you I considered it, just

so that I could be a perpetual irritation to them. But in the end I decided to leave Imre, to seek my fortune. Heh! You might have noticed that I haven't done all that well in this regard."

He inclined his head judiciously. "But then again, not all that badly, either. Since then, I have wandered through the world, doing what I can to stay alive. Briefly, I was a clerk in a spice shop in Estos, but it soon grated on me to be a menial in a trade I had grown up in. So I moved on; and since then I have been a mercenary, an armed escort, anything that would provide me a living without too much restricting my freedom. Having lost everything else, I prize my freedom. If you can understand what I mean."

"You have no idea how well I understand," Alonin said. He drew a breath. "Yet it seems to me that you have grown disillusioned with this life of wandering. Why do you still do it?"

Dalkin appeared to consider the question for a moment. "Yes—it can become wearisome after a while. Still in all, it does have its compensations. I am free. I am not dependant on anyone or anything. And I have been able to see a good deal of this world, which I suspect would not have been the case if circumstances had been kinder to me."

Dalkin paused, filling his pipe from a small leather pouch. "I don't know," he said. "I suppose that I still wander because I have yet to find a place where I could be happier staying, because I haven't found a life that suits me better. I am still looking."

The next morning the sky was heavy and threatening. Dark clouds boiled above the green spires of the pines, and a fierce wind lashed through the treetops. There was a cold, wet, clammy feel to the air.

"It looks as if there's a storm brewing," Alonin said, securing the last parcel to the pack horse.

"Yes, it does," Dalkin agreed. "We'll have rain before noon. Curse the luck."

Indeed, they had been riding less than an hour when the rain began to fall. At first it fell as a light mist, wetting their faces and beading up harmlessly on their cloaks. But as the day progressed, it began to come down harder and harder, until suddenly it was as if the fabric of the heavens had been torn asunder. Rain slashed down at them in coarse streams. In the distance, lightning flashed and thunder roared.

Alonin shivered miserably. His clothes were completely soaked through. Cold water ran streaming down his face, trickled down his chest, flowed along his legs and into his heavy boots.

Dalkin called to him, "If it rains any harder, we'll be breathing water!"

Alonin grinned weakly at his companion. Dalkin's curly red beard was plastered to his face, and a large drop of water hung comically from the tip of his nose. His shoulders were hunched vainly against the elements, and from time to time Alonin could hear him cursing under his breath.

Hours passed. At times the rain would slacken, almost cease, but then inevitably the torrent would begin with renewed fury. The thought of a warm fire and a dry change of clothes became a cherished dream of Alonin, something for which, he thought, had he been given the choice at that moment, he would have traded all of the magic gems and nebulous plans of revenge in the world. He remembered the warm hearths and the sheltered life of Lanfarran Castle with a fondness he would have previously found unimaginable. And he found himself wondering dismally what he was doing out there in the wilderness, what it was he thought he was accomplishing. *Vanity*, he thought, *it is all just vanity*. But even as that thought came into his mind, he rejected it. What he was doing had to be done. Had not wise Mernon himself told him that? And even if there were some way to avoid the fate binding him, he would not do it, for there was still his honor to consider.

Late in the afternoon the two men came over a ridge and down into a shallow valley. Alonin noticed that the trees in the valley were different—smaller, less mature— than those brooding giants to which he had grown accustomed. Scanning the woods, he soon saw why this was so, a scattering of dead, burnt-out tree trunks fingered out from between the smaller living growth. Long ago, he surmised, there must have been a fire which had decimated the valley, and the forest was only now beginning to heal itself.

"Look!" Dalkin said without warning.

"What?"

"Over there," Dalkin said, pointing across the valley.

Squinting, Alonin searched the area indicated. At first he saw nothing unusual and was about to tell his companion so; but then his eyes fell upon a slender gray tower rising from a rocky outcropping, almost invisible against the slate-colored sky.

"By Dinas!" Alonin said. "I would not have believed it. Who would be mad enough to build such a thing in the middle of the wilderness?"

"Who can say? Yet it is a fortunate thing for us that it is there, for it looks to be deserted, and it should provide us with shelter for the night."

Alonin paused, uncertain. "Do you think it wise to leave the road?"

"That all depends on whether you'd rather sleep in the mud tonight."

"You've made up my mind. Lead the way."

There was a faint, narrow trail running along the side of the valley, leading up to the tower. It was too slick and uneven to risk riding on, so the two men dismounted and led their horses carefully along it. The sticky mud adhered stubbornly to their boots, so that after a while they were walking, not on the soles of their boots, but on several thicknesses of caked earth. The two men slipped, skidded, slid along the treacherous trail, falling down with distressing regularity. Soon they were covered from head to toe with glistening patches of thick mud.

The prospect of having a protected and dry place to spend the night, however, so brightened their spirits that they did not greatly mind the hardship of the trail, and they remained in good cheer. They were like children, laughing when they fell.

The rain slackened, and finally stopped altogether by the time that they neared the tower. The clouds lightened, and at last the sun broke through.

"Wonderful," Dalkin said. "*Now* it stops. We're almost there."

The two shook their heads and laughed in the hapless manner of men showing their grudging appreciation for one of the universe's imcomprehensible jests, then struggled onward toward the tower.

By the time they managed to make their way up to the long jut of rock that supported the tower, night was not far off. The temperature was plunging rapidly. In his sodden garments Alonin was bitterly cold. He thrust his white, trembling hands under his armpits—virtually the only warm, dry place on his body—and stamped his numbed feet vigorously on the ground as he and Dalkin circled the rock, searching for a way to scale it.

On the other side of the rock they found the way up—a narrow staircase cut directly into the mottled stone. The two men stood silently at the base of the stair for a moment, peering upward.

"This seems to be the way," Alonin said finally.

Leaving their horses sheltered under a copse of pines, they climbed slowly up the steps, one man after the other. The way was difficult; the steps—little more than a series of hand- and footholds—were too shallowly cut for comfort and were choked with sand and crumbled rock. In order to avoid a misstep, which could be fatal, Alonin planted each foot with the utmost care before moving on to the next level.

Alonin was the first to reach the top. Waiting for Dalkin to join him, he examined the tower, now at close range.

It was very old, weathered and wind worn. Once, it had been opulently jacketed with white marble, but now most of this had fallen away, exposing common gray granite. Heaps of broken masonry lay nearby, suggesting to Alonin that there may have once been an appending building—or, perhaps, buildings.

"It seems you were right," he called back to Dalkin. "It does look to be deserted."

Dalkin clambered up to the top of the rock. He stood for a moment beside Alonin, eyeing the tower appraisingly. "Shall we explore the inside?"

Alonin nodded. They went forward together. The doors to the tower were wide open and half hanging off their rusty hinges. The men passed between them and into the gloomy chamber beyond, stopping just inside.

When his eyes had adjusted to the dim light, Alonin gazed slowly about the room. It was choked with debris. Years of accumulated dust and sand were heaped up against the curving walls. Broken furniture lay scattered and rotting across the dusty stone floor. Gauzy wisps of cobwebs drifted down from the ceiling.

"Not very promising, is it? Let's try upstairs," Dalkin said, indicating a stairwell not far from where they stood.

The second storey of the tower was in a slightly better state of preservation than the one below. It appeared to Alonin to have once been a workshop or study. The center of the room was dominated by a large rectangular table, upon which rested an assortment of strangely shaped vessels and instruments, the purpose of which Alonin could not even guess at. Beyond the far end of the table, there was a small wood-paneled alcove in which there was set an old rickety desk, heaped high with parchment scrolls and leather-bound books.

Curious as to the content of the books, Alonin skirted around the side of the table to the desk and bent down over it.

The years had wreaked a toll on the books; many of them had long since disintegrated into a coarse brown powder, and those that still survived were themselves deep into the slow process of decay. Alonin flipped open one of the less severely damaged volumes and studied its contents. The pages were brown and brittle with age; the ink was faded, making the writing all but illegible. Still, peering down through the gathering darkness, Alonin was able to make out enough of what was written there to determine that the book was a magical text of some sort. It occurred to him that he remembered seeing another copy of the same text in the royal library at Lanfarran, or one very similar.

Alonin remembered then that he had seen implements resembling those on the table behind him in Mernon's house. Had a magician dwelt in this tower once? Very likely, he decided. That would explain the structure's odd location, so far removed from civilization. But why had the magician left without his books and his tools?

Alonin heard Dalkin clear his throat pointedly behind him. He shut the book, sending a thick cloud of dust spiraling into the air. Turning, he said, "Ready to try the next floor, are you?"

Alonin fell in behind Dalkin, and they started to ease their way up the narrow staircase. The stone steps here were loose and wobbly, worn treacherously smooth, forcing them to proceed up them at a slow, even, cautious pace.

As Alonin was climbing the last step, he heard Dalkin, who had already reached the top, whisper, "*Cernon and Dinas!*"

Hearing the hushed note of horror in his companion's voice, Alonin froze for an instant, then quickly ascended the last step to the top. Dalkin stood motionless before him, a dark gray shadow in the semidarkness. As Alonin came to his side, the young lord's eyes caught a glimpse of something white on the floor a few paces ahead of him. He looked closer, and a chill spread suddenly through his body.

Human skeletons—a dozen of them and more—lay carelessly scattered across the floor between where Alonin stood and the open archway leading out onto the balcony. The young lord's eyes lingered morbidly for a long moment on the grisly scene, sweeping back and forth in shocked disbelief. From the varied conditions of the skeletons, Alonin guessed that they differed widely in age; some were so old that even the connective tissue had rotted away, leaving the spearate bones in confused heaps; others were fresh enough that bits of shriveled flesh still clung to them.

Alonin swallowed. "What . . . what could have done this?" he asked in a subdued voice.

"I don't know—but have you looked closely? Some of those bones have been gnawed on, and recently."

"Gods!" Alonin's hand instinctively sought out the pommel of his sword, as if strength could be drawn from the cold metal. "But how could they all have gotten here?" he asked, indicating the skeletons. "This place is a long way removed from anywhere; it doesn't seem likely that this many would find their way here by themselves."

"Perhaps someone—or as I begin to think it more likely, some*thing*—brought them here."

There was a dreadful silence, then Dalkin spoke again. "I just had an awful thought: what if whatever did this is still lurking in the vicinity?"

"Let's get out of here," Alonin said. "I suddenly have a very bad feeling about this place."

"I can imagine."

They turned and started hurriedly for the stairs. Just at

that moment, however, Alonin heard a fluttering noise behind him. His senses alerted, he turned back to the center of the room in time to see a bulky winged shape settle ominously onto the balcony.

"Dalkin!" Alonin cried in a low but urgent voice.

"What?"

Alonin pointed wordlessly at the misshapen creature that was by now sidling awkwardly into the room. He heard Dalkin's breath catch in horror.

The thing came slowly toward them, making a wet snuffling sound and weaving its head searchingly as it went. It walked upright like a man, but, even discounting the tapering batlike wings projecting from its back, there was no mistaking it for anything even remotely human. Its posture was hunched and twisted, and its stiff, gray, hairless hide shone with an unhealthy oily luster in the pale blue light streaming in behind it from the open archway. The tips of its elongated toes and fingers were armed with sharp, wicked-looking claws.

The creature came to the center of the room and stopped. Its slitted nostrils worked eagerly as its head twisted from side to side. The bobbing head finally centered on the portion of the room in which Alonin and Dalkin stood frozen in the shadows, and the creature made a happy cooing noise.

Alonin felt a chill traveling up his spine. It knew that they were there! It knew! His hand grappled briefly with his sword.

Then its eyes fell upon him.

They were a deep, luminous blue, totally unlike anything Alonin would have expected to find in that grotesque face. There was something fascinating, compelling about them. They drew his attention as lodestones draw iron. They glowed softly, softly, like twin pools of light, seeming to grow larger, seeming almost to spin in space.

Soothing sapphire light seeped into Alonin's skull, easing away all tension, all fear. His hand slipped from his sword. He felt as if he were floating outside his body. He did not, could not, move—not because he was paralyzed, but simply because the will to do so had been drained from him.

Nothing mattered but the light, the blue light, sparkling like a cool, clear stream.

Awareness lapsed—

—then returned.

The first thing that Alonin became aware of was a peculiar humming vibration emanating from a spot just below his throat, spreading in rhythmic waves throughout his body. It was an annoying, nettlesome sensation; it disturbed him. Alonin's consciousness rallied weakly around it, and his hand came up to touch his throat, the source of the vibration. The talisman, he thought dully, the talisman . . .

Alonin shook himself, and the intrusive light in his mind faded. The creature was no longer in front of him. Where then? Hearing a soft slithering sound to his right, he turned and saw that the thing was behind Dalkin, seductively sliding its taloned fingers across the red-haired man's shoulders. Cooing gently, it pressed its quivering body closer. There was something horrible, twisted, obscene in its embrace. It raised its head and its loose mouth gaped open, exposing a pair of moist, yellow fangs.

With a hoarse cry, Alonin drew his sword and sprang forward. With the creature pressed so close to Dalkin, he could not risk using the edge of the blade, so he drew back the sword as far as he could in the confined space and, with the flat of his blade, delivered a mighty blow to the creature's back.

Dalkin gave a soft grunt and pitched forward against the wall, while the creature separated from him and whirled on Alonin with an angry hiss, its mottled red maw gaping horribly. It flexed its sinewy wings and sprang into the air.

A cold, crawling terror in him, Alonin retreated hastily to the middle of the room, where he would have room to maneuver.

The winged creature followed, fluttering madly about his head, bobbing up and down, and rending the air with its razor-edged toe claws. Trying to keep the creature in view, Alonin turned and turned again as it circled him. Dodging the raking claws, he slashed blindly at it, missed. He turned again, slashed, dodged.

He lost sight of it for a moment; then, with a sharp spasm of despair, he heard the sound of its wings behind him. Whirling about, he saw it plunging down at him. He took a step backward; his heel came down on something—

a bone, perhaps—and his leg slid out from under him. With a startled cry, he tumbled to the floor, amidst the dust and the bones.

The creature was upon him in an instant. Its sinewy bulk struck him as he was trying to get to his knees; the impact made him collapse forward on his face. The hot reek of its breath grazed his cheek. A sharp, burning pain pierced his neck. Alonin gave a cry born equally of pain, fear, and revulsion, as he fought to free himself.

Then, abruptly, he heard the thing emit a high, keening shriek, and it rolled clumsily from his back.

Alonin struggled to his elbows. A few feet away, the thing was thrashing about wildly on the floor, howling piteously. Black blood gushed in gory spasms from it. Above it stood Dalkin, a dripping blade in his hand, watching the creature warily, a trace of disgust in his eyes.

The creature's convulsions grew steadily less, and its cries became a low moaning. Eventually, both sound and movement ceased.

With a shred of cloth, Dalkin wiped off his blade and sheathed it. He helped Alonin to his feet. "Are you all right?" he asked.

"It bit me," Alonin said, probing the moist wound at the back of his neck with the fingers of his right hand. He examined his fingers, and, seeing the mingling of blood and a milky yellowish fluid, he said, "I think it may have poisoned me."

"Can you travel?"

Alonin nodded. A dull ache was beginning in the back of his skull. He felt drained, exhausted.

"There might be more of those things around. We should get out of here while we can," Dalkin said, sounding almost apologetic.

"Yes." Alonin stooped to retrieve his sword, and his head filled with shooting red sparks.

The two men started down the stairs. By the time they reached the next floor down there was no doubt but that Alonin had been poisoned. His legs trembled with each step, and his whole being was filled with a profound nausea. The world tilted at crazy angles around him. The ache in his head continued to grow worse.

"How are you holding up?" Dalkin asked, clasping Alonin's shoulders with strong supporting hands. Through the growing fog, Alonin could hardly feel them.

Swallowing, Alonin said, "Fine. I'll be . . . all right."

They went down another flight of stairs, and then out into the chill night. The cold wind toyed with Alonin's damp garments. He shivered.

He half staggered to the edge of the rock, then stood staring down at the shallowly cut steps leading to where the horses were tethered. They seemed to be weaving snakelike before his eyes.

"I can't help you here," Dalkin said. "The way is too narrow. Can you make it alone?"

The words flowed by Alonin without meaning. He gaped at his companion for a moment while they washed up again on the lapping sea of his awareness. "Make it alone? Yes . . . yes, of course," he said finally. He was not so sure, though.

Slowly, he lowered himself over the lip of the rock and started down the steps. He had made less than a quarter of the way down when the world started to blink in and out in shimmering waves. He was losing consciousness, he realized. He bit his lip, tasting blood. He could not allow himself to black out—not now. A fall from this height would kill him. He could not let himself die; he had too much he had to do. He had to keep on. Concentrate, concentrate. One step at a time. Now, step. Step. The dragon. The Dylcaer. Keep on. Step, step. The dragon, kill, yes. Step.

Midway down the rock, Alonin had to stop. Black exhaustion weighed heavily on him, pressing him toward perilous darkness. He clung tightly to the stone step, his cheek pressed against the back of his grasping right hand. He did not think that he could make it. It was too far; he was too tired, too sick.

Alonin gave a shuddering sob of despair. He could not die this way. He was the last, the last Lord of Caladon. He could not let it all go for naught.

Alonin took a deep breath, tried to clear his mind. *All right*, he told himself, *you can make it. It's not that far. Just hold on for a few more minutes, hold on. Now, step.*

Painfully, he forced his leaden body to continue the descent. Down he went, one cautious step at a time. Gradually, he lost all track of time, of his surroundings, of any ambitions that he might have had or might have again. All that mattered was that he keep moving. His world narrowed to the demands of his descent, and all else faded from his mind. Step. Step. Step.

Then, after a seeming eternity, his foot touched ground, and he realized that he was safe. The feel of the earth beneath him seemed at that moment the most delicious sensation that he had ever experienced. It was wonderful, indescribable.

Still trembling with relief, he turned and started for the horses. His eyes filled suddenly with grainy redness, and he felt one leg buckling beneath him. He felt himself start to fall, and then his world collapsed into black and crimson, spinning.

8

CAUGHT in the folds of the swirling black cloak of unconsciousness, Alonin tossed fitfully on the narrow bed, unaware.

The fevered, clawing darkness that encased him stretched virtually unbroken from when it had first overtaken him at the base of the tower rock. Since then, it had lifted only enough for a few scattered, vague impressions of the world to leak through: a sense of motion, an uncomprehended babble of voices, discomfort. Only at one point did consciousness return strongly enough for him to become dimly aware that he was draped loosely across the back of a horse. He thought that he heard Dalkin speaking with someone, but he could not make out what was being said. Then darkness clamped down on him once more, blotting out everything but the dreams.

The dreams were fitful, disjointed, frightening. Everything in them was in some way twisted, unproportioned, grotesque. Familiar faces, made suddenly strange and threatening, leered at him from bizarre angles, their voices distorted into the harsh croakings of a raven, or into an echoing bass that made them seem to be coming from the bottom of a deep well. Scenes shifted and melted together alarmingly; fragments of his life, merging and mingling with fantastic images and shapes, washed up again and again on the dark shores of his consciousness, and then were swept away to whatever mental backwater from whence they had come.

After a long while the dreams slowed in their whirling dance; in this comparative stillness, he saw once again the vision he had first had beneath the ancient border stone of the downs of Yggrs. This time it came at him more disjointed and distorted than before, imparting a greater sense of menace. He saw again the knife glinting over him, held in that perfect white hand, saw it descending toward him. He felt the same terror as before. He cried out.

He felt a sudden coolness on his burning brow, and he heard a woman's soft voice speaking over him in a language he could not understand; there was a soothing quality to her words.

Alonin opened his eyes. The woman was sitting next to him on the edge of the narrow bed, dabbing his forehead with a cool, damp cloth. She was young—he could tell that much even by the pallid orange glow produced by the single candle guttering on the small table beside his bed. Her hair and her skin were both very dark; the hair was a sleek, glossy black; the skin was a warm, ruddy shade of brown. The features contained within her wide, heart-shaped face were delicate and finely wrought. The nose was short, straight, and rather wide; the eyes were large and almond-shaped; the lips were generous and nicely curved. The young woman leaned over Alonin to wipe his burning face with the rag, and he caught the scent of her perfume; it was a warm, spicy smell—cinnamon, cloves, and musk.

Alonin stirred slightly, and murmured, "Where am I?"

"You are awake?" the young woman asked, sounding surprised. Her voice was soft, deliberate, lightly accented. "How do you feel?"

"Terrible."

"Here, drink this," she said, taking up a cup and holding it to his lips. When he hesitated, she said, "It will help you."

He drank some of what was in the cup; it was bitter and it made his mouth feel drier than before.

"Now sleep; you are still weak."

"Don't want to. Bad dreams."

"You must," she said, smoothing back his damp hair.

"Where . . . ?"

"Do not worry. You are among friends."

"Dalkin . . . where is he?"

"Your friend? He is resting. No one expected you to wake so soon. You must sleep."

"Your name—what is your name?"

"Marda."

"Marda . . ."

Alonin's eyes fluttered shut. He slept. This time the darkness was complete; there were no dreams.

When next Alonin awoke it was morning, and he was alone. He felt better—his fever was gone—but he was still weak. A faint trace of a headache lingered at the back of his skull, and there was a dullness on his thoughts.

Realizing that he was naked under the blankets, Alonin suddenly wondered who had undressed him. He flushed slightly, thinking that it might have been the young woman, Marda. Then he smiled wryly at himself. What a thing to be worried about!

Propping himself up slightly, Alonin surveyed his surroundings. He discovered that he was not, as he had previously supposed, in the room of a small house. Rather, it appeared that he was in some kind of an enclosed wagon.

It was long and narrow, and was crammed with goods of all description: foodstuffs, bolts of fabric, pottery. The ceiling was set so low that a tall man would have to stoop as he walked through, if he wanted to keep from hitting his head on one of the many curved beams supporting the roof. The walls were of brightly lacquered wood, burnt orange in color. Through a window at the fore of the wagon, Alonin could see part of an attached platform where a driver would sit to guide the horses or oxen; beyond that he could see the end of another wagon.

Wagons, wagons, thought Alonin reflectively. That meant something to him, but it took him a few moments to figure out what it was. "Of course!" he exclaimed suddenly to himself, "the *Kirith-ber-Weirlon,* the People of the Wagons!"

The People of the Wagons; yes, that must be it. That would explain where he was. Alonin knitted his brows and thought. He knew little of the *Kirith-ber-Weirlon,* for they were a secretive and enigmatic folk. An ancient race of nomads, they had wandered Thaerdayne in the manner of their forefathers for countless centuries, their origins sunk in mystery. They shunned civilization, holding to their old ways even after the arrival of the more advanced Acynians and Icthans from across the sea.

The *Kirith-ber-Weirlon!* A superstitious thrill nibbled at

the edges of his mind; he remembered the stories told him during childhood in which the People of the Wagons were portrayed as an enchanted folk, soulless and willful, who would on occasion spirit away misbehaving children. He recalled that his nurse particularly delighted in telling such tales. From the vantage of these many years later, he recognized these as fanciful inventions used to obtain obedience from a wayward child. Still, he thought of the *Kirith-ber-Weirlon* with a mixture of wonderment and fear— showing, he reflected, that though the lessons of early youth may be exposed by adult reasoning, yet they still leave an imprint.

Alonin's ponderings were abruptly interrupted by the sound of the small door opening on the other side of the wagon. Marda entered, carrying a shallow copper bowl. She wore a long blue skirt, very full and gathered at the waist, a white blouse with an elaborately embroidered yoke, a short maroon vest with black piping along the edges. A heavy silver pendant of intricate and unusual workmanship rode between her small, high breasts.

Marda smiled, still standing by the door with the wide-lipped bowl in her hands. "You are awake again," she said. "Are you feeling better now?"

"Yes, much."

"This is good, very good. You are lucky that your path brought you here to my people, for otherwise you would have died of the evil sickness that afflicted you. Even so, there were those among the wise women of the council who did not expect you to survive the bite of the *Urdaeth*. I am pleased that you proved them wrong." She came forward, placed the bowl down on the table beside Alonin, and sat on the edge of the bed. Laying the back of her hand on Alonin's brow, she said, "Your fever has broken."

"Yes," Alonin said. Her closeness to him stirred a part of him that he knew he must keep submerged. To distract himself, he said, "An *Urdaeth*, is that what that thing in the tower was?"

She shrugged. "That is what my people have always called it. Lean forward; I must cleanse the wound."

Gathering the covers about his chest, Alonin did as he was told, while Marda plucked a dripping cloth from the copper bowl and pressed it gently to the back of his neck.

The cloth was pleasantly warm and it smelled of fresh grasses and pine.

"How does that feel?" asked Marda.

"Stings. What is it?"

"An infusion of *kael* and other healing herbs."

After a pause, Marda asked, "Are you an *Ar-kaeth*—a man of magic?"

"No."

"Your friend, then?"

"No. Why do you ask?"

"I know of no other way to account for you being able to defeat the *Urdaeth*. It was very strong in magic, able to place a dread glamour on its victims, fogging their minds and making them blind to danger. We of the *Kirith-ber-Weirlon* have our own magic, so fortunately we could protect ourselves from it, yet we were helpless to destroy it or drive it forth. And still the *Urdaeth* sometimes preyed on those of us who wandered too far from the rest. Yet you and your friend entered the creature's place of strength, and not only were you able to leave with your lives—which in itself has never before been done—but you were able to end its threat forever. How you could do this is a matter of great curiosity among my people."

"It is easy to explain," Alonin said. "You see, I wear a powerful talisman, which was given me by a great wizard—an *Ar-kaeth*?—that fortunately was able to protect me from the creature's power, else I imagine that my bones would also be reposing in the tower of the *Urdaeth*. And even with my talisman, I would be dead now, were it not for Dalkin, my companion."

"I see. Yes. Fortune does indeed smile on you."

"Tell me, do your people know what the *Urdaeth* was, where it came from?"

"We have our stories, but they disagree as to this. According to the old ones, a man strong in dark enchantments once dwelt in the tower. Some say that he raised the creature from some black nether region beyond the ken of normal folk, and that it turned on him and destroyed him; others say that the *Urdaeth* is really the magician himself, transformed by some strange sorcery gone wrong."

Seeing the creature in his mind's eye with terrible clarity, Alonin shuddered. "I can't see how that—that—monstrous *thing* could ever have been human."

"Perhaps it wasn't. It is only one story. You may sit back now; I am finished."

As Alonin was settling back into bed, there came a muted rapping at the door. "Come in," Marda said.

The door opened; Dalkin thrust his red-bearded face into the wagon. Seeing Alonin, he grinned widely. "So you *are* alive," he said, climbing up into the wagon. "I had begun to wonder. So, how are you feeling?"

"Not bad, considering. Weak . . . A little tired . . ."

"*You're* tired!" Dalkin said in mock outrage, wrinkling up his brow in a comical display of incredulity. "Ha! Let me tell you about what *my* night was like, struggling through the mud and muck and whatnot, while you, my friend, remained blissfully unconscious, utterly gone to the world! Why, you weren't even good company!"

Alonin snorted petulantly, picking up the spirit of the thing. "I would have gladly traded places with you!"

"Yes, I expect that you would have," Dalkin said in a more subdued voice. "Well, you're getting better, that's the important thing." He smiled slyly and winked. "Personally, I attribute your extraordinary recovery to the loveliness of your nurse here."

Marda colored slightly, momentarily dropping her gaze. She said to Alonin, "I'll leave you with your friend for a while. Don't let him tire you too much. When I come back, I will bring you some food. Can you eat?"

"I can always eat."

She smiled. "That is a good trait in a man." She got up from the edge of the bed and left the wagon.

When she was gone, Alonin said, "You embarrassed her. That wasn't necessary."

"I did, didn't I? Well, she is a pretty one, isn't she?"

Alonin sighed. "Yes."

"I tell you, I would be tempted to make a try for her, if she didn't like you so much."

"She doesn't," Alonin protested.

"Are you kidding? She's mad for you, boy. Surely you can see that."

Alonin decided to evade the subject entirely. "Have you been keeping yourself busy?"

"Indeed, yes. I'm having a wonderful time. I can do no wrong with these people, we having gotten rid of the—ah—I forget what it's called—"

"The *Urdaeth*."

"Aye, that's it. Apparently they have been plagued by it for as long as anyone can remember. They are grateful to be rid of it at last."

"That's good, anyway."

"Aye," Dalkin said. He patted Alonin on the arm. "Well, I had better be going. That Marda will have my hide, I have no doubt, if I stay too long."

"All right," Alonin said. "I *am* a little fatigued. I think I can sleep for a while."

"I'll drop in on you later." Dalkin got up and turned to go.

"Dalkin."

"Yes?"

"I want to thank you for taking care of me last night."

"Ah, well, think nothing of that. It was the least I could do. After all, I was the idiot who convinced you to go to the tower in the first place. In a way, I was responsible for your condition."

"Mmm. You're right. I take back my gratitude."

Dalkin chuckled. "Very funny. Sleep well."

Alonin slept sporadically through the rest of the day. Marda came in several times during his scattered periods of wakefulness to redress his wound, and once to bring him a brimming bowl of fragrant broth. Even though his hands were still unsteady, Alonin insisted on feeding himself, being disinclined to be treated like an infant by Marda, for reasons that he found perturbing.

He kept trying to distract himself from her attractiveness. He knew that he could not press suit for her, for he had his mission to consider, and she could have no part in that. And it was not in him to attempt a more casual romance. *No*, he told himself, *it is best that I put aside such thoughts.*

Then he thought: *it is foolish to worry about this. I doubt if she has any interest in me, other than as my nurse, despite what Dalkin says. Soon I will be recovered; I will ride away from here, and all of this will be forgotten.*

Night came; he slept once more, and this time it was a

long stretch of darkness that ended only with the light of the next day.

Waking, he discovered that he had slept away the worst of his fatigue. He sat up and stretched. He was bored with staying in bed. Getting up, he found his clothes folded neatly at the foot of his bed and dressed. His muscles felt tight and stiff. Wrapping his cloak about his shoulders, he left the wagon.

The camp of the *Kirith-ber-Weirlon* was set in a wide oval glade, which bulged from the side of a slow, winding river. The camp consisted of a loose circle of eight wagons, painted in varying colors, and a few low canvas tents strung between the wagons, their sides quivering in the light breeze. White wisps of smoke curled lazily from the single stone-rimmed fire pit in the center of the camp.

The livestock—oxen, horses, goats—were kept penned beyond the circle of wagons, in a crude corral made of bleached wood and rope. Among them, Alonin saw his own horses.

Alonin saw neither Dalkin nor Marda in the camp. At the other end of the compound, however, he noticed a small knot of young women—who, upon seeing him, fell back upon one another, giggling and gabbling in their own language, which sounded to his ears as soft, quick, and light as the rilling of a small stream.

Alonin gave them a smile. They returned the smile; some waved. Embarrassed by his sudden status as a curiosity, he turned away and started a red-faced search for his gear.

A brief examination of the area found his possessions stacked neatly beneath the wagon whose shelter he had enjoyed for the last several days. He dug through the packs until he found what he was looking for—a cake of brownish soap and a small towel. Flipping the towel over his shoulder, he started for the river.

Alonin found that he was weaker than he thought; the short walk left him short of breath and slightly dizzy. He stood for a short time on the sandy bank of the river, watching the flow of the water until he was recovered enough to go on. He continued downstream, halting finally at a place he deemed secluded enough for him to be able to carry out his ablutions without fear of disturbance.

Squatting by the side of the river, Alonin gazed into the bright, reflective surface of the water. Seeing his own thin, solemn face staring back at him, he noted with a combination of satisfaction and dismay the weariness rimming his large dark eyes. Those eyes, he felt, were no longer the eyes of the sheltered, inexperienced boy he had been, but those of the man he was becoming. He felt a pride that was tainted by a heavy nostalgic regret.

Alonin dipped his hands into the water; his image distorted and disappeared. Splashing his face vigorously, he felt the skin draw tight across the underlying bones. He manipulated the lump of brown soap in his wet hands, working up a rich lather, which he massaged into the coarse stubble of his beard. Removing his knife from his belt, he carefully ran the sharp blade over the angular planes of his jaw. When his face was shorn of hair, he replaced the dagger and washed off the remaining soap.

The rest of his wash was performed in a more cursory fashion. He would have enjoyed a proper bath, but the water was too cold for him to want to risk it in his weakened condition. He stripped to the waist, laying aside his dark blue doublet and his white linen shirt, and rubbed handfuls of water over his naked torso. Then, shivering, he dried himself thoroughly and dressed hurriedly. He began to feel more himself after that.

He spread his cloak out upon the ground as a blanket and sat on the river bank, his back to a tree trunk. He contemplated the gray flow of the water, while his thoughts turned on nothing, nothing at all.

His reverie was finally broken by the sound of someone calling his name. He turned his gaze upstream and saw that it was Marda. He grinned and waved to her.

It seemed to Alonin that she smiled back, though she was too far away to be able to tell for certain. He settled back, watching Marda traverse the long stretch of river bank separating them. There was a soft, fluid grace to her walk that he could not help but admire.

"Good morning," Marda said as she came to stand a few paces before Alonin. He detected a certain crossness in her tone, which surprised him. "Good morning," he replied.

"What are you doing out of bed?"

Alonin paused, regarding her, then shrugged. "I was bored. I felt the need to be up and around."

"Bored. Fine—you remember that if you get sick again because of this."

"Don't worry, I won't. I feel much better today."

"Well . . ." she said uncertainly, running the moist pink tip of her tongue over her upper lip. "May I sit with you?"

"Of course you may." Alonin got up and made room for her on the cloak. Marda lowered herself down, gathering her long skirt about her legs, and Alonin sat beside her.

At length, Marda said, "I'm sorry if I sounded . . . harsh. When I found that you were not in your bed, I was worried."

"I thank you for your concern—really. It's nice. But, as you can see, I am taking things very easy here. After all, there is not all that much difference between lying in bed and sitting here by the river, is there?"

"I suppose not," she conceded.

"And I really do feel fine. I am quite myself again, thanks to your care."

They fell silent. The river flowed ceaselessly by, making a low, rushing sound. Caught in the current, a bobbing, half-submerged log made its way downstream. Alonin watched it until it disappeared around a bend in the river.

He slowly became aware that Marda was staring at him, a complete singularity of concentration in her eyes. "What is it?" he asked.

"You are no normal man, are you?"

"What do you mean?"

"There are many ways of seeing a thing. Most people see only the obvious, the surface appearance, and even then not all of that. My people have developed a discipline for looking beneath the surface to that reality that shapes the physical. As yet, I have little skill at this, and one of the wise women of the council could tell you more, yet I do see a dark power in you, a great purpose burning in your soul."

"Your eyes are indeed keen."

"I am correct, then?"

"You are. I have such a purpose."

Marda paused for a moment before saying, "I cannot help but wonder as to what this may be, that it burns so fiercely in you. It fascinates me, though it is also a little frightening."

"It is a complicated matter, long in the telling."

She smiled with a delicacy that was almost shyness, and said softly, "I would hear it if you would tell it." Her eyes were like pools of night, yet they shone with a wonderful glow that lit a fire of gladness in Alonin's heart.

Returning her smile, he said, "How could I refuse such a request? Very well, then, I hope you have time for a lengthy tale."

"All day."

He laughed. "I trust that it won't take that long."

"How sad," Marda murmured when Alonin had finished.

"Yes," Alonin said, "sad." Just talking about it had brought a heaviness to sit on his soul. His face was pale and pinched; he gazed gloomily at the river, silently rededicating himself to his quest. From the corner of his eye, he could see Marda watching him.

"I'm sorry if it was painful to speak of this," she said. "I did not mean to make you unhappy."

Alonin gave a dour smile. "I am often unhappy, and often for no reason at all."

Marda shifted uneasily. "You are very shy, aren't you—very . . ." Her voice trailed off; her eyes sought the sky while she seemed to search for a word. She made a gesture of withholding. "Very much inside yourself?"

"Shy?" he said uncomfortably. "I don't know. I've never thought about it before. But . . . yes, in a way, I suppose I am."

Alonin gave a curious glance at Marda; she was staring at the ground, her eyes narrowed with concentration. Suddenly, with grave expression, she looked up at him, searched his face, and reached out and lightly touched his cheek. Without thought, Alonin drew back slightly. Marda did not seem offended, nor did her gaze falter. "Do you like me?" she asked.

"Why, yes. Of course I do."

"No. You know what I mean."

His heart quickening, Alonin let his breath out slowly.

He was confused. He could not seem to find the words to answer her.

"You need not answer if you don't want to; I'll understand."

"No," he said. "Forgive me, but I am just a little overwhelmed. This is difficult for me. I am . . . attracted to you, if that is what you mean. But I can't let myself be."

"Why? I do not understand."

"You know my mission," he said. "I could offer you nothing."

"I ask for nothing. Nothing except what is here and now." She touched his hand.

The last shred of Alonin's resistance fell away with an abruptness that he found surprising. There was a hollow rushing in his head, a warmth spreading through his body. He drew close to Marda and kissed her. Her lips were like silk, and their taste was sweet.

After a time they drew apart, staring into each other's eyes. Marda shook back her flowing raven hair. "Are you sure that you are well enough for this?" she said softly. "Perhaps we should wait."

"Practicality at this late date?" he said, smiling. He felt laughter in every cell of his being. "Oh, yes—I feel fine, better than fine. I feel wonderful."

She smiled, yet her eyes still dwelled on Alonin with that solemn, tender intensity that made him feel that he stood at the very center of the world. He gently took her face in his hands, searching it lovingly, noting with a kind of wonder each perfect feature. He drew her to him, and drank once more of her sweetness.

It was dusk; the pines lining the opposing bank of the river were dark and robbed of color. Alonin lay upon the sandy earth, Marda's warmth pressed against his side. He felt sleepy. He yawned.

"Are you tired?" Marda asked.

"No, not tired. *Very* relaxed, though."

She giggled prettily. "Good. So am I." She sighed roundly, and commenced playing with a lock of Alonin's hair.

Alonin smiled up at the darkening sky—at the universe in general, and at that small corner of it in particular.

Then a thought occurred to him, and the smile faded from his face.

"Marda?"

"Yes?"

"There is something I must say."

"Yes?"

"As much as I may come to want to, I cannot stay with you. Soon I will have to leave, and where I must go I cannot take you."

"I know. Don't you think I knew beforehand?"

"I don't know. I had to be sure. I feel . . . guilty, I guess."

"Don't. I know that there is nothing in this world that lasts forever, not life, even, and certainly not love. This may be the principal wisdom of my people; it is what our life teaches us. We learn to accept things as they come to us."

"That is a lesson that we Acynians can never learn, I fear," Alonin said. "Always we strive to order the world to our liking, and it is a bitter thing when we find we cannot . . . Well, I just wanted to make certain that you understood."

"I do. Now let's not speak of it anymore."

"All right."

They lay together wordlessly for a time, life against life, warmth against warmth, watching the slow advance of night. The river gurgled darkly by, and the birds in the trees made their melancholy nighttime cries.

From the direction of the camp the sharp peal of a horn split suddenly through the dusky air. Startled, a flight of doves burst from the underbrush and veered off over the trees. Faint and faraway, a vague mingling of shouts and laughter came to Alonin.

Marda stirred and sat up abruptly. Leaning forward, she slipped on her shoes.

"What is it?" Alonin asked. "What's happening?"

"The hunters return. It sounds as if they were successful. We will feast tonight!" Straightening her garments, Marda rose to her feet. "Your friend is among them. Come!" She extended her hand to him.

Alonin got up with a grunt, gathering up his cloak, and took her outstretched hand. They started off along the river's edge, Marda setting a brisk pace and Alonin lumbering along a little behind her.

When they reached the camp, it was aflurry with activity; people milled about the wagon-enclosed circle, talking and laughing with cheerful animation. Most of them had gravitated to the long wooden pole from which a dead stag was suspended by its thong-bound hooves. Several of the hunters pointed to the stag and made spreading gestures with their hands, indicating, Alonin supposed, its great size.

"I will see you in a little while," Marda said, giving Alonin's hand a little squeeze. "Enjoy yourself in the meantime." She set off lightly through the confusion.

With a mixture of admiration and bemusement, Alonin watched Marda walk away from him. Then, finally losing sight of her, he started wandering across the busy encampment, idly looking for Dalkin.

In the center of the circle, a vast pile of firewood had been laid; a red, sparking torch was put to it, and long tongues of flame lapped greedily through the layered branches. Meanwhile, the stag was shorn of its hide and dressed, and the carcass was spitted and propped up over what was by now a glowing bed of coals.

By this time, however, Alonin had succeeded in locating Dalkin. The red-haired man was, as Alonin might have expected, wholeheartedly involving himself in the festivities. His arms about two women—one young, one not so young—he was engaging in an odd, hopping impromptu dance, laughing merrily.

Seeing Alonin, he broke from his dance and came toward him, grinning broadly. "Ho! You're out of bed. Good, very good!"

"That is quite a stag you brought in."

"Not me. I just stood by and watched. You should see these people hunt. There is not their equal in all the Acynian Kingdoms!"

"I'm sorry to have missed it."

"Oh, well. We can all share in the spoils."

Just then, Alonin felt a pair of arms come around from behind him, encircling his middle. He smelled the familiar scent of cinnamon and cloves. Alonin turned slightly and saw Marda's smiling face, lit with the ruddy glow of the fire.

"Surprised?" she asked.

"Well, what's this? Marda, isn't it?" Dalkin beamed, his eyes sparkling mischievously. He said to Alonin: "Sick or not, you seem to be doing well enough for yourself, my friend. Well indeed."

Alonin felt a flush come to his cheeks. He grunted gruffly in an attempt to offset the effect.

"I have just come from Loness," Marda said. "She is Oldest. She wishes to see you."

Marda's reverential tone told Alonin that Loness, whoever she was, held a high position of respect among her people, so he agreed at once to see her. Marda set off through the crowd, and Alonin followed.

As they went, Marda said, "I didn't embarrass you in front of your friend, did I?"

"Not at all," he said with a weak grin. "Actually, he seemed delighted."

Slowly they threaded their way across the circle. The festive atmosphere was becoming contagious; Alonin felt a peculiar buzz of excitement coursing through him, a tingling glow of energy behind his eyes, a racing of his heart.

Indicating an old woman sitting by herself in a high, wing-backed chair of wood and leather, Marda whispered, "That is Loness."

The old woman sat motionless in her chair, observing the proceedings with an implacable dignity. Her wrinkled face was as hard and dark as old oiled leather. Deep crescents of gray ran beneath the heavy pouches under her eyes, and her cheekbones were sharp peaks in her sunken cheeks. Her hair was grizzled with gray, and was drawn neatly back and fixed behind her head with a silver clasp.

"Wait here for a moment," Marda said. Going to the old woman's side, she leaned over and conferred with her in low tones. Loness turned her head slowly to Alonin. She raised one hand, beckoning to him with a two-fingered gesture. "Come here, young man."

Alonin came forward. Uncertain of the proper etiquette with which to treat the woman, he went down on one knee before her and bowed deeply. "Oldest," he said deferentially.

"That is not necessary, young man," Loness said, "Although your respect does speak well for you. Rise, let me

look on you." Either she knew the language of the Acynians less well than did Marda, or else she was accustomed
to speaking very deliberately; she spoke slowly, carefully,
giving each word equal weight, as if she were considering
each syllable before she spoke it.

Alonin rose and stood by stiffly, while Loness regarded
him piercingly, her dark eyes glinting in the firelight. Her
gaze made Alonin slightly uncomfortable; he was not used
to being scrutinized with such unabashed intensity.

"Yes," she said finally, as if coming to a decision. "I see
much unhappiness in you, much pain."

Alonin started to speak, to protest, but he could not induce the words to come. He remained silent.

Loness continued, "Yes, much unhappiness. I read the
flames of your soul. There is a dire *sintas*, a—" She turned
abruptly to Marda and said, "A *sintas*; what is the word?"

"Fate, destiny . . ."

The old woman's hard gaze came back to Alonin. "A
dire fate is upon you. There is trouble before you, great
trouble, perhaps death." Her heavy-lidded eyes drew shut
for a moment and her brows lowered with concentration.
"Beware of what you want," she said in a husky voice.

"What do you mean?"

"I see what I see," Loness said, subsiding. "That is all.
Think you on the meaning."

"I will."

Loness shifted slightly, and the chair groaned protest-
ingly under her. "You are well enough to travel?"

"Within limits."

"Good. Your companion says that you are traveling
through the mountains to the sea. This is so?"

"Yes. Why?"

"The day after tomorrow we will be leaving this place. If
you wish, you may travel with us, for our path will be the
same as yours until the mountains. It will be safer for you."

Alonin wrinkled his brow. "How so?"

The faintest flicker of a smile crossed her face. "None
dare molest the *Kirith-ber-Weirlon*—or those who enjoy
our protection. Our curse is widely and justly feared."

"I see. Well, then, I thank you for your offer—and I
accept."

"Good. Then you may rejoin the celebration."

Alonin gave a slight bow, backed away a pace, then turned and started to make his way through the rowdy celebrants, Marda hanging on his arm. He felt a thick bemusement on him. He could not shake the feeling that the woman he had just met knew things about him that he did not know himself.

The crowd grew suddenly quiet; Alonin noticed that everyone was looking to the center of the circle. Following their gazes, he saw a man in a flowing red shirt, a battered old lute hanging about his neck by a wide leather strap.

"It is Orda," said Marda. "He is going to play."

Twisting a wooden knob at the top of the instrument's neck, the man plucked experimentally at the strings. He frowned, turned another knob, plucked again. Then, apparently satisfied, he looked up with a grin, and called out something to the crowd. They responded with laughter.

The man bent down his head, fitted his fingers to the strings, and began to play. The song came slow and simple at first, sounding sad and sweet—but as it continued, it began to change, growing both in speed and complexity, until the musician's fingers were flying furiously over the instrument. The man threw back his head and began to sing in a warm, sandy tenor.

Now, at scattered points throughout the audience, people started to clap their hands in time with the music. The clapping spread rapidly through the crowd, until it embraced everyone, including Alonin.

The song finally ended in a wild flurry of strumming. The rhythmic clapping gave way to enthusiastic applause. His face glowing happily, the musician bowed to his audience, then stood by until the applause subsided.

The musician then exhorted something to the crowd in their shared language, and received good-natured hoots in return. He smiled crookedly at them, and started to play again.

This time all of the *Kirith-ber-Weirlon* took up the song, singing loudly, boisterously. The camp, the glade, the surrounding woods echoed with the sound of their joined voices.

Marda leaned toward Alonin. "You are not singing," she said.

"I don't know the song," he answered. "I don't know the words."

"But it is not the song that matters—it is the singing!"

Alonin gave her a sharp sidelong look, then laughed. He started to sing. One more voice was lost amongst the rest.

9

ALONIN drew his horse over to the side of the road and sat watching as the long line of wagons rolled past him, rocking and creaking as they went. He looked off to his right, where the harsh, jagged-topped mountains rose magnificently over the thick canopy of trees. Above them, fluffy, lemon-colored clouds sailed serenely by.

The last wagon rolled past him, spitting broken stones from under its wheels, and Alonin coaxed his horse forward once again, catching up with the rest of the line.

It had taken them almost two weeks to reach the mountains—twice as long as it would have taken Alonin and Dalkin, had they ridden alone. Far from begrudging the lost days, however, Alonin felt the time too brief. He liked the *Kirith-ber-Weirlon* and their life. He had grown used to them, had come to depend on their presence. It filled him with sadness to think that soon they would no longer be there for him.

Alonin turned his eyes once more to the mountains; they stood there immovable and immutable. Running an idle hand through his hair, Alonin considered his chances of making a successful crossing through the mountains. There had been some snow in the higher peaks, but not much. If he could get across before any more fell, he would not have much trouble. If not . . . Well, then, it would be more difficult, but he would still have to chance it. His only other option was to bend his way far to the south and find a crossing there—but that would take him a hundred leagues or more out of his way, through some very wild and dangerous territory.

Looking ahead, he saw that Dalkin had stopped by the side of the road. Spurring his horse to a faster pace, Alonin joined him there.

"The crossroads are about a half an hour ahead," Dalkin said, his hands crossed loosely over the front of his saddle. "We will be making camp there."

"It's still early in the day."

Dalkin shrugged. "I suppose that they decided to stop there for the night out of deference to us." He smiled wistfully. "They're good people; they lead a good life. Had I an extra lifetime, I might spend it riding with them. The gods know, I could do worse."

"Much worse."

"Oh, well, nothing lasts forever, as they are fond of saying. Come, let's ride on together—they're getting ahead of us."

As they rode on, Alonin said, "How do you estimate our odds of getting across the mountains?"

"Hard to say," Dalkin said, shaking his head. "We'll just have to see how our luck holds out."

Sitting on the edge of a massive outcropping of volcanic rock, pitted and gnarled from the violence of its creation, Alonin and Marda gazed down on the newly set up camp of the *Kirith-Ber-Weirlon*. The sky was clear, and lightly washed with orange. A vast sea of pines, dark with the coming twilight, stretched into the misty west for as far as they could see.

"Such a lovely evening!" Marda murmured.

Alonin agreed. It was fitting, he felt, that their last night together should be as this one was—clear and somber, full of fragile beauty and dying fire.

Alonin tightened his arm about Marda's slender waist. There was a melancholy mood on him. He felt terribly alone, isolated—a feeling that no amount of human contact could change. He wished that he could forget his quest and be as other men, living life as it came to him.

"We should be getting back soon," Alonin said. "It will be dark soon; they will be worried."

"I know."

A long moment passed, in which they sat silent and unstirring, both huddled beneath Alonin's dark cloak. Finally Alonin said, "Marda, these last weeks with your people—with you—it has been—" He broke off, scowling, for the words sounded suddenly stilted and false to him.

A lazy, subdued smile passed over Marda's face. "I know what you mean. It has been good for me, too."

Alonin sighed. "If only I did not have to go; if only I could stay."

"But you must go, so it is useless to discuss it."

"You are right—as always."

Marda stirred. "Come, let us start back," she said, rising to her feet.

Alonin stood, gently grasped Marda by her shoulders, and pulled her to him. He reached out and cupped her dark, lovely face in his hard and clumsy-feeling hands. Leaning forward, he lightly brushed her soft lips with his own. Marda, gazing solemnly at him, pressed his hand more firmly against her smooth cheek. Then, abruptly, she smiled, taking his hand.

"Come," she said.

In the bitter early morning cold, Alonin stood by his horse, pounding his gloved hands together in an effort to keep the blood flowing to them. The wagons of the *Kirithber-Weirlon* were already lined up and ready to depart. The shouts of the men making the final preparations sounded thin and distant in the chill wintry air.

Old Loness stood solemnly before him, looking like a small, hunched doll; Marda stood to one side of her.

"We part ways at last, O lord of a distant land."

"Aye," Alonin said. "I would that it were not so. The great hospitality of your people makes one wish never to leave."

Loness accepted the compliment with a stately inclination of her head. "It is always a pleasure to serve one such as you, outland lord. Farewell."

She drew her frail old body into a more formal posture, and she intoned, "May the road before you be an easy one, and may it always run true. May you find contentment along the way, and wisdom, and may you go in peace."

"Thank you, Oldest. Farewell."

Loness turned about slowly, nodding briefly to Dalkin, who stood readying his horse a few yards away. Limping slightly, she went to one of the wagons and disappeared inside.

"We have only a moment," Marda said, coming forward

to take Alonin's two hands in her own warm grasp. "The wagons are almost ready to go."

"So little time, so much to say," Alonin said. "I want you to know that I shall always think of you, no matter where my trail should lead me."

"And I you. Farewell, my lord. I do not think that we shall ever see each other again." She shivered from the cold, and perhaps from something else as well.

Alonin pressed Marda's small body to him and he kissed her. "Farewell, my love," he said softly in her ear.

A shout came from the train of wagons. Marda broke from Alonin's embrace. "It is time. Good luck, my lord. Good luck and good-bye."

She turned abruptly and ran lightly from him, back to the waiting wagons of the *Kirith-ber-Weirlon*, her thin skirts flowing in the wind.

Alonin stood motionless, his hands bunched down at his sides, watching as she sprung up onto the driving platform of one of the wagons and sat down on the bench beside a small, sun-weathered man. She did not look back.

A cry went up, one that Alonin knew well from his wandering with the *Kirith-ber-Weirlon;* the wagons started to roll away slowly, their wheels crunching against the stone-strewn road.

Alonin watched the train rolling away into the south, feeling immobilized, as if his feet were mated with the thick, armored crust of the earth.

"Good-bye," he said softly.

"Well," Dalkin said in a slightly subdued voice, "shall we ride?"

"Aye. Aye, that we shall!" Alonin turned quickly to his mount, fitted his foot to the stirrup, and boosted himself up into the saddle. The two men wheeled off toward the mountains, the wind whistling in their faces.

At the top of the first crest they halted and swung their horses around to face in the direction from which they had come. Seeming as small as a child's toys, the wagons of the *Kirith-ber-Weirlon* were lurching away into the forest, on to newer and fresher hunting and grazing lands. The road they followed turned sharply, and the wagons began, one by one, to disappear behind a dense screen of pines.

Alonin suppressed a shiver as the last wagon turned the

bend in the road and vanished. He was left gazing down on the empty, unmoving forest. He bestirred himself finally. "Onward," he said hoarsely.

The narrow, winding highway that the two riders followed into the harsh, pine-studded mountains was old, older than were the Acynians in Thaerdayne. It was generally thought to have been built by the ancient Agnari, that mysterious race of sorcerers, whose origins were whispered to have been beyond the world.

Few in numbers but rich in power, the Agnari had once ruled over both this land and the lost Western Lands of Ictha and Acynia. They had built and striven mightily for a time, mating with Alonin's race, and then finally fading out as a pure line and living on only in their works and in the veins of younger Acynians. These many centuries later, the Agnari were still regarded by many with a superstitious awe. Some even said that they were gods.

The highway twisted up into the misty blue heights, winding sometimes between the peaks, at other times cutting directly along the sharp inclines of the mountains. The road was beginning to succumb to the vast weight of years. Everywhere it was worn; in places it was crumbling away to dust. Given its immense age, however, the wonder was not that it was decaying but that it still stood at all.

As Alonin and Dalkin ventured farther into the forbidding upper reaches of the mountains, the cold grew increasingly bitter. Icy winds roved tirelessly through the knife-edged peaks, whipping into the young men's faces, and piercing through their heavy winter clothing, causing a constant pain that alternated between numbing and burning.

A week passed, then another; the two men lost track of time. Each day was colder than the last; each day the trail grew harder; each day they awoke a little more weary. Alonin longed for the shelter of the meanest inn, but he knew that there would be no more inns until they reached the far side of the mountains, if ever they did.

Throughout this time they could still count themselves fortunate, for at least the sky remained clear, and no snow fell. As they began working their way up the loftiest spine of the mountains, however, a dark mass of clouds began to boil ominously out of the north. Dalkin was first to notice the storm clouds, and he pointed them out to Alonin. "Just look at that—it seems our luck has finally run out."

The clouds drew across the sky like a dirty woolen blanket; by nightfall they covered all the heavens. No snow fell that night, and Alonin prayed by all the gods he knew that it would continue thus. But either the gods were not listening, or else they did not greatly care for his prayers, for with the dawn came the first fluttering flakes of snow, drifting lazily from the heavy, steel-gray sky.

The snow continued light and inconstant throughout the morning and into the early afternoon; most of it that fell was devoured by the residual warmth contained within the hard crust of the earth. Alonin continued to be apprehensive, but he began to hope that perhaps it would grow no worse.

He was wrong. As the cloud-shrouded sun was sinking below the low peaks they had left behind them, the snow began to fall fast and heavy. Blown by the sweeping mountain winds, the fallen snow whipped about to collect in thick drifts across the road.

The two men pressed ahead, but finally it became too dangerous to continue on; they were forced to make camp in a small rock hollow in the side of the mountain, to await the storm's end.

The snow continued unabated for several hours, then gradually tapered off, and finally stopped. An icy rain followed briefly; a numbing blanket of cold descended.

The two men could do nothing but sit silently by the side of their small fire, its size restricted by the amount of fuel they had carried with them that day. Even without speaking, both of them could be only too aware of the trouble now facing them. They were at almost the precise center of the mountains, with the distance that they had already come nearly as great as that which was before them. There could be no turning back now. If the storm should begin anew—or worsen—they would be trapped, and then it would only be a matter of time before they died of starvation or exposure.

Weary from the day's struggle against the elements, and firmly depressed by the knowledge of their predicament, Alonin and Dalkin wrapped themselves in their blankets and tried to find solace in the dark embrace of sleep. But the raw cold made sleep all but impossible. At three separate times during the night, the fire having burned low, Alonin was awakened by the chattering of his own teeth. Each time he shuddered, threw a few sticks of wood on the dying fire, and then burrowed deeper into his tangled pile of blankets.

When Alonin awoke the next morning, he found that the sky was less threatening; though still overcast, it seemed lighter than it had the day before, and the cloud mass was breaking up in patches, allowing an occasional glimpse of sky to show through.

Alonin pulled himself from his heap of blankets, shivering. He called to Dalkin to awake. The red-haired man answered with a mumbled curse, then sat up and looked blearily around him.

While his companion was pulling himself together, Alonin studied the results of the previous day's snowfall. The snow, the rain, and the terrible cold had combined overnight to create something that was in many ways worse than the snow itself: ice. It was a thick, hard, crystalline stuff, slick and dangerous. Everything in sight was covered by it.

His boots crunching on the hardened snow, Alonin went to the edge of the road. Peering along it, he shook his head blackly. The ice was all over the roadway. Barring a sudden thaw, it would slow their progress for many days to come to an uncertain crawl.

When Alonin returned to camp he saw Dalkin patting at the side of his head, giggling weakly. "What is it?" Alonin asked with a quizzical look.

"My hair. Look at it. It's frozen!"

Despite all of his anxieties, Alonin could not suppress the laugh that came bubbling up his throat. He said, "Well, it could be worse, you know. You're lucky that that's all that is frozen!"

That afternoon they lost the pack horse.

They were slowly working their way up the highest pass of the mountains. To their left was the sheer side of the mountain, a hard wall of speckled granite; to their right there was nothing at all, save for a quick hundred-foot drop to the jagged rocks below. It was a bad stretch of road that they were on, narrow and crumbling. Alonin and Dalkin had dismounted, and were leading their horses in a long column.

Without warning, as they were going around one of the many sharp turnings of the road, the pack horse stumbled on the uncertain footing of the ice-encrusted stone. With a wild neigh of alarm, it slipped back and slid to the outer edge of the road. It held there for a brief, terrible moment, with the distant peaks framing it, then skidded once more and fell from the side of the mountain, still struggling to regain its balance.

A long leather thong led from the back of Alonin's mount to the pack horse; when the falling horse reached the end of this tether, the jolting interruption of its descent snapped its neck.

The dead weight of the pack horse jerked back on Alonin's mount, causing it to slip backward toward the edge of the chasm, unable to find purchase on the hard, unyielding ice.

Almost without thinking, Alonin drew his dagger from its sheath at his belt and slashed savagely at the thick leather thong. The thong gave with a loud snap; a moment later Alonin heard the heavy thud of the pack horse's body striking the rocks below. With the strap broken, Alonin's mount stumbled forward a few steps, before regaining its balance, then stood there with its shaggy sides heaving with terror.

Without a word, Alonin and Dalkin picked their way gingerly to the edge of the precipice and, kneeling, craned their necks to see down into the wide chasm below. The carcass of the horse lay broken at the bottom, its legs sticking out at odd angles. All around it, their supplies were scattered among the rocks.

"I don't see any way down there, do you?" Dalkin decided.

"No," Alonin said, the palms of his hands crunching against the thick crust of ice.

"Damn! Food, blankets, everything—*gone!*"

"Well, there's nothing we can do about it now."

Dalkin scowled. *"Cernon's horns!"* he muttered blackly.

The two men drew back reluctantly from the edge and stood glumly by the remaining two horses.

Alonin laughed suddenly, and Dalkin shot him a bleak look. "What have you found worthy of laughter, may I ask?" he demanded.

"I just remembered—one of your reasons for coming with me was for the regular meals."

"Hmph. So it was. It looks like I've been had," the red-haired man admitted, half grumbling, half chuckling.

As arduous as the days prior to the loss of their supplies were, those that followed were infinitely worse. Hunger and cold, two twin specters, haunted them ceaselessly. It was difficult to say which was the worse visitation.

Hunger. It gnawed at them constantly, filling even their dreams with the need for food. It became an obsession with them, something that occupied the major part of their thoughts and their conversation. Alonin never would have believed before this how important eating was to him; suddenly he realized that he would be capable of killing a man over a morsel of meat, and he understood for the first time how thin the veneer of civilized behavior was.

Cold. It went with them always, cold that was carried with the sharp, blasting mountains, cold that gathered in the still, shielded places the men sought out to make their camps, cold that sucked greedily on the marrow of their bones. Cruel cold, terrible cold, unyielding cold.

Even worse than the deprivations the men endured was the suffering of the horses. The supply of hay had gone over the cliff with the rest of the provisions, and there was nothing at all for them to eat until Alonin and Dalkin led them across the lofty spine of the mountains and down again below the snow line. Were it not that they were stout, rugged beasts, bred for hard trails, long use, unfriendly climes, and short rations, they would not have survived the ordeal.

When Alonin and Dalkin reached the far side of the mountains and descended through the trees beyond the snow, they began setting aside a portion of each day for the purpose of hunting. Their luck was meager—hard, stringy rabbits, all bone and sinew and fur, and seemingly no fat at all. As ungracious as this fare may have been, however, it did keep them alive, and for that they were grateful, although their lot was still hard enough that their gratitude was not without bounds.

As the two men wound their way down the tortuous mountainside, the trees began gradually to die out, to be replaced by sparse yellow grass and low, spiny shrubs. Finally, after more than a month in the mountains, the sharply heaving convolutions of the earth eased, smoothing to a casual roll.

A soft, white overcast lay over them constantly now; the surrounding hills were partially obscured by a thin, pearly mist. There was a chill, moist feel to the air.

The two men had been riding over the sandy hills for several days when they began to hear a faint, distant roaring. Dalkin pulled back on the reins of his horse, and sat listening intently for a moment. A wide grin suddenly split his face.

"The sea!" he said. "Do you hear? The sea!"

With a wild laugh, he gave spur to his horse and shot across the somber green hills. Alonin called after the rapidly receding figure, then sped after him at the same frantic gallop.

The dunes flashed quickly by. Alonin could hear, over the rush of the wind and the pounding of his mount's hooves, the shrill, distant cries of sea birds. An astringent smell of salt water filled his nostrils.

By the time that Alonin caught up with him, Dalkin was stopped at the top of a wide crest; he was sitting motionless in his saddle, staring off before him. Alonin pulled up beside his companion. And suddenly there it was.

The sea!

Alonin had never seen the sea before; and he found himself awed by its vastness, its incredible power. It stretched out before him for as far as he could see, disappearing at last behind a diaphanous curtain of mist. Rank upon rank of waves burst upon the jagged shore, sending up explosions of foam. Above, a lone white gull wheeled, filling the air with shrill, plaintive cries.

The sea! It was huge, overpowering, compelling. Its sprawling, unquiet vitality demanded attention, respect, even reverence from Alonin. Beside it, he felt himself suddenly dwarfed to insignificance.

"It looks wrong," Dalkin said slowly.

"Wrong?" Alonin asked, uncomprehending. "How so?"

"I don't know, exactly. I grew up beside the Western Sea, but this . . . this is different, somehow. I can't describe how. It's just a feeling, an atmosphere."

Alonin nodded, hunched in his cloak against the damp air. "Still, it is . . . impressive."

Dalkin breathed in with satisfaction. "*Impressive* isn't half the word for it."

The two men fell silent, their eyes and their minds drawn to the rushing gray waters before them. After a time Dalkin turned to Alonin. "I suppose that we should be pushing on. If we ride hard, we might be able to reach Tulin by morning. And if the truth be known, I am uncommon anxious for a hot meal and a roof over my head."

"Oh, that sounds so good I can't tell you. Lead on, my friend," Alonin said.

Dalkin grinned; the two men wheeled about and rode southward along the rolling shore toward the port city of Tulin.

10

His legs spread wide apart, the captain of the *Gray Swan* stood on the dock, laughing. Behind him was his ship—a stout, round-bellied craft—rocking beside the broad, sea-slimed dock. Before him were Alonin and Dalkin.

"You say that you want to go to Agiza-Saligor, and you want *me* to take you? *Agiza-Saligor!*" he said incredulously. Booming with laughter again, his leathery face split into wide, hard seams. "Now what would two fine gentlemen like you be doing going there?"

He held up his callused hands in a gesture of denial. "No, don't tell me. It don't make no difference, it don't. The answer would still be no. A man'd have to be a fool to take his ship there, and nobody can call Captain Moritara no fool—a bit of a rogue, I'll admit, but no fool."

"You would be well paid," Alonin said.

"I don't care if you could afford to pay me the loot of the temple of Artis, I surely don't. Money's no good if you're not alive to spend it."

"All right." Alonin sighed. "We'll just have to find somebody else, then."

"You won't find nobody fool enough on these docks."

"If you don't mind, we'll determine that for ourselves."

"Go ahead. Let me give you a timely piece of advice, though. If a man wants to live a long and healthy life, he don't drink no salt water and he steers clear of Agiza-Saligor."

Alonin and Dalkin turned and walked away from the harbor, their boots slithering on the slimy cobblestones. As they turned the corner around a squat, weathered warehouse, they could still hear the captain clucking and chuckling to himself. "Agiza-Saligor! Ha! Do I look mad?"

"It is nice to be able to brighten someone's day," Dalkin remarked dryly.

"I don't know," Alonin said wearily, rubbing his smudged eyes. "Maybe he's right. We have been scouring these docks for the last two days, and we have met only with derision and blank looks."

He sighed. "What do you suggest we do now?"

"Me, I suggest we go back to the inn and have dinner. My belt still buckles an inch too loose, after the mountains."

A wan smile crossed Alonin's face. "Done," he said.

The public room of the inn was more spacious and better lit than most. The walls were plastered white; the ceiling was low, and was ribbed with dark oaken beams. The inn catered mainly to a low, rough sort of clientele: sailors, seedy merchants, dock workers, petty thieves. In a dim, isolated corner of the room, Alonin and Dalkin took their evening meal.

Dalkin was soaking up the last of his fish stew with a crust of coarse brown bread when Alonin said, "Why don't we just buy a boat and sail to Agiza-Saligor ourselves?"

Dalkin munched thoughtfully on the dripping bread crust, swallowed, then said, "Not a good idea."

"Why not? It is not far."

"Because neither of us is a seaman, that's why. In all likelihood, we would either get lost, or capsize the boat, or run aground on a reef. Even for an experienced sailor, the sea is a perilous place; for us, it would be doubly so."

"It can not be that difficult," Alonin insisted. "I think that we could learn what we need to know. At any rate, it is an option worthy of consideration."

"You can say that because you were raised inland, far from any sea. I, at least, know enough to realize how totally ignorant of seamanship I am."

His fingers laced tensely about his ale cup, Alonin stared stonily across the room. He felt resentment for Dalkin flare within him, as if the red-haired man were in some undefined way responsible for his inability to find transportation to the island. "In any case, you need not accompany me. Our arrangement ended when we reached Tulin. You are free to go your own way, if you wish."

Dalkin's face froze. His eyes studied Alonin for a long moment. Slowly, with measured voice, as if selecting his words with great care, he said, "You must know that I want to go with you. After all we have been through, I would like to see this thing through to the conclusion. And besides, we are friends—or so I thought."

Alonin sighed, and some of the tension left him. "I'm sorry. I did not mean to insult you. Of course we are friends, and you are welcome to stay with me for as long as you like. It's just that—" He grimaced, wrestling with his frustration. "—I can't abide this waiting, this inactivity. We've come so far—and now, to be stopped now, when we are so close . . . I cannot believe that in all of Tulin there is not one captain who would be willing to bear us to our destination."

"It is understandable in a way, though," Dalkin said. "Agiza-Saligor thrives on one thing only—piracy. What captain would be anxious to risk his ship, his men—not to mention his own sweet hide—on so dubious a venture?"

"If no ship will give us passage to Agiza-Saligor and we cannot sail there ourselves, how do you propose we get there—sprout wings and fly?"

Dalkin laughed. "A neat trick, if we could manage it. But no; I think that if we are patient, we will sooner or later find someone brave enough or foolish enough—or broke enough—to take the risk."

"I hope you are right."

While Alonin and Dalkin were engaged in this conversation, another man had come into the room. His complexion was dark with a slightly grayish cast, indicating that he was of Icthan origin. He wore a purple silk shirt, tight black breeches, a wide-skirted jerkin of shiny black leather. Numerous gaudy rings bespangled his thick fingers.

The stranger conferred briefly with the proprietor of the inn, then nodded, and sauntered off across the crowded room, heading toward Alonin's table. He carried himself with a catlike ease, but there was an inbred wariness in his eyes, and his hand never strayed far from the heavy cutlass hanging at his side.

Weaving his way between the tables, he came to the gloomy corner in which Alonin and Dalkin sat finishing their meal. He stood silently at the table until Alonin finally looked up at him, then he smiled cooly. "Good evening, gentlemen. Do you mind if I join you?"

Alonin scanned the stranger's face for a moment. He felt an instant dislike for the man, but he was curious as to his business, so he said, "Go ahead."

The stranger pulled up a chair and sat, thrusting his legs out before him and clasping his fingers together over his stout belly. "I understand that you are looking for passage to Agiza-Saligor," he said easily.

"And what if we are?" Alonin asked, eyeing the man blandly.

"My captain might be willing to take on the voyage. The price, you understand, would be high."

"How high?"

"Say thirty turlons of gold."

"Thirty!" Dalkin burst in. "We could buy our own ship for that!"

"And who would pilot it?" the stranger drawled lazily. "Thirty turlons, that is the price, gentlemen. Take it or leave it as you please."

"Very well," Alonin agreed, after a moment's consideration. "Thirty turlons it is."

"Fine. I am happy that we could come to an agreement so easily, without a lot of unseemly wrangling."

"I'll bet," Dalkin said.

The stranger smiled benignly. "May I ask what business you have in Agiza-Saligor?"

"We are paying you thirty turlons of gold; it is not necessary that you know any more than that."

"As you wish," the stranger said with an indifferent shrug. He rose and stood by the table. "We sail on the morning tide."

"Aren't you going to tell us the name of the ship?" Alonin asked.

"Of course. Captain Corla's ship, the *Akabeth*. Be on time—and bring the gold."

As the stranger was walking away from the table, Dalkin asked, "How could you agree to that? Thirty turlons!"

"I would pay more than that to reach my destination, although I must admit that it does cut badly into my capital."

"I certainly hope that you don't trust him," Dalkin said.

"Why? Don't you?"

"Not for a moment. Let me ask you something: who do you think would be most likely to set sail for a den of pirates?"

"A pirate."

"Precisely."

"I take your meaning; and I have considered this possibility myself. Yet if this Captain Corla is a pirate, it does not seem likely that he will do us any harm, seeing as how we wish to be taken to his stronghold. If anything, he should be more likely to deliver us safely to where we want to go."

"That is a rather chancy bit of speculation, isn't it? I mean, considering that we are staking our lives on it."

"I just don't see that we have any other choice. Do you?"

Dalkin made a slow exhalation through his nose. "No," he admitted reluctantly, "I don't suppose that we do."

The two men arose the next morning well before the first glimmer of dawn had broken over the black and troubled sea. They dressed themselves in fresh garments purchased during their stay in Tulin. Alonin put on a patterned brocade doublet of black, silver, and blue, ingeniously puffed and slashed, so that the crisp white fabric of his shirt sleeves showed through. His boots and hose were black, as was his long cloak, which he fastened with a clasp in the shape of a silver hawk.

Alonin turned to Dalkin, who now wore a rust-colored doublet of utilitarian cut, butter-soft boots of ruddy brown leather folded over at the knees, and a white linen shirt, the small, square-cut collar of which showed over the tight throat of the doublet.

The two men carefully examined each other, clucking their approval. "I find us suitably attired to face the Pirate Queen," Alonin said. "Shall we?"

Leaving their room, they padded downstairs, and then out into the dark streets of Tulin.

At that early hour of the morning, Tulin seemed a city of the dead. Silence was everywhere, and even the thieves and other denizens of the night had long since slunk off to bed. The honest citizens of the town had not yet risen, and the windows of their houses were dark and blank.

As they walked through the eerie streets, their footsteps sounding loudly between the buildings, Dalkin asked, "Have you decided on a course of action yet?"

"A course of action?"

"On how to gain the Dylcaer from Queen Urganni."

"Not yet. As I see it, either I must buy it from her, or I must persuade her to give it to me—or, failing either of those, I must steal it."

"Stealing from Urganni, now there's an original idea."

"I will acquire it somehow. I must."

By the time the two men found the ship that was to bear them to Agiza-Saligor, it was almost dawn, and the sky had turned from black to a deep, vibrant shade of purple. In this light the *Akabeth* was but an ominous shadow, a ghost ship.

"This all could be a trick, you know," Dalkin said in a low voice. "It could be that they will take your gold and then turn around and sell us to slavers. That is, if they aren't slavers themselves—I didn't like the looks of that Icthan last night."

"I know," Alonin said. "Stay alert and keep your hand by your sword."

The *Akabeth* was, they saw as they came nearer, a sleek, sharp-prowed galley, holding low to the water. It was a trim ship, a fast ship, a suitable raider or warship, but a curiously poor choice for a trader; it could have very little space for cargo.

There was a lone sailor stationed at the base of the gang-plank, shivering miserably in the damp cold. When he saw Alonin and Dalkin approaching him, he stiffened, clutching at the handle of his knife. "Who goes there?" he asked warily.

"It is all right," Alonin answered. "We have booked passage on this ship. This is the *Akabeth*, isn't it?"

The sailor relaxed somewhat. "Aye," he said, "it's the bloody *Akabeth,* all right. Go on with you, then. The captain'll be expecting you. You'll find him on the quarter-deck, most likely."

"Thank you," Alonin said, starting up the boarding ramp. When he reached the top, he turned to Dalkin and murmured, "The quarterdeck, where's that?"

Dalkin shot him an amused look. "And you were going

to try and sail to Agiza-Saligor yourself?" he queried. "Amazing."

"Where?" Alonin repeated stiffly.

"This way."

Alonin followed as the red-haired man led him beyond a huge oaken mast, past scattered knots of seamen struggling with thickly corded rope, to a large square of open deck. At the fore of this area, attached to a low housing, there was a small raised platform on which stood two men. One of the two Alonin recognized as the swarthy Icthan who had approached them in the inn the night before. The other was a big, beefy, dark-bearded man, dressed all in black and crimson. He kept scanning the activity on the deck and in the masts with a keen eye, no less keen for the negligent attitude he maintained. From time to time he would say a few terse words to the Icthan, and the other man would relay them to the rest of the crew in a series of sharp barks.

"Unless I miss my mark, that is the captain," Dalkin said.

Alonin nodded. Taking the lead, he went to the platform on which the two men were stationed. As he was ascending the steps leading to the top of the platform, the Icthan gave a look in his direction and grinned wolfishly.

The swarthy man touched the captain's arm lightly. "Captain," he announced, "I do believe our passengers have arrived."

"Captain," Alonin said, stepping onto the platform.

"Did you bring the gold?" the captain asked, swiveling an expressionless gaze in Alonin's direction.

"Yes." Alonin reached into his pouch and brought out a small doeskin bag, which he deposited in the captain's outstretched hand. The captain upended the bag, spilling its contents into his palm with a heavy *clink*. He counted the square lumps of gold with an appraising eye, then, apparently satisfied, he poured them back into the bag and tucked the bag into his belt.

"You may have the freedom of the deck," he told them. "Try not to get in the way." The corners of his mouth and eyes showed a sour disdain but, rather than a personal affront to Alonin, it seemed that this was more a matter of general disposition.

"When should we reach our destination, Captain?"

"With favorable winds, shortly before noon."

Alonin nodded briskly. "Very good. Thank you, Captain." He turned and started down the steps.

"One more thing," the captain said abruptly.

"Yes?"

"I can't help wondering what truck the likes of you could have with Agiza-Saligor."

"Your man here asked the same question. I told him that it was none of his business."

"I know that. But I am captain of this ship, and when I ask a question I expect an answer."

"Very well. If you must know, I seek an audience with Queen Urganni."

The captain gave out a short, barking laugh, and his eyes filled with a nasty sort of humor. "Urganni! You *want* to see her? That's good! That's rich! I know of many men who have devoted much time and effort to avoiding precisely what you claim to seek!"

Staring woodenly, behind a slight protective smirk, Alonin said nothing.

"You may go now," the captain said finally. An unwholesome chuckle sounded deep in his throat.

Alonin and Dalkin made their way to a quiet corner of the deck near the prow and waited. The sun was a small white disc peering through the fog when the lines were finally cast off and the oars unshipped and plunged into the lapping water. The command was given, and, to the pounding of kettledrums, the *Akabeth* was maneuvered from the dock and pointed out to sea. Looking over the curved side of the ship, Alonin could see the oars turning rhythmically in clockwise circles—the stout blades descending, biting into the water, coming up again, pausing, beginning the cycle once more.

When the *Akabeth* had cleared the two horn-like projections of land that enclosed the port of Tulin, the sails were run up, and the oars shipped once more. The flowing white sails filled with wind, and the sleek ship cut swiftly across the dancing waves.

Tulin was but a shadow in the mist behind them before either of the two spoke. Dalkin said, "We're lucky—we have a calm sea."

"*This* is calm?" Alonin gasped. It seemed turbulent enough for him. The sharp prow of the vessel heaved and fell ponderously as it cut over the peaked swells, sending up geysers of foaming white water. Groaning, the deck rolled uneasily beneath them. All this constant motion combined queasily in Alonin's stomach. He licked his dry lips, and swallowed sour-tasting saliva, wishing for something stable beneath his feet.

"You look terrible," Dalkin said, watching him carefully. "Seasick?"

Alonin nodded miserably. "I guess so. How can I stop my stomach from churning so?"

Dalkin grinned crookedly. "I have found that throwing up often helps."

"Thanks, I'll try and remember that."

The morning progressed; the sun rose high in the sky. The ship remained shrouded by fog, with a bubble of clear visibility spanning perhaps a hundred yards traveling along with them. Alonin and Dalkin stood near the bow of the ship and gazed into the blank curtain of mist before them, the wet wind rushing into their faces.

Finally Dalkin pointed off eagerly before and slightly to the right of the ship. "Look! I see land, I think. Do you see it?"

Alonin strained his eyes into the mist. After a few moments he succeeded in locating it—a vague, gray shore rising steeply from the edge of the sea. Alonin thought for an instant that he could see buildings, but then the swirling fog closed in and made it impossible for him to tell for certain.

Moments later, calling down from the rigging of the mainmast, a lookout confirmed their sighting.

"It won't be long now," Dalkin said. Alonin noted the apprehension in his companion's voice.

Gradually the ghostly outlines of the island began to solidify, and Alonin was able to see what a dismal, inhospitable land it was. Pounded by the relentless surf, sheer, deeply-fissured cliffs of tortured stone were thrust up directly from the slate-colored sea. There was no shoreline that Alonin could see, except for a narrow strip fronting on the small U-shaped harbor. Alonin counted five ships in the harbor, slim raiders, much like the *Akabeth* itself.

Squatting high on the glistening cliff tops, partially hidden by the fog, a huge, dark fortress dominated the island with its grim presence.

Alonin now thought he understood why Agiza-Saligor had for so long been a base for pirates and raiders; surely no other living could be had from that barren land.

As the *Akabeth* slid quietly into the harbor, Alonin's dreams of stealing the Dylcaer were dashed upon the uncertain shoals of reality. The island was too well fortified to allow him any hope of succeeding in any such venture. A blank-faced tower guarded each side of the harbor, and another occupied a small, rocky island in the center of the bay. Dour-faced men, armed with crossbows or pikes, peered down from the slit windows of the towers or patrolled the stone quays. The massive fortress that stood on the ridge behind them seemed, on such inspection as Alonin was able to give it, proof against an invader. The entire island was an armed camp.

The *Akabeth* was still being moored when the Icthan, whom Alonin now supposed to be the first mate, came to the young lord and said, "The captain wants to see you."

Alonin nodded. He followed the oily fellow back to the quarterdeck on which the captain still stood. The captain remained motionless, his hands clasped behind his back; he did not even deign to look at Alonin when he spoke. "Well, how do you find our little island so far?"

Noting that "our" with the twitch of an eyebrow, Alonin said, "I find it quite . . . imposing."

"I thought that you might," the captain said with a faint, sour smile. "Is it still your wish to go farther?"

"Certainly."

"Very well, I shall escort you myself."

"Thank you, but I do not require an escort."

"You think not? I am afraid that without my presence you would not make if off the dock. The guardians of Agiza-Saligor have keen eyes and nasty dispositions."

"Well, since you put it that way . . ." Alonin shifted uncomfortably. "May I ask just what your association with Agiza-Saligor is?"

"Let us just say that our futures are firmly entwined, its and mine."

* * *

When the ship was securely moored, Alonin and Dalkin were conducted down the gangplank, led by the captain of the *Akabeth* and followed by a small gang of heavily armed seamen. Alonin had a strong suspicion that these last were not intended for his protection, but rather for his containment.

The men guarding the harbor were a bad lot, if looks were any sign of character—and Alonin thought they were in this case. They regarded Alonin and his companion with a mixture of curiosity, suspicion, and hostility; they seemed to know the captain, however, for they gave him a wide berth, as if they had cause to fear him.

Alonin and the rest of the party slowly navigated the long stone ramp that twisted up through the blasted rock cliffs. When the party came finally within sight of the ugly iron gates of the fortress, Alonin was suddenly taken back by the enormity of the structure. Even Castle Lanfarran— a place now grown more than a little dim in his memory— seemed dwarfed by comparison. The castellated walls reached up more than fifty feet above the base-rock and stretched out for hundreds of yards on each side. The northernmost wall was matched with the soaring sea cliff, so that it seemed even more impossibly immense. Where the sections of the wall were fitted together there were set massive watchtowers, each so tall that it made Alonin dizzy to contemplate it.

The stone comprising the walls and the towers was a smooth gray, and the surrounding hills and cliffs were of an abrasive volcanic substance—also gray. Even the sky was a mottled slate in color. Only by staring at the red trim of the captain's cloak could Alonin shake the eerie feeling that color had somehow been banished from the world.

In front of the fortress gates there lounged a small contingent of guards, leaning on their pikes and commenting among themselves as they watched the approach of Alonin's party. Despite the guards' undisciplined appearances, Alonin felt that, given cause for contention, they could be formidable opponents, for they were hard, cruel-looking men, doubtlessly well-schooled in the use of the weapons they held so casually.

One of the guards—the leader, Alonin supposed— advanced to intercept them. He was a large man, dressed in mail and a breastplate of intricate design. His face was difficult to see, being partially obscured by the iron nose and cheek protectors riveted into his heavy helm.

The man halted before the captain, touched his brow, and bowed. The bow was awkward and abbreviated—due, Alonin thought, to the weight of his armor. Addressing the captain, the man said in a low, grating voice, "Lord Moridar."

"*Moridar!*" Dalkin muttered, stiffening. "Gods!"

"Moridar?" Alonin whispered, sensing that Dalkin attached some significance to the name that he could not. "Have you heard of him before?"

"Haven't you? Moridar—Red Moridar!"

It came to Alonin suddenly. Red Moridar! Of course! Chief among Urganni's pirate lords, and most feared of that fearsome society, he was an almost legendary figure—a dire spirit haunting the gray coasts of the east, raiding, burning, spreading anguish and ruin wherever he went. Red Moridar!

"O gods—Red Moridar!" Dalkin repeated.

With a sardonic smile, Red Moridar pointed a thick thumb back at Alonin. "This one wishes to see Queen Urganni."

The guard made a laugh that sounded oddly like the grating of metal on metal. "Hrr hrr hrr," he said, "maybe 'e'd be satisfied with a tour of 'er dungeons. Hrr hrr."

Alonin saw then that he had to take quick control of events, or risk being unceremoniously thrown into some dank cell beneath the fortress, with never a chance to complete his mission—or even to articulate it. He stepped forward stiffly, and snapped commandingly, "You will inform your queen that Lord Alonin, sole sovereign of Caladon, requires an audience with her." He used a tone which he had often heard his grandfather use with good result on one recalcitrant lordling or another. It was a hard-edged, utterly confident thing, that tone, demanding obedience.

As Alonin had hoped, the guard was one used to responding to orders from his superiors; Alonin saw him flinch involuntarily to attention. But then the guard regained some control over himself and he offered, a little lamely, "And if I don't?"

"Then I imagine that when she finds out, Urganni will have out your swollen guts to make her potions with," Alonin replied with icy calm.

The guard glowered at Alonin in a manner which he probably intended to be intimidating, but which Alonin knew to be only a cover for uncertainty. Alonin smiled back evenly at the man, maintaining his guise of unflappable confidence.

The guard finally weakened; he gave a look to Moridar for guidance. Moridar, who also seemed affected by Alonin's display—though certainly to a lesser degree—gave a curt nod.

"Well, I guess there'd be no 'arm in checking if she wants to see you," the guard said grudgingly. "Come with me, then."

Alonin and Dalkin were brought through the wide gates of the fortress, guards on all sides of them, and then across a gloomy courtyard and into a squat, ungracious building. There they were left in a cramped, vile-smelling cell, and told to wait.

More than an hour passed; Alonin became filled with trepidation. He was hoping that Urganni would be sufficiently intrigued by his presence to wish at least to hear what he had to say. But by all accounts, Urganni was capricious; he could not predict with any surety what her reaction would be. He might yet end up in her infamous dungeons.

The guard at last returned, thrusting his way into the cell with exaggerated self-importance. He growled, "The queen will see you now."

Paradoxically, Alonin felt both relief and a sharpening of anxiety. He and Dalkin were taken from the cell and were led through the twisting maze of corridors that apparently riddled the fortress. As they went, the halls became gradually more and more ornately decorated, until finally they glittered with sumptuous luxury. Fine Thurian tapestries, in shades of green, red, and gold, hung on the ugly stone walls, and gold statuary occupied the shallow niches between their shimmering lengths. Silk draperies from Narbia and Borinor were drawn across the narrow slit windows. The loot of a hundred ships was thus displayed.

Alonin could not help but be impressed by such wealth,

so casually exhibited, but at the same time, he felt that the effect that it created, far from being one of elegance, was garish and ill-conceived. It seemed grotesque, somehow, in its very opulence.

At the doors to the throne room, which were elaborately carved and gilded, Alonin and Dalkin were stopped and relieved of their weapons. After a moment's hesitation, Alonin cooperated readily, for he knew that, should matters take an ugly turn, there was no way that he and Dalkin could hope to fight their way free—and even if they could, there was no escape from the island, except by pirate ship.

Dalkin seemed more distressed by this turn of events, however, and he surrendered his sword only when it became clear that he had no other choice in the matter. He shot Alonin the look of a trapped animal, to which the young lord could respond only with a helpless shrug.

The doors to the throne room were then thrown open, and the two men were led inside.

"Lord Alonin of Caladon and companion," announced a young page in a tabard of purple silk, his shrill voice echoing through the cavernous hall.

Queen Urganni sat hunched impassively on her enormous throne, watching as Alonin and Dalkin were brought down the center of the great room. The queen was old, Alonin knew, incredibly old. She had occupied the throne of Agiza-Saligor for more than a hundred years, her life sustained—so it was said—by dark and gruesome sorceries. But although her powers had enabled her to live much beyond a normal span of years, yet they were apparently not sufficient to maintain her youth, for she looked every day of her age.

Her silk-shrouded body was slight and shrunken, her arms so thin that it seemed that a man could snap them easily between thumb and forefinger. Her face was greatly ravaged by time; the cheeks were deeply sunken, the teeth worn small and brown, the skin covered with crisscrossing wrinkles, so that it seemed like a piece of parchment that had been crumpled into a ball and then stretched out flat again.

Yet as old as she was, she was not beyond vanity, for she had made great effort to disguise the depredations of time.

She wore an elaborately coiffed black wig, woven with strands of pearls. A thick layer of bone-white powder coated her face; her cheeks and lips were rouged scarlet; a lavender pigment adorned her heavy eyelids.

But these adornments—the rouge, the powder, the cloth of gold—could not conceal from Alonin her physical decay, no more than did the sumptuous furnishings of the fortress hide from him its utilitarian ugliness.

"Ah, Lord Alonin," said Urganni. "This is indeed a pleasure. We do not usually entertain guests of your quality here on our little island. Welcome." Her voice was surprisingly strong; it was fire and steel, all wrapped in velvet. It served to remind Alonin that this was no vain, foolish old woman he faced, but a powerful queen, renowned for her cunning and her cruelty.

Alonin made a deep bow. "I thank you for agreeing to this audience," he said.

"How could I refuse a brother sovereign?" Alonin detected a slight ironic twist to that "sovereign." "Now what is it you wish from us? I imagine that it must be a thing of some import, to bring you all this long way."

Alonin paused, taking in a deep breath. Suddenly he had a hundred misgivings for the way in which he was approaching matters. It was necessary for him to play this just right, or all would be lost. He wondered if he could carry it off, and the only answer he could give himself was that he had to, for he had left himself no room to back out. He was committed.

Drawing himself up very straight. Alonin said, "I have come to ask a boon of you, your Majesty."

"A boon!" The idea seemed to amuse Urganni greatly. "My reputation in the world must be slipping, for never before has anyone come to ask me such a thing."

"On the contrary, I can assure you that what you have labored so long to create is still quite intact. Nevertheless, I have come to ask a boon."

"I am intrigued. Go on, then, ask."

"There is a gem, a great gem, which I believe to be in your possession."

"There are many great gems in my possession."

"The one of which I speak is very distinctive. It is a stone nearly as large as my fist, and I believe dark in color.

It is not set in gold, as one might expect, but in pure silver. The setting is shaped in the form of two entwined serpents."

Urganni paused for a moment, arching up her painted eyebrows. "I know the stone," she acknowledged. "Am I correct in assuming that it is the boon that you seek?"

"You are."

She studied him intently. "Why do you want that particular gem? It is not of any great worth, yet you have gone to much trouble for it, which I find strange."

Here was the difficult part. Alonin had to tell Urganni enough to make his quest seem plausible, without alerting her to the gem's dark potential. There would be gaps in his story, but he hoped that, if he made himself seem ignorant enough, Urganni would not think to challenge him on them.

He said, "Are you aware of the terrible circumstances under which Caladon, my rightful realm, has labored these hundred years?"

"You are speaking of course of the dragon Thudredid."

"Yes."

"Then, yes, of course—for who has not heard of this, save fools and savages?"

"Then it follows thus: long ago, my great-great grandfather stole this gem from Thudredid; in revenge, the dragon took Caladon, killed my great-great grandfather, and laid a curse upon my family. It is very confusing, and I admit that I do not understand it all myself—but I am told that by returning the gem to Thudredid I can void the curse and regain Caladon."

Narrowing her eyes, and stroking her chin reflectively, Urganni said, "I see . . . I see . . . Yes, that does make sense."

Hoping to distract the queen from questioning him further on the matter, Alonin put in, "Naturally, I do not expect you to give it to me without due compensation. I would pay you well for it."

"How much?"

"Two hundred turlons of gold seems a fair price to me."

She gave a dry chuckle. "More than fair, more than fair! You could afford to pay so much?"

"The treasury of Caladon contains many times that

amount. Once Thudredid is slain and I sit in Castle Caladon, two hundred turlons shall be delivered unto you."

"But what if you are slain in the attempt to regain your realm? Would I not be cheated of my just payment? Are you so confident that you have never considered the possibility?"

"In that event, I have arranged for your interests to be protected. I have here—" He reached inside his doublet and withdrew a folded sheet of parchment. "—a paper signed and sealed by my grandfather, King Clemmth of Yggrs, guaranteeing this sum, should I for any reason fail in my attempt."

Alonin passed the sheet to a page, who in turn brought it to the queen. She perused the document, frowning. Abruptly she crumpled it in one clawlike hand. Alonin watched in horror; he restrained himself from giving out a cry of protest.

Urganni smiled sweetly, showing a mean amusement at Alonin's obvious discomfort. "I like you, Lord Alonin," she said. "I really do. It took a great deal of courage to come to me with such an absurd proposition. I respect that. Therefore, I shall not require this bond of you."

She clapped her hands together sharply. "Lord Moridar!" she called out.

The pirate lord oozed out from the shadows behind the throne. "My Queen?" he said.

"Are you familiar with the jewel which Lord Alonin has described?"

"Aye, your Majesty."

"Bring it hither."

"Aye, your Majesty."

Moridar departed from the throne room. Alonin could scarcely dare to believe that things were going as well as they seemed to be; it was all too easy. Even when, after an absence of several minutes, Moridar came back into the hall and placed a carved teakwood box in the queen's hands, Alonin still had misgivings. He suspected that Urganni's apparent cooperation might simply be an elaborate ruse to make mock of him. Such was not beyond her, he knew.

The queen opened the case, giving an indecipherable smile to Alonin, reached inside and brought out something clenched in her hand. She extended the hand to Alonin, and unclasped her fingers.

The jewel that rested exposed in the queen's palm was exactly as the wizard Mernon had shown it to him, those many weeks ago, yet still it came as a disappointment to Alonin. The setting, it could not be denied, was of extremely fine workmanship. But the stone itself was quite another matter. It was a dull blackish lump, devoid of luster, its surface irregular and pitted. It was an ugly thing, of no value or significance that Alonin could see. He found it hard to believe that this was what he had come so far to claim.

"Take it with my blessings, Lord Alonin," the queen said.

Alonin hesitated for a moment, then reached out and took the gem. Once in his hand, an extraordinary thing happened to the stone; its color, which had been a dead black, became suddenly suffused with a brilliant sapphire blue, and a murky glow began to throb from its heart. Then, suddenly, Alonin's talisman began to tingle, and the light in the gem faded, becoming once more dark with slumber.

Cupping the Dylcaer to him, Alonin looked up, fearful that someone else might have noticed the transformation; no one showed any sign of having seen it. Sucking in a breath of relief, he took the teak case from the queen and restored the Dylcaer to it. He said, "I thank you, O Queen. You are indeed generous."

"Do you think so?" the queen asked with a crooked smile.

There was something in her gaze that Alonin did not like. The strain of this audience was beginning to tell on him; he was damp with nervous perspiration, and blood pounded in his ears. "Aye," he said. "What else could I think?"

Urganni did not say anything. As casually as he could, Alonin said, "Now, if you would consent to provide transportation for my companion and myself, we will trouble you no more."

"But I could not possibly let you go without tasting the hospitality of Agiza-Saligor. You and your friend must stay with us as guests for a time."

"Your offer is most kind, of course, but I do not wish to impose on you."

"It is no imposition."

"Still—"

"I am afraid that I must insist," she said, the hard edge in her voice cutting off all possibility for further discussion.

"Your Majesty," he acquiesced finally.

"The guards will show you to your quarters," Urganni said. "Guards!"

A knot of men armed with pikes closed about Alonin and Dalkin. With a sick feeling, Alonin inclined his head to the queen. "Your humble servant," he murmured.

As they were being taken away, Dalkin leaned to Alonin and muttered through his teeth, "I don't believe she means to let us go. Not ever."

"No," Alonin agreed grimly, "I don't believe she does."

11

A day passed, then another, and still Alonin and Dalkin remained imprisoned on Agiza-Saligor. In all respects they were treated as honored guests, housed in comfortable quarters, treated with deference, given all they had wit to ask for—with one exception, and that was their freedom. They were kept confined to their apartments, a guard outside their door; when Alonin asked when they would be allowed to leave, he was met only with polite shrugs. They had not seen Urganni since leaving the throne room.

With each seemingly innocuous moment that passed, the tension grew in Alonin, and he became increasingly aware of the menace that hung vague and unspoken in the air. He took to wandering restlessly through their apartments and through the rank and somber garden that occupied the small, enclosed court adjoining their rooms.

This behavior finally moved Dalkin to say, "What's the matter with you, Alonin? You have been prowling around here like some lost soul for days now."

"What do you think is the matter?" Alonin asked with a dark scowl. "I am worried. I can't fathom what Urganni is up to. She has held us here for nearly three days—three days! We see no one; even our meals are brought here to us. Why? Why should she go to all this trouble? What is she after?"

"Well, if she's trying to make you apprehensive, she's succeeding," Dalkin said. "Relax. Whatever is going to happen will happen whether or not you worry about it."

"Doesn't it bother you at all? Don't you find our position the least bit uncomfortable?"

"Well, not as uncomfortable as I had feared it might be. I rather expected that Urganni would have us thrown into her deepest dungeons. This—" Dalkin made a sweeping gesture to encompass their apartments. "—came as a pleasant surprise to me."

"In a way, I might have preferred it if she *had* confined us to the dungeon. At least then we would know where we stood. This way, I keep waiting for the other boot to drop."

"Obviously you have not spent any time in a dungeon." Dalkin paused in front of a large bowl of fruit and selected a pear. "You know, it is just possible that there is nothing sinister in all of this. Maybe Urganni just has rather stringent standards of hospitality. Eventually, she may let us leave."

"Do you really think that likely?"

Dalkin shrugged. He bit into the pear, chewed "How do we know? I mean, what can she possibly be up to? We've not even seen her since that first day."

"I don't know—I just have this feeling inside me. There is something strange going on here. I am afraid."

"I really think that you're letting your imagination get the better of you."

Alonin shook his head. "Perhaps, but I think not. You are forgetting Urganni's reputation for dark sorcery. There are other threats besides the purely physical ones, you know."

"That may well be. But I know of no way to protect against them. Do you?"

"No. But we had better give the matter serious thought while we still can." Alonin fell into a deeply cushioned chair and began to ruminate blackly on the situation. There was something very wrong in all of this, he knew. Urganni was playing some sort of game with them, but what was it? What on earth could it be? Alonin felt that he was trying to assemble a puzzle while lacking most of the pieces.

There was a bitter irony in his position. Urganni had freely given him that for which he had asked, then kept him. Perhaps this wicked joke was all that the queen intended, but somehow Alonin knew there was more to it than that.

Alonin spent the rest of the day pacing and fretting, without coming any closer to the answer and, when night came and he tried to sleep, he was unable to turn his mind from the problem. Toward midnight while he lay in bed staring up at the ceiling, he was suddenly gripped by an overwhelming desire to get up and go into the garden. He fought the urge for a while but, with sleep farther away than ever, he finally gave into it. Crawling from bed, he dressed hastily in the dark; he started for the door to the garden.

"What is it?" Dalkin asked sleepily from his bed.

"Can't sleep. I'm going out for a breath of fresh air."

Confined on three sides by tall buildings and on the fourth by the great outer wall, the garden was a small, dreary, sharply enclosed place, crowded with a vast profusion of trees, shrubs, and plants—willow, eucalyptus, myrtle, lilac, fern, and many others that Alonin was unable to identify, all tangled together in a lush green chaos. Near the center of the garden there was a stone fountain, stippled with dark moss, around which there were arranged three low benches.

The garden had long ago been left to grow wild and untended; an atmosphere of shabbiness and melancholy hung over it. What drew Alonin there this night he could not guess.

Restless, Alonin prowled the borders of the small square. Perhaps twenty minutes passed; he decided finally to go back inside and try his luck with sleep again. But, as he was turning to go, he caught a glimpse of movement from out of the corner of his eye and he stopped. He looked closer and saw that he was no longer alone—a woman had joined him. She was standing a few yards away, gazing off toward the towering outer wall, seemingly unaware of his presence. Moonlight glimmered on her long, golden hair and shone on her pale and lovely face. A faint breeze ran rustling through her silken garments.

Alonin realized with a start that he knew her, but he could not think how or from where. Then it struck him. It was *she*, the woman from his dream!

Suddenly spellbound, Alonin took an uncertain step toward her. His foot snapped a small twig. Attracted by the noise, the woman's face turned to him.

Her vivid blue eyes locked momentarily with his own. Feeling the shock of that contact, Alonin hesitated where he stood. He opened his mouth to speak and started forward once more. But even as he did so, the woman had already turned from him and was making her way rapidly across the garden, her gown flowing in shimmering waves behind her.

"Wait," Alonin called hoarsely, his voice barely audible. "Wait!" he cried again, more loudly.

But she was already gone, vanished through a door in one of the buildings. Alonin followed, but when he tried the door he found it locked.

Furious at his own blundering, Alonin slammed his balled fists into the heavy oaken door frame. "Idiot!" he said. "Idiot, idiot! You frightened her!"

He continued to rage at himself for several moments, but then he felt himself relax. Suddenly he realized that he would see her again. He had to. Somehow, for better or worse, she was the key to his predicament—that much of his dream was clear to him now. They would meet again.

His mind working busily on this new complication to his situation, Alonin returned to his room. When he opened the door, he saw that it was no longer dark inside. Dalkin had lighted the lamp and was sitting propped up in bed, wearing only his shirt and hose. Resting on his lap was the small carved case in which the Dylcaer was kept. The case was open; the gem rested in Dalkin's outstretched hand, glowing softly with a faint azure light.

When Alonin came inside and saw this, a fierce possessiveness flared abruptly within him. "Put that down," he said sharply.

"What?" Dalkin asked, looking up with a bemused expression.

"You heard me. Put it down."

Dalkin's face became pinched with a sullen resentment. "Why?" he demanded. "I was just looking at it."

"Because I told you to," Alonin said in a low but deadly voice. "You have no right touching what does not belong to you." He stalked over to Dalkin and extended his hand. "Give it here."

Dalkin glared defiantly at Alonin for a moment. He snorted, then dropped the heavy jewel into Alonin's open palm. "There," he said thickly.

As the Dylcaer came into contact with Alonin, it began to blaze brilliantly; immediately his talisman pulsed into activity once more, and the light in the gem died utterly. Odd!

He restored the Dylcaer to its case and snapped down the lid. His anger had abated abruptly; he felt astounded by his vehemence, and he was embarrassed and remorseful. "I am sorry, Dalkin," he said, rubbing his temples wearily. "I don't know what came over me to speak to you so. But it is dangerous to handle the Dylcaer or to look too long upon it—or so the wizard Mernon told me. I should have explained this to you before, but it did not occur to me, and for that I am sorry."

It was a long time before Dalkin responded. "It's all right. It was my fault," he said finally. "I should not have touched your property without asking—but I couldn't seem to help myself. Curious, I guess."

Alonin sat on the bed, his back to Dalkin. He pondered on the Dylcaer. Why was it, he wondered, that the stone had caught fire in Dalkin's hands, burned brighter in his own—until his talisman had neutralized the effect—but had been dead and cold when Urganni had held it? Alonin remembered suddenly that Mernon had told him that the Dylcaer had been wielded by the Dark Master of Heggoth, last and most dreadful of the ancient Agnari lords. This brought a possible explanation to mind. Alonin, like most of the Acynian nobility, had a large proportion of Agnari blood in his veins; Dalkin, being an Acynian, also might conceivably have some, too. Urganni, however, was derived from Icthan and various local bloods, and therefore would probably not have any Agnari in her lineage. Could it be that the Dylcaer responded to people in a manner that was proportional to the amount of Agnari blood in them? If the Dylcaer were a creation of the Agnari, and it was reasonable to suppose that it was, then this seemed to make sense.

Finally satisfied that he had penetrated the heart of the matter—or if not, that it was beyond his present capacity to understand—Alonin broke off his deliberations and turned to Dalkin. "Friends?" he asked.

There was a slight, sulky silence. "Friends," came the answer at last.

Alonin returned to the garden late the next night. It was a pleasant evening, cool and still. The odors of growing things mingled with the subtle musk of decay. The moon cast a faint silvery radiance upon the garden.

Would she come? He felt somehow that she would. Sitting on one of the stone benches encircling the fountain, he settled down to wait.

Who was she, this living embodiment of his dream? What influence would she have on the events of his life soon to come? Alonin recalled his dream, and he shivered. It was ambiguous, but it contained a terrible overlay of dread. He, lying imprisoned, bound hand and foot—possibly a representation of his present confinement. She, leaning over him with a slender blade in her hand, but did she mean to cut his bonds, or . . . ?

Alonin heard the soft rasp of a door being unlatched. He stood and faced the door.

It opened slowly, and she appeared. The woman took a few steps into the garden, then saw Alonin and froze.

"Don't go," Alonin said softly, so as not to frighten her. "I mean you no harm."

"Who are you?" she demanded, studying him.

"I am Lord Alonin of Caladon. I am a prisoner here."

Her vibrant blue eyes continued to search his face for a moment, then she seemed to relax. "I am the Princess Elayse," she said, "and I too am here against my will."

"Come, then, and sit with me. Let us pass some part of our confinement together."

The princess gave a smile that dazzled. She came across the garden to him. Never had Alonin seen such flawless, elegant beauty in a woman. She was, he decided, like one of those fine porcelain figures for which the city of Kos was so justly famous. It was difficult for him to remember that she was flesh and blood. She seemed too nearly perfect to be real.

It gave him an eerie feeling to look on her. He almost felt that he knew her—and not only because of his dream—for her beauty seemed to be the embodiment of that image of the ideal woman that he, like most young men, carried in his imagination. He could not help but desire her.

Feeling a strange, insistent pulsing in his body and mind, Alonin took in a deep breath, trying to keep himself from being swept away by his emotion. Yet the pulsing grew stronger the closer she came to him.

Alonin tightened his jaw, willing his thoughts to stillness.

He had never felt this way about anyone before, and it was a little frightening.

With perfect grace, the princess sat upon one of the benches, and Alonin sat beside her.

"Are you being held for ransom, too?" she asked.

"No. To tell the truth, I have no idea of why I am being held here." He paused for a moment, feeling her closeness to him exerting an almost irresistible force on him. More to distract himself than to satisfy any curiosity, he said, "I take it, then, that you *are* being held for ransom."

"Yes."

"How came you here?"

"Ah, my lord, that is a long tale, sad to tell. Yet here it is in brief: I was to be married to Prince Vorsak of Borinor, a match arranged for reasons of state by my father, who is king of Kyre; I was on my way to the wedding, which was to be held in Borinor, when my ship was attacked and taken by one of Queen Urganni's pirates; now I am being held for a ruinous ransom, which thus far neither my father nor the prince have been able to meet."

She paused briefly, then said, "In a way, I am almost grateful. I do not even know the man to whom my father betrothed me. He is said to be much older than I, and an Icthan besides. I am not anxious to be bound to a man I do not love, yet Urganni has threatened that if the ransom is not raised soon, she will have me sold into slavery. Thus whatever happens, I am faced with bondage."

Alonin expressed sympathy for her double plight. At length he spoke of his own situation: of the deaths of his parents, of his life in Yggrs, of Caladon, of the dragon Thudredid, of his quest, and of the wonders he had seen since leaving Yggrs. He talked on and on, feeling as if a charm had been laid on his tongue. He was aware that the conversation had somehow become a monologue, yet it was impossible for him to stop. He felt drunk with the night, with the beauty of Elayse, and with her obvious interest in his words.

Even so, he kept himself from talking about the Dylcaer, of its power and history, for he knew that as long as he remained in Agiza-Saligor this must remain a secret. If ever Urganni learned the true nature of what she had given him, she would never allow him to take it off the island.

Finally he said, "But I must be boring you."

"No, no," the princess protested, her eyes flashing splendidly. "I find it all fascinating. I myself have lived a very sheltered life until now. Go on."

At her urging he continued, speaking at last of his frustration at his confinement. "Here I am. I have succeeded in completing the first half of my mission, and this done despite great hardship and peril—and here I must sit, and sit, until Urganni decides otherwise."

Elayse narrowed her eyes slightly. "I know how you must feel," she said, "but there is nothing you or I can do about it. There is no escape from Agiza-Saligor."

"Now you sound like Dalkin."

"Who?"

"The friend who accompanied me here."

Alonin paused, thinking of the dragon, which even now occupied Castle Caladon. "I will escape," he stated, an edge of finality in his voice.

Elayse gave him a long, piercing look—and that vague throbbing that had been with Alonin ever since meeting the princess quickened. There was something about this sensation that almost reminded him of something, but he dismissed it as simply a sign of his great desire for her. Speaking rapidly, Elayse said, "How will you escape? Have you a plan?"

"Not yet—but I will think of something, that I can promise you."

Elayse subsided somewhat and said, "When you do, will you take me with you?"

"I cannot promise, but if I can, I will."

"*Please.* You must. I cannot remain here, and I cannot return home without submitting to another sort of prison."

"I will try, that is all I can say."

Alonin leaned back and contemplated the sky. The night was almost over, he noticed suddenly. The sky glowed with the faint gray light of false dawn. It was much later than he had thought. Stretching wearily, he said, "We have talked the night away. Look! It is nearly dawn."

Elayse gave a start, and glanced up at the sky. "I lost track of the time," she said. "I must go." She rose hastily from her place on the bench.

Alonin stood. "Now?"

"Yes, now," she said. There was an urgency in her voice.

"Stay awhile yet. I would have you meet my companion, Dalkin. He should be up and around soon."

She shook her head emphatically. "I cannot. I must go. I will explain later." Her voice dropped low. "Meet me here again tomorrow night."

"Of course I will."

Elayse looked up at Alonin. Her eyes, so clear and blue that Alonin felt himself lost in them, were filled with an unvoiced expectation. Alonin felt his desire for her flare violently within him, and he took her abruptly in his arms. She melted softly against him, and he kissed her, roughly, clumsily.

Alonin was unprepared for what happened then. His talisman suddenly throbbed an urgent warning, and he felt desire drain from him. Elayse must have felt it too, for she gave a small gasp and staggered back from him. A confused look clouded her face. "I—" she said, then gave a quick glance at the brightening sky. She shook her head, as if to clear it. She looked at Alonin, bewilderment in her eyes. Her lips moved soundlessly for a moment, then finally she said, "Tomorrow night. Remember." She started away rapidly through the shadows.

Alonin said nothing. He stood motionless in the early morning darkness, one hand pressed to his talisman. It struck him in that instant that the throbbing sensation he had felt all night, which he had confused with lust, had actually been caused by the talisman, operating at too low a resonance for him to recognize it in his distracted state of mind.

Startled into stillness, he watched Elayse go to the door, fit a key to the lock, and disappear into the interior of the building. The door was swinging shut when Alonin suddenly leaped forward, vaulting over a low hedge. He caught the door just before it could snap shut. He hung there for a few moments, as silently as he could, then eased the door open and peered inside.

Elayse, he saw, was proceeding rapidly along an ornate, lamp-lit hallway, her shoes clattering on the bare marble floor. When at last she turned off into a side corridor, Alonin slipped inside, silently closing the door behind him. He followed as quickly as he dared, afraid that Elayse

would hear his approach, and even more afraid that he
would lose her trail among the winding web of corridors.

That Elayse was one of Urganni's agents Alonin now
had little doubt. He trusted the warning of his talisman
implicitly—it had, after all, saved his life once. He remembered the keen interest that Elayse had shown in his plans
for escape. At the time he had found nothing odd in that—
he had thought that it stemmed from her own desire to
gain freedom from Agiza-Saligor. Now he saw that she
wished to know his plans only so that she could report on
them to Urganni. Alonin raged at himself. He had been
such an easy dupe, despite the warning of his dream, despite his talisman. Suddenly he recalled that he been given
another warning of this, by Loness, Oldest of the *Kirith-
ber-Weirlon*. "Beware of what you want," she had said.
Alonin had not understood at the time, but he thought that
he did now. He was amazed at the extent of his stupidity.

The only satisfaction he could gain from his behavior
was that at least he had not told her of the true nature of
the Dylcaer; that much sense he had shown.

Coming to the corner that Elayse had turned moments
before, Alonin flattened himself against the wall and eased
cautiously around the corner, so that he could see into the
corridor without being seen.

As far as he could tell, the corridor was a dead end;
there were no doors on either side of it, and it ended after
some twenty feet in a narrow window, which looked out
over the sea. Perplexed, Alonin watched Elayse. Why had
she come here? he wondered.

His question was quickly answered. The princess—if indeed she were what she claimed to be, which appeared
doubtful at the moment—halted about three-quarters of the
way down the hall, turned to the left, and reached up and
deftly depressed a small carven face that stood out on the
wall. There was a loud *click*, and a mahogany panel slid
abruptly aside, revealing a gloomy space of undefined di-
mension behind it. Elayse slipped quickly inside, and the
panel rolled back into place.

Alonin smiled tightly, feeling for once the hunter instead
of the hunted. He went to the secret panel and paused for a
moment, giving Elayse time to get far enough ahead of him
that she would, he hoped, not notice his presence in the

hidden passage, then he reached out and manipulated the stone face in the same way that Elayse had done. The panel slid open, and Alonin blinked against the darkness, as his eyes adjusted slowly to the gloom. Hearing footsteps falling away to his right, he followed the sound, feeling his way along the claustrophobically narrow passage.

After perhaps a minute of this painfully slow progress, Alonin came around a sharp bend in the passage and saw, a few feet before him, a drawn curtain across what appeared to be a doorway. A bright nimbus encircled the edge of the curtain, showing him that whatever lay on the other side was better lighted than the passageway.

Alonin crept stealthily to the curtain. Scarcely daring to draw a breath, he plucked aside one edge of the heavy fabric, just enough so that he could see what was on the other side of it.

Beyond the curtain was a large room, almost bare of furnishings. A long, marble-topped sideboard ran along one wall, and near it was a large chest, with fittings of antique brass. There was only one other item that Alonin could see.

It was a mirror; it stood next to the window, near to where Elayse was standing. It was a huge, oddly fashioned thing. From floor to top, it measured more than six feet in height. It was framed by a thick molding of gold, studded with precious and semi-precious gems. Around the frame, spaced at regular intervals, elaborate, twisting glyphs and symbols were etched.

A powerful, uncanny aura surrounded the mirror. It filled the room with a feeling of heaviness, of inertia, which Alonin did not think he felt with any of the five normal senses, but which seemed to impress itself directly on his mind. The very space around the mirror seemed, in some way that the young lord could not quite define, twisted and torn from its natural shape.

Some sort of dark magic was attached to the mirror; even Alonin, with his limited knowledge of such things, could sense it.

Alonin shifted his eyes uneasily from the glass to Elayse. She stood before the open window, her hair blown back from her face by fresh sea breezes. Her arms were held out slightly from the sides of her body, palms forward. Her eyes were closed, and her brow was slightly furrowed, as if by deep concentration. Her attitude was one of waiting.

The window she faced peered out over the main wall of the fortress onto the gray, swelling sea. Only minutes remained until dawn; the misty sky was streaked with silver, and on the horizon the crests of the waves glistened dully.

What was she doing? Alonin wondered. That it was something that held deep significance for her he could tell by the rapt expression on her face. Beyond that, however, it was a mystery to him. He had expected her to go directly to Urganni, to report on her meeting with him; he had planned to eavesdrop on the conversation and perhaps learn what the queen expected to accomplish with him. But this had not happened, which was as odd as it was disappointing. Now all he could do was wait and hope for eventual enlightenment.

Alonin stood watching for what seemed a very long time. Nothing in the scene altered; Elayse still stood as before, in her ritualistic attitude, as if she were offering herself to the sea or to the growing dawn. Alonin's nerves were becoming strained by the fruitless waiting, but somehow he sensed that something extraordinary was about to happen.

The sun broke over the horizon. When its first rays struck Elayse, a thing happened that Alonin could not begin to comprehend or explain.

She began to change.

A blazing red aura of curdled energy flared up around her, enveloping her like a fiery eggshell. Within it, her form began to ripple, shift, distort. The effect was unpleasant to watch; it made Alonin feel sick and disoriented, so that after a few moments he was forced to look away. From the corner of his eye, he caught sight of the mirror. It seemed to loom larger than it had before and it was infused with some of the same energy which surrounded Elayse; within it he could see a vague figure, which he did not think was a reflection.

Alonin suddenly sensed that whatever had been taking place was now over. He brought his eyes back to Elayse, and what he saw made a harsh gasp tear from his constricted throat.

Where only moments before Elayse had stood, there was

now a very different shape—old, shrunken, withered, marked with an ancient evil.

It was Urganni.

A prickly horror engulfed Alonin. His face twisted with revulsion. He wanted to gag, but he choked back the desire. A bottomless disgust filled him, for now he realized what it was that Urganni had planned for him, why she had kept him on the island. Recalling how close he had come to playing out his own part in the queen's obscene drama, he could not contain the full extent of his loathing within himself. If not for the talisman . . . No, he could not think about it.

Unable to stop himself, Alonin whirled about and fled blindly back along the dark passage. He made his way to the outer hallway, then to the door that led out into the garden.

By this time, the first rush of panic had receded somewhat; he had the presence of mind to disable the door's locking mechanism before he went out.

He paused for a moment in the garden, trying to regain possession of himself. He closed his eyes and took a long, calming breath, then opened his eyes again. He remembered with perfect detail how Elayse had stood there, so cool and so beautiful. Too beautiful to be real, he had thought. How right he had been! Recalling the kiss, he shuddered and wiped his mouth with a convulsive gesture.

Returning at last to his room, he found that Dalkin was awake. The red-haired man was standing beside the basin, naked to the waist, splashing his face with clear water. The sight of his friend performing this mundane act returned to Alonin some sense of normality. Clenching his jaw, he tried to drive out the nightmarish terror he still felt.

"Morning," Dalkin said, glancing briefly at Alonin through water-streaked eyes. "Have you been out there all night?"

"Be ready to leave tonight," Alonin said hoarsely. His voice sounded strained, even to himself.

"Eh? What's that?" Dalkin rubbed his face dry with a length of towel, then examined Alonin closely. His expression slowly changed. "By the goddess!" he exclaimed, "you look as if you've just seen the ghost of Seriphas!"

"Worse, worse than that. But I don't want—I can't talk about it now."

"But what's this about leaving tonight?"

Alonin made a tense, dismissive gesture. "Later. Just be ready."

Apparently realizing that Alonin was in no mood to talk, Dalkin shrugged and said no more.

Alonin collapsed wearily onto his bed. His brain whirled furiously, but with peculiar efficiency. A plan had begun to take shape in his mind. It was a desperate venture, he realized—there were a hundred things that could go wrong, but it was the only way, his only chance to leave Agiza-Saligor.

Alonin thought for a long time, trying to approach the matter from every conceivable angle. Then he smiled slightly.

With any luck, it would work.

12

LATE the following night, while the moon was rising high in the sky, and an hour before the usual time for his meeting with the bogus princess, Alonin slipped from his room into the garden. He halted for a moment and sniffed the air, trying to steady himself for what was to come.

It was a gloomy, sinister-seeming night; the silvery brightness of the moon twisted the garden with eerie shadows, and the distant thundering of the surf sounded sad and doleful. Alonin started forward once more, crossing the garden to the building into which he had followed the "princess" the night before. With stealthy care, he pulled open the door. He paused momentarily to restore function to the lock, so that Urganni would not be able to detect his passage, then he entered the building and proceeded along the deserted corridor, going as quickly and quietly as he could.

Turning off into the side corridor, he went to the secret panel and pressed down on the carven face. The panel opened, and he slipped through into the darkness, which became more complete as the panel slid shut behind him. He crept slowly down the passageway.

When he reached the heavy curtain which divided the passage from the room beyond, he drew it aside slightly and peered out. Finding the room unoccupied, he came out from behind the curtain and confronted the huge mirror standing by the window.

As he studied the mirror, Alonin could feel a chill working its way down his spine. As before, he could feel its dark, evil energies pulling at him.

He was proceeding on two basic assumptions. The first

was that Urganni obtained her shape-shifting ability from the mirror. From what he had observed of her transformation, he was reasonably sure that this was the case. The second and more questionable assumption was that he would be able to suborn the mirror's power to his own use. He was not at all sure of this point, but it did seem within the realm of possibility, and therefore worth a try.

If either of these assumptions proved incorrect, all of his planning would go for naught and he would be dead soon, in all probability, for refusing—as he most certainly would—his part in Urganni's odious game. Of course, he could gain time by playing along with Urganni, but— Alonin made a grimace of distaste—this seemed a high price to pay for a few extra days of life.

Alonin turned from the mirror and scanned the room for a place to hide; if everything went according to plan, Urganni would be arriving soon, and he did not want to be found there when she came. Once she completed her transformation, the queen would probably leave by the secret passage, so Alonin needed someplace else, but someplace that still commanded a clear view of the mirror. He flipped aside a nearby tapestry and found that a shallow alcove lay behind it. This should do well enough, he decided.

Secreting himself behind the tapestry, he waited. Long minutes passed. He grew increasingly anxious, afraid that Urganni would not appear, even though on another level he was sure that she would. Then, finally, he heard a slow, shuffling fall of footsteps outside the door. He stiffened against the back of the alcove, sucking in a tense breath. The door creaked open.

From a narrow gap between the tapestry and the wall, Alonin saw Urganni enter the room. The door closed behind her with a muffled thud. She cast a long, suspicious gaze about the room, as if suspecting that she was not alone. Alonin tensed, getting ready to spring, should she discover him. But she scanned the room for only a moment more, then shrugged slightly and limped to the mirror.

Heart quickening, Alonin watched her confront the silver face of the glass. Urganni looked deep into the heart of it, squinting with concentration. She brought her frail body into the star position—legs spread wide and arms out parallel to the floor. She drew several long, slow breaths.

Then, in a monotonous voice, she began to chant: *"Ditha! Ditha! A'bir na dol! Aerin na dol! Na ditha, na dol!*

She repeated the chant several times, with Alonin struggling to engrave it on his mind. Then she paused and brought her arms up over her head. *"Ma'kee atu s'drae!"* she pronounced vehemently.

Suddenly her eyes rolled back in her sockets; violent convulsions shook her thin body. A shrill wailing arose from nowhere, filling the chamber. Alonin clamped his hands over his ears, vainly trying to lock out the piercing squeal. The discordant sound grew louder and more penetrating, until Alonin feared his head would split from it. He fell against the rear wall of the nook, gnashing his teeth in anguish. Pinned against the back of the alcove, he lost sight of Urganni. A fulgent redness invaded his hiding place; the air filled with a cutting brimstone stench.

The wailing ceased abruptly, and with it the light. Alonin lowered his hands from his ears—slowly, for he was not yet sure whether the sound had stopped or merely paused. A few moments of silence convinced him that it was over, and he let out a small, shuddering gasp of relief. He shook his head to clear it, and then went back to his observation point.

Urganni once again wore the guise of Princess Elayse. She smiled coldly into the mirror, her new beauty making her seem all the more wicked. She smoothed back her now golden hair. "Now, my young lord, my pretty one," she murmured. "There is a mystery about you, but I shall penetrate all, shall I not? Yes, now, tonight, my pretty young fool."

Wary, Alonin shrank back into his nook, watching with cold revulsion as the woman went to the secret passage, threw back the curtain, and left. Alonin sighed out his withheld breath, glad to be out of Urganni's presence. He waited for a moment, then came out from his hiding place.

He went directly to the mirror, and stood studying it for a time. Then, coming to his inevitable decision, he spread out his arms and legs as he had seen Urganni do and visualized, as vividly as he could, the form of Red Moridar in the bright face of the mirror. Haltingly, he began to speak the words of the spell he had overheard Urganni say, ending at last with the words, *"Ma'kee atu s'drae!"*

He fell silent, feeling a strange churning sweep through his body. A lightness grew in his head; his flesh crawled. But then, his talisman began to throb, driving out these sensations with its dull, steady beat. When the talisman ceased its throb, and when he returned his gaze to the mirror, he was disappointed to find his own familiar countenance staring back at him.

The realization of defeat tugged downward on his spirits, and he pursed his lips together grimly. Reaching up with one hand, he toyed thoughtfully with his talisman. It was just possible that the talisman had somehow worked against the spell he had tried to place on himself. If this were so, he knew of only one way to remove the impediment.

Alonin hesitated, reluctant to make the required action. But finally, seeing no other way, he reached up slowly and drew off the talisman. Holding it suspended by its chain he went to the sideboard and placed it carefully on the polished marble top. Deprived of his lucky charm, he felt naked and vulnerable.

As soon as the talisman left his hands, the oppressive forces woven about the mirror seemed to redouble. A ponderous weight descended crushingly on Alonin. Against incredible pressure, he struggled back to the mirror. The air seemed to thicken to oppose him.

Facing the glass, he slowly raised his arms, his every muscle protesting against the gesture. Again he projected Moridar's visage into the silvered surface of the mirror; once more he took up the chant—but now the words seemed to be forcing themselves from his lips, and he did not think that he could stop their flow, even had he wanted to. When the last of the spell had been uttered, he paused expectantly. The silence was unnatural in its completeness. The room went suddenly dark, then blazed with blinding light. A rushing grew in Alonin's ears, and a great churning within him. Powerful forces tore at him from all directions; he felt he was being torn asunder. He was on the verge of losing his consciousness and he would have fallen, had he not been held bolt-upright by the hideous powers that swam about him. Fixed there, seemingly forever, he was pulled at, pummeled, and shaped. Then, without warning, there was a great explosion in his ears, and the assailing pressures ceased abruptly. With a ragged cry, Alonin sunk nervelessly to his knees.

Stunned, Alonin cupped his face in his hands, uttering a low sob. Suddenly he noticed that the geography of his face felt strange to him; the nose was too blunt, the cheeks too full, the jaw not long enough. Alonin uncovered his face and peered into the mirror.

Staring back from the silvered glass was the dark, saturnine face of Red Moridar. Alonin studied wonderingly the familiar yet unfamiliar visage, probing the flesh with his fingertips. He noticed that his hands were altered also: the fingers were too thick, dark, and blunt to be his own.

Alonin tugged experimentally at the short black beard that had sprouted along his jawline. Seeing his flesh pull away with the beard, he realized that this was no simple illusion he had worked upon himself, but a true changing, a complete alteration of the very stuff of his being.

Rising shakily, Alonin examined his full length in the mirror. He had lost several inches in height, gained perhaps twenty pounds. Even his clothes were those of Red Moridar. It was a peculiar feeling to find that he was someone else.

Alonin tried speaking then. He found that, while his voice was now of the proper timbre for Moridar, the manner was all wrong. He tried once more, imitating the pirate lord as best he could. The effect this time was better, though still far from perfect. Well, he thought, it would have to do.

Going to the sideboard, Alonin made to retrieve his talisman—but when his fingers touched it, such an intense feeling of dislocation twisted through him that he was forced to drop it.

Withdrawing his hand, he chewed thoughtfully on two fingers. Even now, it seemed, the talisman was in conflict with the spell he had put upon himself. If he tried to wear it, he risked loosing the guise he wore. Alonin scowled. He could not leave it behind.

Then he remembered that when Mernon gave it to him, the wizard said that it would only have effect if it touched directly on his skin. Therefore, all he had to do was keep it from doing that. Alonin looked around for something to wrap it in and found nothing. Then his eyes fell on the drape that covered the entrance to the secret passage. *Of course!* he thought.

Going to the curtain, he swept up a portion of it in his hands. The fabric of the drape itself was too heavy to tear, and he had nothing with which to cut it, but it was backed with a thin, silky stuff. Alonin managed to rip away a patch of this.

Returning to the sideboard, Alonin covered the talisman with the torn fabric and picked up both in his hand. He made sure that the talisman was tightly wrapped, then placed it in the bottom of his belt pouch. There! He was ready.

Alonin glanced back to the mirror. Strong was the temptation to destroy it before he went, but that could prove extremely dangerous. It might remove the spell of transformation from him. Worse, it might lock him into his present shape forever. It might even kill him. *I can't take the risk,* Alonin thought. *Best just to leave it be.*

Alonin stirred himself to action. He would have only a short time before Urganni grew suspicious, and there was much to do.

Going to the door, he let himself out into the hallway. He appeared to be in the main section of the fortress, rather than the isolated wing in which he was housed. He peered along the corridor in both directions. The way on his left he recognized as leading toward the throne room, so he set off briskly in the other direction.

After a few minutes he came to a place where two corridors crossed one another. Standing at the junction, pike in hand, was a solitary house guard. Seeing Alonin striding toward him, he gave a loose-mouthed look of astonishment.

Alonin walked boldly up to the man, imitating as best he could Moridar's slouch-shouldered swagger. "Is there something wrong, guard?" he asked in a voice not his own.

The guard swallowed, clearly terrified of him. "No, nothing, my lord. But . . ."

"But?"

"Well, my lord, it's just that I saw you go to your quarters—" He pointed lamely down the side corridor. "—not more than an hour ago. How did you . . . ?" His voice faded away, leaving the question hanging in the air.

Alonin accepted the information with a thin smile. He had been simply attempting to find his way back to his own apartments where Dalkin waited for him, but now he was reminded that he still had unfinished business with Moridar. "Accompany me to my quarters," he said.

The guard looked around indecisively. "I'm not supposed to leave my post."

"Not even if I command it?"

"Well . . . I suppose that would be all right. If you command it, Lord Moridar."

"Lead on, then, guard. Lead on," Alonin said.

"Aye, my lord."

The man turned and started unhappily down the corridor, Alonin following along close behind. About a hundred feet down the hall the guard stopped in front of an anonymous door. "Here we are, my lord," he said.

With a bland look, Alonin said, "Lend me your poniard."

Bemusedly, the guard said, "Eh . . . ? Aye, my lord." He unsheathed his dagger and handed it to Alonin.

"Very good. You may return to your post now. I may require your services later, however."

The man hesitated. Alonin could tell that he wanted very much to know what was going on, but was afraid to come out and ask. Curiosity warred briefly with caution; caution won. "Aye, my lord," he said in a subdued voice.

With a faint smirk, Alonin watched the man go. Things were going amazingly well. If his luck could hold another hour yet, he would make good his escape.

Alonin tried the door. It was unbolted—yet another piece of good fortune. He pushed it in slowly. The door made a slight groaning sound as it swung inward; Alonin winced at the noise.

The room beyond the door was dark. Alonin slipped inside and closed the door behind him. His eyes probed the gloom, until they fell on a large fourposter bed on the other side of the room. On the bed, under a thick mass of blankets, a man lay busily snoring.

Stealing silently across the dark chamber to the bed, he studied the slumbering shape for a moment. It was Moridar, all right, mouth hanging slackly open. Very good.

Alonin sat suddenly on the edge of the bed, putting most

of his weight on his one arm that ran across Moridar's
beefy chest and arms, pinioning them. His free hand held
the dagger at the man's throat.

Moridar awoke and immediately began to struggle.
Alonin bore down harder on the man's chest. He said in a
low, menacing voice, "Be good, or I will slit your miserable
throat."

Moridar ceased his struggles. Peering up through the
gloom at his captor, his eyes widened, then narrowed.
Alonin wondered what was running through his head,
seeing his exact double holding a knife at his throat.

"Urganni!" Moridar exclaimed, "what is this?"

"I'm not Urganni, fool!"

"Who, then?"

"You should remember me, Lord Moridar. I paid you
well enough to deliver me to this accursed island."

"*You!*"

"Indeed, Lord Moridar, me. Now, I have but one question to put to you: where are our weapons?"

Moridar's face set with stubborn hatred. "I know not,"
he said.

Tickling the man's throat with the point of his dagger,
Alonin said, "Come, Moridar, I should hate to kill you over
so small a thing."

"You will kill me no matter what I do."

"Not so. I may have your appearance now but, thank the
gods, I don't have your disposition. I do not kill unless I
must."

Moridar deliberated over this for a moment, then he
said, "Very well. Your sword is here in my room—see,
over by the chest. It took my fancy. The rest of your weapons . . . I don't know . . . They are probably in the ar-
mory."

Alonin turned his head warily, directing his gaze across
the room. As Moridar had said, his sword was standing
upright in the corner. Turning back, he said, "Many
thanks, Moridar—and pleasant dreams!" So saying, he delivered a stout blow to the side of the man's head with the
heavy handle of the dagger. Moridar gave out a low groan
and went limp.

Alonin crossed the room and retrieved his sword, lofting
it in one hand, grateful to feel its deadly weight in his

grasp again. He sheathed the ancient weapon at his side, then shifted his attention to the oaken chest in the corner.

The chest was large, stoutly built, reinforced with thick fittings of tarnished brass. A small iron padlock hung through a metal loop on the front of it, sealing the chest against casual inspection. Alonin knelt by the chest; with his borrowed poniard, he tore the lock fitting from the splintering wood. Opening the chest, he saw that it contained, as Alonin had suspected, some part of Moridar's personal collection of plunder—gold, silver, rings, jewels, chains, finely inlaid boxes, rare spices and essences, sumptuous fabrics. After removing from this glittering store thirty turlons of gold—the price he had paid Moridar for his passage to Agiza-Saligor—Alonin shut the lid on the rest of the treasure.

With ragged strips torn from the bed sheets, Alonin trussed and gagged the unconscious Moridar. He took Moridar's own sword from where it hung on the back of a chair and thrust it into his belt; it would have to do for Dalkin.

Alonin left the room and returned to where the guard stood sentinel. Handing the dagger back to the man, Alonin said, "Thank you for the use of your weapon."

"Uh, you're welcome, my lord."

"Do you know where the outland lord and his companion are being held?" Alonin asked.

"Aye, Lord Moridar."

"Good. I want you to conduct me there."

The man's face registered no change; he was resigned, it seemed. "Aye, my lord," he said.

Another sentry was stationed in the hall outside Alonin's apartments. After having the man unlock the door, Alonin told him and the other man to wait. He went through into the rooms.

Dalkin was sitting propped up in bed. When he saw Alonin come through the door, he stiffened and half rose. "Moridar!" he cried.

"Not so, my friend. Despite all appearances, it is I, Alonin."

Dalkin's deep-set eyes narrowed. "What sort of trick is this? What kind of fool do you take me for?"

Alonin gave him an ironic smile. "Are your two brothers

and the rest of your merchant family in Imre also this suspicious?"

A look of dawning realization swept across Dalkin's face. "Alonin! It is you! I'll be damned! You told me you were up to something, but I never imagined anything like this. How did you manage it?" He gaped at Alonin in amazement.

"I didn't tell you about this before because I wasn't sure it would work. I'll give you the whole story later—right now, we had better get out of here. By the way, I brought you a present." Alonin pulled Moridar's blade from his belt and handed it to the other man.

Hefting the sword, Dalkin frowned. "Too heavy for my taste," he said. The sword was much larger than his customary weapon. Its blade did not quite have the reach of Alonin's sword, but it was almost as wide.

"It will have to do for now. I couldn't get your own blade."

"Just so, just so."

"Hurry now, get yourself together. We haven't much time."

" 'Twill be done in a nonce."

While Dalkin was collecting his meager possessions, Alonin went to his bedside and took up the case containing the Dylcaer. He opened the case, just to make certain that the stone was still inside. Within, in its bed of black velvet, the jewel flared like a pocket of blue fire. This time the light did not fade, but grew ever brighter. Alonin was struck motionless. Dancing before his eyes, the Dylcaer swelled and grew larger; his eyes were drawn deep into the heart of it. Gradually he began to perceive shadows amidst the blazing light. He looked deeper; the shadows resolved themselves into a pattern. A face! it was long and as sharp as the edge of a sword; its brow was heavy, and two small bony projections stood out on its forehead. Its burning eyes fell upon Alonin. The coldness of the eternal void touched him. The face smiled, a triumphant smile.

Alonin heard Dalkin's voice. "Alonin, are you all right? Alonin! What's the matter?"

Alonin tried to speak and found that he could not. Perspiration burst out on his forehead. Suddenly, with the psychic equivalant of a snap, the Dylcaer let him go. The unnatural gleam in the gem dulled, but did not go out.

Alonin gasped, his head reeling. He sat shakily on the edge of the bed. His memory of the last few moments faded rapidly, as with a dream; he found that he could no longer recall what the face in the gem had looked like; he could not even say that it was not a work of his own imagination.

"What's the matter?" repeated Dalkin.

"I'm . . . I'm not sure. I'm all right now. Are you ready to go?"

"Ready, if you are."

"Just a moment." Alonin snapped shut the Dylcaer's case and slipped it into his doublet, near his heart. He went to the window and peeked out into the garden. Elayse/ Urganni was pacing furiously between the benches and the fountain. She chose just that moment to shoot an impatient look in Alonin's direction. He avoided her gaze by flattening against the wall. He slipped from the window.

"Come," he said to Dalkin, "we have but a brief time."

Alonin ordered the two guards waiting outside in the hall to conduct Dalkin and himself to Moridar's ship, the *Akabeth*. Once aboard the quiet ship, he dismissed them both, then went below deck, found the first mate's cabin, and roused the swarthy Icthan from his sleep.

"Awake! Awake!" Alonin ordered loudly, nudging the rickety bunk with his knee.

"Eh? What?" the bewildered Icthan mumbled, sitting up suddenly in bed.

"Awake, I say!"

The Icthan's puffy red eyes found Alonin's face. "*Uumph.* Moridar," he said, rubbing his face with the heels of his hands. "What is it, Captain?"

"I want you to get the crew together. We sail for Tulin."

"Now? Tonight?"

"Yes, *now*," Alonin said sardonically. "This one—" He jerked his thumb back toward Dalkin. "—has a mission for Urganni on the mainland which cannot wait."

"Mmm. All right. Give me a minute to pull myself together."

"I mean to be underway within a half an hour," Alonin said, making for the door of the cramped cabin.

"All right! All right! Give me a minute, will you?"

Alonin and Dalkin went up on deck into the damp night air and watched as the ship came alive. Sharp and insistent, a bell rang. Sleepy-eyed sailors came pouring out onto the deck, roused from their dark warren bellow; there was an exchange of shouting; the sails were inspected and made ready; men took up their stations at the oars; lines were cast off.

The Icthan came finally to Alonin and said, "All is in readiness, Captain. What are your orders?"

Alonin hesitated. There was a major problem with his passing himself off as a sea captain, he reflected, and that was that he would be expected to know how to sail. Alonin, whose knowledge of the sea and of ships was, to say the least, limited, found himself at a loss. He hemmed for a moment, then said brusquely, "Carry on. There is much that I must discuss with this one before we reach port."

The Icthan cocked his eyebrows slightly, but answered obediently, "Aye, Captain."

After the first mate had left to take control of the ship, Dalkin murmured, "Well, that came off pretty well."

"Yes," Alonin said. "Fortunately, he has no reason to believe that I am anything other than that which I appear to be. Anything strange in my behavior he can easily explain away. With luck, we will be off this ship before he can become suspicious."

"Let's hope so."

Sharp commands cracked through the lazy air, and the *Akabeth* was backed slowly away from the dock and brought about to a seaward heading. The sails were run up and they filled with a brisk wind.

The moon was full that night; its radiance made the clouds scudding overhead show as tarnished silver against the stark black sky. Gazing up, Alonin tried to gauge the time remaining before dawn. Five hours, maybe a little more. Ample time for them to reach Tulin.

Behind them, from the now distant island, came a wild clanging of bells, drifting thinly on the wind. "It sounds like our escape has been noted," Dalkin said. He laughed, a little wildly. "For all the good it will do them. Before they can get a single ship from the harbor, we will be halfway to Tulin."

"Don't let's celebrate yet," Alonin said, looking back with apprehension at the island. "Urganni may yet be able to stop us with powers we cannot even guess at."

"Witchery?"

"Witchery."

The next hour passed uneventfully. The ship made good time, cutting neatly over the night-darkened waves. There was no sign of pursuit. All was going well. *Why, then, this feeling of dread I have?* Alonin wondered gloomily.

Somehow he knew that their voyage could not be without incident, that there must come something to block their way. And he was not wrong in this, for a few minutes later the first mate came forward again from where he had been directing the progress of the ship. "Captain!" he said, his voice crackling with excitement.

"What is it?" Alonin asked.

"Look!" The man pointed off to the northwest, where Alonin could just barely discern a fat band of black clouds boiling toward the *Akabeth*, sealing off the star-flecked sky with astonishing rapidity.

"A storm, Captain," the Icthan said. "It looks to be a beauty. It is cutting right across our course, and it's bearing down fast. What should we do?"

Alonin ground his teeth together. "Do? Make sure everything is secured, and hold to your course. I mean to make Tulin before dawn."

"Captain, are you certain? This be dangerous weather we're heading into."

"You have your orders."

"Aye, sir," the man said without much spirit; his left cheek gave a tic of repressed emotion.

"Poor fellow thinks I've gone mad," Alonin observed as the Icthan trudged away once more.

"Who knows, perhaps you have," Dalkin said, for he was watching the approach of the storm now, and he looked gravely worried.

Alonin shot a glance in the direction that his companion was looking. "I wonder if this is of Urganni's creation?"

"Do you think she has the power to block our path in this manner?"

"I don't know, I truly don't, but I can't say that she hasn't."

The storm struck a bare half an hour later. First an ominous calm descended upon the ship. The sails went slack, and a stale, dead smell hung in the air. The seamen on the deck all stopped whatever they were doing and looked with dread expectancy to where the rolling storm clouds were drawing across the sky. A long moment passed. A breeze came like a sigh. Then, with sudden fury, a howling wind raked across the sea, lashing into the side of the ship. Shimmering black swells arose, broke over the railing and onto the deck. The angry clouds massed overhead to lock out the stars and the moon. Lightning cut searing zigzag scars against the blackness.

Alonin had to clutch a rail to keep from being swept overboard. He called out to Dalkin: "By the triple goddess, this is unbelievable!"

"What?" Dalkin cried, his voice lost to the winds. Alonin merely shook his head, tightening his grasp on the rail.

The storm steadily increased in intensity. The wind roared with fury, then moaned piteously, Through the gale Alonin could hear the cries and curses of the frantic seamen, sounding vague and far away, as if in a dimly remembered dream. The rain struck against his face with stinging force. Groaning, the deck rose and fell violently beneath him.

After a seeming eternity of being lashed by storm and sea, Alonin saw the Icthan first mate lurching slowly toward him across the wave-swept deck. Making his way painfully to where Alonin stood clutching the railing, the Icthan shouted, "This is lunacy, Captain. We must turn back before it's too late!"

"Must you insist on questioning my orders?" Alonin roared in mock fury. "I say we go on!"

"But Captain—"

"You have your orders!"

"Captain, you know that I have never questioned your orders before, but—"

"Then don't start now!"

The Icthan's face twisted with a dire emotion. "As you will," he said in a dead voice, "but you are wrong."

"Get out of my sight and do as you are told!"

The Icthan wheeled about angrily and started to make his way laboriously across the tossing deck.

Watching the man go, Alonin said tensely to his companion, "We're not going to make it."

"We'll make it," Dalkin assured him. "Despite his lack of faith, that Icthan knows how to handle a ship. It will just take us a little longer, that's all."

Alonin felt sick with despair. "No, you don't understand. It can't."

Dalkin frowned. "Why not? If there are any ships following us, they will be as discommoded as we are."

"That's not what worries me. This is difficult to explain, but at dawn the guise I wear will fall from me. Gods, at least I hope it will—I do not relish the thought of being locked into this form forever. Can you imagine what he—" Alonin indicated the slowly departing form of the Icthan. "—will do when he discovers I'm not his precious captain?"

Dalkin looked suddenly thoughtful and troubled. "Dawn! That will be cutting it close."

For hours the *Akabeth* struggled onward, making little headway against the raging tempest. Eventually the winds grew so fierce that the sails had to be run down in order to save the masts, and from then on the ship had to proceed by the straining sinews of the oarsmen alone.

During the complicated process of lowering the sails, one unfortunate young lad slipped from the wet rigging. He fell screaming and was broken upon the heaving deck. When this happened, the first mate turned to glare pointedly at Alonin, as if to say, "Because of you, so may we all meet such an end."

Alonin was pierced through by guilt, thinking of how he was using these men for his own purposes, without the smallest consideration for the peril in which he placed them. But then he reminded himself sternly that they were all pirates, raiders, their souls besmirched by the blood of countless innocents. It eased his guilt to regard the matter in this way, though it did not purge it.

The storm began to abate with the first gray light presaging the dawn. By this time, however, the gale had done its work. The *Akabeth* was still far from shore, and the terrible winds had forced it many miles south of its goal.

Holding onto the rail with tense, bloodless fingers, Alonin gazed despondently across the tossing sea to the stark black outline marking the shore. *So close*, he thought, *so very close*. Too close to allow him to admit defeat, and yet for all practical purposes the shore might just as well have been a world away. Within minutes, the sun would rise over the horizon, and Alonin would be revealed as himself. He pursed his lips together and thought. There had to be some way out.

Dalkin stirred suddenly beside him, bringing his fist down lightly on the polished wood of the rail. He uttered an exclamation of triumph. "Come on," he said, "I think I have an idea."

"What is it?"

"No time. Follow me."

Having no plan of his own, Alonin could not but do as he was told. He followed Dalkin along the unstable deck, the rain and the salty spray of the sea stinging his face. Dalkin ducked through a hatch leading into the main housing; Alonin followed close behind.

"Aha! I thought I remembered seeing these beauties earlier." Dalkin said with obvious delight, going to the three wooden barrels lashed together in the corner. They were large, bulky, potbellied casks, made of stout staves of seasoned oak and banded by thick rings of brass. "Help me cut one loose," he said.

"I still don't understand what your idea is," Alonin said, stooping to help the other man cut the barrel free.

"It is my idea that when this cask is emptied, it should float extraordinarily well."

"Of course!" Alonin exclaimed, Dalkin's plan coming suddenly into his mind. He was afflicted with a sudden skepticism. "But do you think that we'll have a chance on so rough a sea?"

"I couldn't say. But do you have a better idea?"

"No," Alonin confessed.

Working quickly, the two men pried the lid from the barrel and spilled out its contents—well over a hundred pounds of coarse, brown flour—and then pounded the lid back on.

"That should make it fairly watertight," Dalkin muttered. "Now, what we need are some handholds."

With a long length of rope, to which they tied loops made from several shorter lengths, they tightly wrapped the barrel. Dalkin tugged firmly on each loop, testing it for strength, and then finally grunted in satisfaction. "All right," he said, "let's get this monster out on deck."

Straining and grunting, they lifted up the bulky barrel and lurched to the hatch, and then out onto the deck.

During the time they had spent in the housing, it had grown much brighter outside. The ship was bathed in the somber light of the coming day; in the eastern sky, the clouds had caught the ruddy fire of the rising sun. There could only be minutes before dawn broke over the horizon.

Alonin felt a faint tingling sensation thrilling through his limbs, and he heard a distant buzzing in his ears. His strength drained suddenly from him, and he stumbled on the uneven deck. *It's starting*, he thought

"Hurry!" he said urgently to Dalkin.

They carried the heavy oaken cask to the edge of the deck, hefted it higher, and balanced it on the railing.

At this inopportune moment, the Icthan appeared around the corner of the housing. Seeing them, he started forward, a confused look on his face. "Captain!" he said. "What are you—" He stopped abruptly in his tracks, gaping in wonder at Alonin—for at that instant, the sun broke over the edge of the sea and its golden radiance fell upon the young lord.

Alonin fell back against the railing, his frame shaken by a series of violent convulsions. The intense feeling of dislocation, the painful hum in his head, the sense of crawling evil assailing him, all told him that he was changing back into his own form. He gasped, trying to force himself back from the rail, but he did not have the strength to defeat the immense pressure holding him back. He saw a flash of light from behind his closed eyelids, heard a resounding *crack*, and then the force pressing down upon him ceased abruptly. Dazed, Alonin staggered forward a step.

He glanced down at his hands, reassuring himself that he was indeed back in his own body. The sight of his own familiar slender fingers—one of them banded by the gold signet of Caladon—gave him a tremendous rush of relief.

This feeling, however, was not long-lived for just at that moment the voice of the Icthan bellowed out, "Seize those two!"

Alonin looked up just in time to see three burly sailors racing at him and his companion, one a little behind the other two. When the first sailor came within reach, Alonin dealt him a terrific backhanded blow to the jaw, and the sailor fell back stunned against the wooden storage housing. Dalkin caught the second sailor with a slashing blow to the windpipe; the man sank slowly to his knees, gasping for breath, his face congested and purple. By the time that the third sailor reached them, Alonin and Dalkin were poised unsteadily on the railing beside the barrel. With a snarl, Dalkin dispatched him with a well-placed kick. By this time, however, reinforcements were reaching the fray, some brandishing weapons. In a rough semicircle, the seamen closed slowly on Alonin and Dalkin.

Pushing together, the two men tipped the barrel from the rail into the gray flood below. "Jump!" Dalkin cried, immediately following his own advice.

On an impulse, Alonin paused to pat the case containing the Dylcaer, to verify that he had not lost it in the excitement. In that instant, perhaps emboldened by the fact that Alonin was now alone, one of the seamen dodged forward with a loud whoop and seized Alonin by his left arm; the young lord was very nearly pulled from the rail. He struggled to tear free, but the sailor was strong, and Alonin's precarious balance put him at a disadvantage. Seeing Alonin thus caught, the rest of the sailors closed in quickly for the kill, uttering sounds of animal triumph.

The inexplicable chose this moment to intrude. A powerful pulse of energy passed from the Dylcaer's box into Alonin's hand; he felt his desperation turn to arrogant fury. Not knowing how he did it, he reached skyward with his mind. In response, a bolt of searing, violet lightning arced down from the heavens. There was a blinding flash, a throbbing boom, and the man who held Alonin fell back senseless against his comrades.

Chaos broke out on the ship. Those of the crew who had been closest to Alonin now lay stunned on the deck; the rest milled about in panicked confusion. The storage housing was on fire; dancing flames and thick black smoke shot from it. Certain of the seamen tried frantically to smother the flames with their cloaks, to no noticeable effect. The Icthan shouted orders, which were largely ignored.

Alonin noted all of this in the barest fraction of an instant; he did not pause to reflect upon it. He turned immediately and leaped from the rail. There was a moment of free-fall, then the shock of plunging feet first into the icy water. A wave caught him and pounded him against the hull of the *Akabeth*. His breathed battered from him, Alonin was jerked beneath the foaming waves, where he was spun about by the churning currents. No longer sure of which way was up and which way was down, he thrashed out desperately with his arms and legs, lungs bursting. At last one arm broke the surface, and he felt a hand grasp it. He was pulled up, and his head broke through into the air. Gasping, choking, Alonin sucked the sweet air greedily into his burning lungs. Through blurred, salt-stung eyes, he saw Dalkin bobbing beside him on the barrel, his hand extended out to him. Alonin swam a stroke, still trying to get his breath, and caught at one of the loops of rope.

"Are you all right?" Dalkin asked.

Coughing up water, Alonin nodded.

"What happened?"

"I . . . I don't know, exactly. Something to do with the Dylcaer . . ."

"Tell me about it later. Now we swim."

Clutching the barrel before them, the two men started kicking toward shore. The gale-tossed waves rose and fell about them, curling and breaking over their heads. The barrel proved an unwieldly craft; it kept trying to roll in the water, plunging first one man then the other beneath the surface.

After several minutes of struggle, Alonin cried out: "Stop. I must take my boots off before I can go any farther."

Linking his arms with the coarse loop of rope, Alonin reached under the water and pulled off his boots, abandoning them to the swirling currents. He momentarily considered forsaking his sword which hung heavy at his side, but he decided to bear the weight rather than lose the ancient weapon.

Alonin shot a glance back to the *Akabeth*. The fire had

spread; the entire storage housing was ablaze, and the flames had leaped up to involve the mainmast. Hoisting up great leather buckets of sea water from over the side, the crew was desperately trying to quench the blaze, but Alonin could see that their efforts were destined to meet with failure. The *Akabeth* was doomed.

Alonin drew a long breath. "All right," he said, "let's go!"

They started once more toward the shore, lashing the water with quick, powerful kicks. The sea raged all around them, fighting them for each yard gained toward their goal. Alonin grew exhausted; his breathing became ragged and labored, and often what he breathed in was not air but water. His legs grew heavier and heavier; they seemed joined to him only by the pain it cost him to move them. Each kick was a minor agony, but he kept doggedly on.

The rugged coastline hung tantalizingly before him: sheer cliffs, narrow strips of sand, gnarled fingers of sea-pitted rock. Alonin held it longingly in his fatigue-blurred eyes, watching it grow closer with agonizing slowness.

Whether it took hours or minutes to reach that grim shore, Alonin could not say. Pain and exhaustion made his mind too small to contain the concept of time. All he knew was that he had to keep moving, keep kicking, or perish.

Alonin and Dalkin propelled their makeshift craft painfully into a small inlet. A giant swell caught them, battering them against the sharp rocks, with the barrel taking the brunt of the impact. There was a loud *crack* and the sound of splintering wood, then the primitive craft shattered into jagged shards.

Alonin scrambled onto the rocks. The rough, glistening stone was studded with clinging black mussel shells; Alonin made use of the black shellfish for handholds. Just as he secured himself to the rock, the sea began to recede, doing its utmost to pull him out with it. Alonin clung with all of his waning strength to the mussels, until finally the waters withdrew entirely, and he could loose his frantic grip.

"Come on!" he gasped out to Dalkin. He took off, running unsteadily through the ankle-deep water. He made it several yards down the shore before the tide began to rush in once more. Grabbing onto the rocks, he was struck by a fresh assault of waves. These, too, then began to recede, and Alonin, knocked from his feet by the pounding force of the sea, was kept from being swept away once more by his hold on the shiny black mussels. As soon as the tide stopped pulling at him, he got up and began slogging his way along the shoreline.

It was in this way that he made his slow, tortuous progress to safety. Finally, he reached a long finger of rock that jutted far out to sea. With the very last of his strength, Alonin clambered up wearily onto the jutting rock, his feet cut and bleeding from the sharp, abrasive stone. On the other side of the rock Alonin saw a small, sandy stretch of beach beckoning to him. With a vast sense of relief, he leaped down, collapsing face first into the soft, damp sand.

Alonin heard Dalkin come down behind him. "Alonin? How are you?" he heard him ask.

Alonin rolled over onto his back. A great gasping sigh tore from him. "I'm fine, just great. You?"

"I'll live."

Dalkin stood towering over him. A red, burning sun was at his back, lending him a bloody cast. The play of light and shadow on his face sculpted it into something dire and fantastic. "And the Dylcaer—do you still have the Dylcaer?" he asked quickly, with ragged breath.

Alonin felt a brief spasm of alarm. A pat to his doublet reassured him. "I have it," he said.

Dalkin dropped limply to his knees. He began to chuckle crazily. "Gods!" he said. "We made it! I don't believe it!"

Alonin looked askance at Dalkin. Seeing the man's wet, steaming clothes, his drowned hair and beard, his red, congested face, Alonin began to laugh giddily, unable to control himself. "Neither do I," he said weakly, writhing with laughter. "Oh! Neither do I!"

13

"THIS route seems to be our best bet," Alonin said, stabbing down with one finger at the grease-spotted map resting on the dark-grained oaken table. "To the south. To be sure, it does take us out of our way—but in the long run, I believe we will be better off, what with snow blocking the northern passes. See, we can cut through this gap here, skirting the wastes of Klu."

Dalkin studied the map, nodding slowly. "I agree. We should go south."

"Good," Alonin said, folding the map into a small square and inserting it into the pouch that hung at his belt. "Well, that settles that. Shall we eat?"

A huge lunch consisting of various cold meats, cheeses, bread, and fruit was spread before them, and the two men devoted themselves to the eating of it. It was two days now since their return to Tulin, but they still maintained the tremendous appetites created by the long and comfortless trek to the city from where they had washed ashore.

After the meal was finished, the dishes were taken away, and Alonin and Dalkin settled back before the comforting smoky yellow glow emanating from the soot-blackened fireplace, sipping at their wine—a rough local vintage. Dalkin lit his pipe. He sat puffing wordlessly for a time, his head wreathed by pale blue smoke. Finally he said, "So. To Caladon."

"To Caladon," Alonin agreed.

Dalkin stared pensively into the crackling fire, eyes slightly unfocused. He drew a long, noisy breath through his nose. "I have been wondering about something," he said.

"Yes?" Alonin asked. "What is it?"

"Mind, it is just idle curiosity—you don't have to answer

if you don't want to—but . . . It is about the Dylcaer." He sucked again on the stem of his pipe and cleared his throat. "Now that you have obtained the gem—a difficult proce- dure, to say the least—why give it away to the dragon Thu- dredid? Why, the Dylcaer is priceless, absolutely priceless. From what you told me about how it helped you on the *Akabeth*, it would seem that its power is immense. Just think if one could harness that power . . ."

"No . . . no. It is evil."

"Evil? Why then did it come to your aid when you were in need?"

"I don't know."

"I'll tell you what I think. This wizard, this Mernon, he filled you with a lot of nonsense about the Dylcaer, so you wouldn't try to penetrate its secrets. He wants you to give it up, because then he can take it for himself."

"No," Alonin said. But there was uncertainty in his heart.

"I mean, give it up—for what? With it you could carve out a dozen realms to equal poor ruined Caladon!"

Tensing his jaw, Alonin said, "Even supposing that what you say is true, certainly you must be aware that the recla- mation of Caladon is not my sole motivation in this. In- deed, it is not even the greatest of them. There is also the matter of revenge."

"Yes, revenge. Here is something else that I am hard put to understand. Why this overwhelming compulsion to avenge the deaths of men you never even knew?"

"These men you speak of are my ancestors—and one of them my father. This seems adequate cause for vengeance, do you not agree?"

"Yes, yes, of course," Dalkin said briskly. "But still in all, you owe them nothing. They are dead, and you cer- tainly cannot change that. But think! Are you so eager to surrender the Dylcaer?"

"The loss will only be for a brief time. After I slay Thu- dredid, it will be mine once more."

"Assuming, of course, that the dragon doesn't kill you, instead of the other way around. This is by no means a safe assumption. The course you follow smacks of folly; I tell you this because I am your friend and I love you well. In getting the Dylcaer, you have already succeeded beyond all expectations. Can you not be satisfied with your gains? Must you risk all in a reckless adventure?"

Alonin glowered at his companion. In truth, Dalkin had said nothing that Alonin himself had not considered; he too had wondered at his motives; he too had entertained the attractive notion of keeping the Dylcaer for himself, of delving its power. Still, it angered him to have Dalkin parroting his own deepest desires to him, perhaps because he knew that he could not allow his sense of purpose to be eroded any more than it already had been.

He said stiffly, "I do not expect you to understand my feelings in this. Suffice it to say that I am resolved to follow this course I have set for myself."

"Yes," Dalkin said, "but—"

"I do not wish to discuss the matter any longer. The subject distresses me," Alonin snapped. Almost immediately, he regretted the sharpness of his tone.

Dalkin glared at him for a moment, anger tightening the corners of his eyes; then he shrugged sullenly. "As you will, Lord," he said.

The two men spent the rest of the afternoon among the teeming market stalls of Tulin, replenishing their stores for the long journey to Caladon. All the while, Dalkin remained sulky and withdrawn. In irritation, Alonin made no attempt to humor him. As the purple shadows of evening grew, they returned to the inn, ate dinner in silence, and retired early to their room.

Alonin could not sleep that night. In him there was a restlessness, a nameless anxiety. He tossed in bed for an intolerable period of time, then gave up. Propping himself up in bed, he poured himself a glass of wine from the half-full bottle at his bedside, hoping that it would relax him.

Sipping the tart red liquid, Alonin gazed glumly at the curtain-shrouded window. The weather outside was stormy and unsettled; the bare, wind-blown branches of an old oak moved restlessly, casting ominous, shadowy claws against the curtains.

On the nightstand next to the bed rested the case containing the Dylcaer. Alonin was painfully conscious of it now. More and more, it was becoming difficult to put the gem from his mind. He wanted badly to open the box, gaze upon that which it held, and it required a firm act of will to keep himself from doing this.

But why should he not take it up? If he could master its power, what could he not accomplish? Surely it would give him the strength to void the dragon's curse, even to destroy the dragon itself. Thudredid would shrink before his terrible might . . .

"No," he murmured to himself, squeezing his eyes shut. "I must not even think it."

Alonin drained his glass and put it aside, then settled back and tried to purge his mind of thought. He had finally succeeded in gaining that vague realm occupying the space between wakefulness and sleep when, without warning, a sharp, incoherent cry rang out. Jarred awake, Alonin sat up quickly. The shout had come from Dalkin, he saw; the red-haired man was tossing feverishly in his bed, muttering violently, evidently in the thrall of some troubling dream.

Alonin hesitated for a moment, wondering whether to wake the man or let the dream run its course. The decision was taken from him when Dalkin uttered a startled cry and heaved abruptly upright, eyes snapping open. He stared forward for a moment, face taut, eyes darting.

"Take it easy, friend," Alonin said quickly. "You were having a nightmare. It's all right now."

Dalkin swiveled a curiously blank look in his direction. He shivered suddenly, then covered his face with his hands. "Yes," he said hollowly, "a nightmare."

"Want to tell me about it?"

"It was . . . No, I can't remember. It was nothing." Dalkin settled back against his cushions, supporting his head with one arm. "It was nothing," he repeated. In his eyes, however, there was a hooded, haunted look that refuted his words.

The two men departed Tulin early the next morning. For the next several days they journeyed southward along the rugged coastlands, going from bare dunes to mist-haunted cypress woods, then inland to low, wind-scoured hills. On most mornings a thick gray overcast hung overhead; this usually burned off early in the afternoon, to return again near dusk.

A certain tenseness lay between Alonin and Dalkin; gone were the days of idle chatter and easy banter. They rode along silently, each sunk in private thoughts. Such conversation as they attempted was strained and halting, frequently falling off into irritable words. Eventually they ceased to speak at all, except when they had to, preferring silence even while sitting idly around the campfire at night.

Alonin slowly found himself growing resentful of Dalkin's presence. The red-haired man suddenly seemed to him bloated, distorted, strange. His face had become a twisted demon-mask—eyes glittering evilly under the shadow of his heavy brow, mouth drawn into a sour line, skin blotched and grainy. There were times that Alonin felt that he could come to hate the man.

Alonin had not the strength to wonder at or regret what was happening between him and Dalkin. He was tired all the time now. He rode along dully, his mind vague and foggy, his body full of small aches. He slept poorly at night, his slumber being full of feverish dreams which he found himself unable to remember in the morning. Even his waking hours began to take on a dreamlike quality, and every day the landscape through which he traveled looked to his eyes ever more flat and lacking in depth.

Increasingly, his thoughts were drawn to the Dylcaer, and the temptation to take it in hand and use it against Thudredid grew greater. To distract himself, he tried thinking about other things—his former life at Lanfarran Castle, the dragon, Marda—but all these subjects, as important as they once had been for him, seemed curiously empty, pale, drained of vitality. Only the Dylcaer, it seemed, could excite him now.

Alonin kept feeling that there was something he had forgotten to do, and this nagged at him for a long time. Hard as he tried, however, he could not make his mind close on what this might be.

On the fifth day out of Tulin the two men came upon a small, dusty town clumped in a fold between some equally small and dusty hills. Weary of spending their nights sleeping on the ground, they decided to stay that night at the local inn.

The inn was a dismal place. The structure was old and in poor repair. Wind whistled in through a number of cracks between the timbers; a thin film of dust lay on everything; cobwebs hung wavering in the corners.

Dinner was a bowl of greasy, vile-smelling stew, with some stale bread on the side. "We seem to have wonderful luck in our choices of accomodations," Alonin observed, in a forced attempt at humor. Dalkin merely grunted, his mouth quirking down at the corners. He shoveled down another spoonful of the odious stew.

For some reason, the innkeeper, a lean, anxious-looking man, became immediately suspicious of Alonin and Dalkin. He hung over the two men, watching them with keen, beady eyes as they ate, his mouth pursed with sour disapproval. What deviltry he must have thought them capable of accomplishing during dinner Alonin could not guess.

Throughout the meal Dalkin seemed agitated. He fidgeted with his food, stroking his beard nervously. When he had finished eating, he thrust himself back from the table and declared, "No point in hanging around down here. I'm going up and try to get some sleep."

"Wait a minute—I'll go with you."

"Very well."

The two men climbed the rickety stairs to the second floor and entered their room. The room was small, cramped, poorly appointed. Alonin removed his doublet and boots, but retained his hose and shirt, as the room was cold and drafty, and there was no fireplace. He spread his cloak over the single thin blanket provided him by the inn and crawled into bed.

When Dalkin was established in his own bed, Alonin said, "Good night."

"Good night," Dalkin replied.

Alonin extinguished the candle and turned over. For once, he fell almost immediately asleep.

Abruptly he found himself awake again, his mind instantly clear and aware. His nerves tingled a vague warning. Without moving, the young lord opened his eyes. He was startled to see someone standing over him in the darkness. Straining his eyes into the gloom, he discovered that this someone was Dalkin. Relaxing somewhat, Alonin said, "Dalkin! What the—"

A look of alarm flashed momentarily over Dalkin's features, before they set in an aspect of grim resolve. "Sorry," he mumbled, slightly averting his feverish gaze.

Alonin saw Dalkin raise up his hand. There was something held in that hand. Too late the young lord apprehended what was happening. The red-haired man's hand dropped rapidly, falling hard against his skull, striking first fire, then blackness.

Awareness returned gradually to Alonin. At first all he was conscious of were the lightning flashes of pain throbbing through his head. Stirring, he moaned. His hand came up hesitantly to probe the spot from which the pain emanated; his fingers came away sticky with blood. He tried weakly to sit up, but the resulting dizziness forced him back down.

Staying as still as he could, Alonin tried to form his thoughts around the pain filling his skull. What . . . what had happened? Something . . .

Suddenly he remembered; memory brought back the dizziness to him. *Why?* Alonin asked himself, *why should Dalkin—*

Alonin felt a surge of panic quicken in his veins. Despite the extreme vertigo it caused him, he pushed himself up laboriously, swinging his legs over the side of the bed. He reached out desperately and felt over the top of his nightstand. His hands met with nothing.

Unwilling to accept the evidence of his senses, he searched over the stand again, to the same effect. The Dylcaer was gone.

With a choked cry, Alonin lurched up and rushed half-undressed from the room. He clattered down the stairs, then outside into the open air. Running to the stable, he flung open the door.

He gave out a roar of rage and despair.

Dalkin's horse was gone. The red-haired man's guilt was unquestionable, yet still Alonin could not bring himself to believe it. *No!* he thought. *Impossible! It can't be!*

Wheeling about, he bolted from the stable and ran reeling down the dark, dusty road. "Dalkin!" he shouted, "where are you? Dalkin! *Answer me!*"

In the darkness, he took a misstep. His ankle twisted,

and he fell heavily to the ground. He climbed dazedly to his hands and knees. The realization of Dalkin's betrayal at last sinking in, Alonin gnashed his teeth and cried tears of rage. He slammed his fists repeatedly into the ground, mad with fury, ignoring the pain it caused him. "Thief!" he howled over and over again. "Thief! Thief! *Thief!*"

When his anger at last burned itself out, Alonin fell in an exhausted heap on the ground. "Thief," he rasped out once more in a broken voice.

Above, the stars burned as brightly as ever, indifferent, uncaring, fixed, inalterable.

14

Warm, golden sunlight slanted down over the steep, tree-grown wall of the canyon and played upon the gently lapping surface of the creek. Dismounting, Alonin dropped the reins of his horse's bridle so that the animal might drink of the creek's lime-colored waters. With a small packet of dried bread, Alonin settled beneath the shade of a large tree, near a patch of blackberry brambles. As he munched his simple meal, he studied his map.

He scowled. There could no longer be any trace of a doubt; Dalkin was headed straight into the barren wastes of Klu. This canyon could lead no place else.

Obviously Dalkin must suspect that he was being followed, else he would be giving Klu as wide a berth as possible; it had an evil reputation among travelers, and was justly shunned by all honest men. Dalkin probably hoped to lose Alonin in the blasted wastes. But if this were indeed his intention—and Alonin had to give a grim smile at this—then he would be sorely disappointed. For Alonin did not track his former companion by a means that could be confused by stealth or trickery, but rather by an unusual affinity that had somehow grown up between the Dylcaer and himself, which drew him to the gem as to a magnet. Somehow, unerringly, he knew in what direction it lay. He could feel it.

This peculiar rapport had first become apparent the night that the Dylcaer was stolen from him. In the fullness of his wrath, Alonin had hastily gathered together his things and taken off in pursuit of his treacherous friend. He had been traveling for more than an hour before it struck him that he had passed by other branches in the road without a moment's thought, that he did not even know if he was headed in the right direction. Alarmed, he had paused to examine the road he followed, and had discovered the evidence of the recent passage of a man on horseback. It was then that he realized that he could actually feel the Dylcaer tugging at some deep, barely accessible part of his mind, drawing him on.

No matter how far Dalkin ran, no matter how he tried to avoid pursuit, Alonin would find him. And then there would be a reckoning, such a reckoning!

Thinking of Dalkin, the muscles of Alonin's face constricted and tensed; he felt afresh his terrible rage. His anger and bitterness had not diminished with time, but had merely become a cold, hard kernel in his heart. There was no retribution too harsh with which to meet such treachery as Dalkin had shown him. Alonin trembled with barely controlled passion when he thought of how he had once called this spotted and inconstant man his friend.

Finishing his joyless meal, Alonin folded his map and replaced it in his pouch. As he did this, his hand brushed against something wrapped in a patch of silken fabric. Alonin realized immediately that this was the talisman, still reposing where he had put it that night on Agiza-Saligor. He had not given it a thought since then, but he knew now that this was what had been bothering him before the theft of the Dylcaer.

He considered putting it on again. A wave of lethargy swept over him. No, he thought vaguely, it could be of no use to him now. It might even have the undesirable effect of blocking out that which drew him toward the Dylcaer. Best to leave it be for the time.

Rising, Alonin drank a few handfuls of water from the sluggish creek, then filled his waterskins. Remounting, he set off once more along the narrow trail that cut through the center of the densely wooded canyon.

Alonin rode for the rest of that day and well into the next before he came to the end of the canyon. Taking to the rising ranks of the hills, Alonin found himself pushing his mount harder and harder. He tried to restrain his impatience, lest he kill the poor animal. It was hard, though. He knew that he was closing on Dalkin; he could feel the pull of the Dylcaer increase with each passing hour.

The hills through which he rode were at first covered with a sparse carpet of dry, spiny grass and wavering clumps of weed, but as Alonin rode further they lost even these somber traces of life. He was left in a bleak, colorless world of bare stone and sand and blowing cinders.

The hills gradually gained in elevation, and the weather grew steadily warmer—so much so that Alonin became uncomfortable in his thick winter clothes. He doffed his cloak and unfastened the front of his doublet. But then from time to time clouds would drift across the sun, a sudden gust of wind would moan through the hills, and he would feel a dreadful chill being driven into his bones.

After three days of journeying through the hills, Alonin came over a steep crest and saw, stretching out below him, the grim, mysterious valley of Klu. Iron-gray, flat and hard it was, and absent of any visible sign of life. The sight of it made Alonin shiver with an inward dread, for an aura of desolation and doom hung heavy over the leaden landscape.

Putting fearful intuitions aside, Alonin scanned the great rocky plain below for his quarry. Eyes narrowed against the sun, which was a burning white globe in the west, he was able to pick out a small, dark dot moving against the dreary barrens. It could only be Dalkin, he knew; no one else would venture into that dismal land.

Setting his mouth in a determined line, Alonin spurred his steed over the crest and down the side of the hills; presently he gained the plain. In the loose, sandy soil the hoofmarks left by Dalkin's horse were easily visible. Alonin followed them at a furious pace, although by this time the pull exerted upon him by the Dylcaer was so powerful that he scarcely needed their guidance.

Strong, hot winds gusted over the plain, throwing up dense clouds of choking dust. Alonin ignored them, possessed as he was by his monomaniacal compulsion to regain the Dylcaer.

Night came, and Alonin was forced to make camp. He himself had no desire for rest, but he knew that he would be risking injury to his horse if he went on in the dark across the tortured plain.

He spent most of that night pacing restlessly around the borders of his camp. He could not rest; he could not think beyond his absolute need for the Dylcaer, and his need to avenge the wrong done him by one he had trusted.

It was not until very late that he felt a great weariness assail him. He curled up on the ground beside a tall pillar of rough wind-cut rock, without even his cloak for a blanket, and fell abruptly to sleep.

He dreamed.

He found himself standing in a place of ultimate darkness and prismatic fire. The sky above was filled with flowing whorls of light, which came together, merged, divided once more.

A fiery geyser flared before him, staggering him, and the flames gathered slowly into the shape of a gigantic face, which pulsed and wavered before him. It was the face he had seen in the heart of the Dylcaer, Alonin immediately knew, now made huge, brilliant, masklike. The face regarded him for a long time with eyes that made naked the very center of his being. Its jaws moved wordlessly for a moment, then its voice issued forth. It came as a thin, windy whisper, not as the bellowing boom Alonin somehow expected. It said, "Come to me."

Wild winds that Alonin knew were not winds rushed by his ears. He shouted, "What . . . who are you?"

"I have waited long for one such as you," the face said. "Come to me and we shall do wonders, such wonders as have not been seen in this world in three times three generations of man. The world shall be ours. Your will shall be law. He who has taken me from you can not bear my full power. He is a fool and he must be destroyed. Do this, and you shall be as the greatest of the great."

"Who are you?" Alonin asked again.

The face did not answer him. Instead, it began to grow larger, swelling hugely. One dark eye socket came gradually to fill all of Alonin's vision. Blue light flickered dimly within the aperture, and Alonin saw inside a distant landscape, which seemed to grow ever closer as he watched, until finally he was able to see a hunched figure sitting with its back to a dark boulder. Alonin realized that it was Dalkin he saw.

"Come," whispered the voice.

There was a sudden explosion of light, a deafening roar, then darkness closed about him, silent, peaceful . . .

An unknown period of time passed, and he awoke with the sun shining in his face. Opening his eyes, he gazed up for a moment at the blazing yellow orb, feeling its heat leaking luxuriously into his body. Only a few senseless bits remained of his dream, which began to fade as he tried to think about them.

Alonin got up stiffly, stretching his cramped muscles, and he prepared his mount. After breaking his fast on a piece of hard journey bread and a cup of lukewarm water, he mounted his horse and set off once more across the dry wastes.

In shades of brown and gray, the endless sea of sand and stone flashed by him. The sun hung high in the sky, beating down with ever increasing heat.

Early in the afternoon he came to a small, turgid stream, the first he had seen since entering Klu. It was contaminated and foul, and an overpowering sulfurous stench rose from it. Wrinkling his nose in disgust, Alonin bent his trail aside from it as far as he could. Even so, he was forced to ride beside it for a time before he could cut away from it and continue along a ridge of warped and blasted stone.

In a sudden spasm, the Dylcaer's pressure on his mind seemed to increase threefold. Dizzy, Alonin almost fell from his saddle. His eyes misted red and his head throbbed painfully. Alonin shook his head to clear it, and the pain eased somewhat. He felt oddly disconnected from the world; the landscape around him seemed to fade and drain of substance. He halted his mount and held his face in his hands for a moment. The feeling of unreality receded, but did not vanish.

As Alonin took up the reins of his horse again, he noticed that his hands were shaking. He could feel perspiration beading coldly on his forehead. Coaxing his steed to a brisk walk, he wondered dully about what was happening to him. He reasoned that the increased power of the Dylcaer upon him could not be due solely to his proximity to it, since he had held it in his hand without experiencing anything like this.

Then he remembered; it was through Klu he rode. Klu—where, according to the wizard Mernon, the Dark Master of Heggoth, Antirides, had maintained his place of power in those days when he had wielded the Dylcaer. It was said that a power lingered still over this land from those days, a power that hated life and the good things of the earth, a power that Mernon thought originated with the Dylcaer. If this were so, then perhaps this site of ancient magics had reawakened in the Dylcaer its latent energy.

Alonin broke abruptly from his speculations; they were too difficult for him to sustain. Besides, in the end they did not really matter. All that was important was that he track Dalkin down, recover the gem, fulfill his mission.

He spurred his horse onward. Hot, stale-smelling winds rushed into his face, and the naked sun cast his shadow out before him like a grim, twisted demon. The pressure on his mind continued to grow mercilessly. He began to feel that he would go mad if it were not relieved soon.

At times it seemed to him that his consciousness was blinking in and out—fading away, and then returning minutes, perhaps hours, later. He could not verify this suspicion, however, since the wastes were so flat and unchanging that it was impossible for him to tell the difference between where he was and where he had been.

How long he went on like this he could not say; it seemed a very long time. Finally, though, he came to the top of a rocky, dun-colored bluff and, looking down from this escarpment, he saw the ancient, time-wearied ruins of a great city, buildings all overthrown, foundations half buried by shifting dunes of sand and ash. At the outskirts of the ruins, standing beside the unmoving form of his fallen horse, which he had apparently ridden to death in his eagerness to escape pursuit, was Dalkin.

Alonin felt a fierce joy. *At last!* he thought. Giving a savage smile, he maneuvered his mount over the side of the bluff, sending up great clouds of dust.

As Alonin was guiding his horse down to the lower ground, Dalkin turned and looked in his direction, shading his eyes with one hand. He leaped back, then, taking to the high mounds of rubble, where Alonin would be unable to reach him on horseback.

Once on level ground, Alonin galloped to the edge of the ruins and there halted. From his saddle, he stared at Dalkin for a long, tense moment, not speaking. At last, in a cold, hard voice, he said, "Give it to me."

"No."

"Do not be overhasty. If you give me the Dylcaer now,

without incident, I will allow you your freedom and your life."

Dalkin gave out an explosive laugh. "I must say, that's big of you!"

"The Dylcaer is mine!"

"By what right? Why should it be yours and not mine?"

"You stole it!"

"Even as did Agwid, your great-great grandsire."

"I did not follow you to this place to debate with you," Alonin retorted angrily. "If you will not return what is mine, then there must stand a challenge between us." The young lord slid down from his horse and drew his sword. "Come, what is it to be?"

"You are being foolish. You know that you are no match for me with a sword."

Alonin made a negligent gesture. "Nevertheless."

Dalkin's face suffused with redness, and his features set belligerently. "Let the challenge stand then!" he said. And he started to climb down from the pile of rubble on which he stood.

Alonin took advantage of that moment to evaluate his position. Apart from that fierce spirit in him that raged and burned for revenge, there was still a small kernel of reason, overpowered and half forgotten, that knew that what Dalkin had said was quite true; he was no match for the red-haired man in skill with a blade. Alonin would need great luck to defeat the other man.

Luck. That stirred something in the murky depths of Alonin's memory, and he recalled the talisman, which had always protected and preserved him. Now, in this moment of uncertainty, Alonin wished again for the safety represented by the talisman. But, even as his hand moved toward his belt pouch, something stopped him. Alonin frowned, his hand still trembling over the pouch.

Suddenly he realized that some force outside himself was preventing him from moving, and this knowledge was enough to arouse in Alonin his stubborn core, and he gathered his scattered will, slowly forcing his hand to obey him. The power opposing him grew steadily greater as he made himself reach down into the pouch, until it was almost unbearable. His fingers touched the talisman's silken wrapping, and painfully he forced them to work their way through the tight folds of fabric, until at last they touched on bare metal. The pressure assailing him ceased with an abruptness that caused him to stagger a step. Freed, he took in a great gulp of air, then withdrew the talisman and pulled it quickly over his head.

The talisman pulsed against Alonin's breast, giving a slow, steady beat. Abruptly he realized that not only was the pressure gone, but also that that which had led him there, to that place, drawing him on with its irresistble force, had vanished. Alonin looked up and saw that Dalkin was finally free of the city's ruins. The red-haired man had his sword out and he was coming at Alonin, a fierce gleam in his eyes.

The murderous hatred that Alonin had felt toward his former companion had left him. The days he had spent pursuing Dalkin seemed to him now a fevered nightmare, which he recalled with a curious detachment. The Alonin who had come to this place, aflame with rage and desire, was a stranger to him. His lust for the Dylcaer had afflicted him with a madness, and Alonin could easily see now how twisted his thinking had been.

But this realization had come too late, for the same deadly power that had controlled him also had command of Dalkin. The red-haired man had come to stand before Alonin, eyes strange and burning. He slashed the air twice in challenge, then centered his blade on Alonin.

"Dalkin . . . wait."

"The time for talk is finished," the other said. "Defend yourself!"

With this, Dalkin leaped at Alonin, launching a furious attack, which drove back the young lord, parrying wildly. Alonin realized that he was in desperate trouble; not only was he the inferior swordsman, but he no longer had any desire to hurt Dalkin, while the other man was clearly after his blood.

Alonin fell back rapidly, fighting a purely defensive fight. As the minutes passed, Alonin became surprised that he was doing as well as he was. So far he had not had any great problem defending against the other man's attack. It seemed to Alonin that Dalkin was just a trifle slow and unsure with his blade, and he guessed that this was because the red-haired man was fighting with an unfamiliar weapon, the one taken from Red Moridar on the island of Agiza-Saligor.

Alonin decided that he could not maintain his unaggressive stance for much longer without Dalkin becoming aware of his reluctance and being emboldened by it, forcing the young lord into the difficult position of kill or be killed. He determined to try an attack or two on his own.

Parrying Dalkin's next cut, Alonin made a riposte that stopped short, then circled around as the other moved to parry him, nicking the other's wrist. Blood flowed from the tiny wound, and Dalkin snarled, pressing the attack with renewed ferocity.

Retreating once more, Alonin wondered at his success. Unfamiliar sword or not, Dalkin should not have been that easy to touch. The young lord resolved to keep a more careful watch on his opponent, to try to discover the cause for his surprising vulnerability.

The two men's blades whirled and flashed, and perspiration slicked their faces. Alonin noticed that Dalkin had developed a tendency to hesitate slightly after each touch of their blades, and after a long exchange he would pause, a look of vague befuddlement on his face. This was odd, for it was far from his usual style. It took Alonin a few moments to form an explanation for this: suppose that the power of his talisman was being transmitted from him to Dalkin though their blades? In such case, it might not be powerful enough to defeat the influence of the Dylcaer, but certainly it could cause the red-haired man some confusion, as opposing impulses fought within him, and this would be enough to slow him to the extent that Alonin saw. The more that the young lord thought about this the more sure he became that this was the explanation. The only question left was how this effect could be exploited to bring an end to the fight.

Somehow, he would have to increase his physical contact with Dalkin, so that the Dylcaer's control of him could be undermined enough that he could be reasoned with. Alonin searched for a means to accomplish this; after a short time he saw his chance. Dalkin came in with a slashing head cut, which Alonin caught by bringing his sword up lengthwise over his head. There was a crash of metal on metal, and the young lord quickly slid his weapon down his opponent's blade, until the hilts of their swords were matched together. Alonin brought up his left hand and took hold of Dalkin's wrist; the red-haired man did the same to his. The two men heaved and pulled at one another, grunting with effort, the smell of their perspiration rising and mingling in the air.

As they struggled, Alonin kept a careful watch on the other man, searching for some sign of a weakening of his resolve. At last the young lord thought he glimpsed something in the other's face that showed him this—a blankness in the eyes, a confused, lost quality.

"Dalkin," Alonin said, gasping with exertion. "You must listen to me. You don't want to do this. You are being used. It is the Dylcaer that forces you to this. You must fight it, resist it, or you will be lost."

Awareness flickered in Dalkin's eyes, and for an instant the contortions of his face eased. He ceased to struggle against Alonin. "I . . . Alonin," he said vaguely.

"It is not me but the Dylcaer you must fight!"

A violent spasm crossed Dalkin's face. "*No!*" he roared, hurling sudden desperate strength against Alonin. Caught by surprise, Alonin was thrown backward. He stumbled, barely managing to stay on his feet. He looked up and saw Dalkin's blade coming at him and he tried to dodge aside from it. He was an instant too slow, however, for the glimmering blade raked the side of his ribs, inflicting a molten pain. Off-balance now, the young lord made an awkward cut, attempting to hold the other man back, and the tip of his sword just barely grazed the other's chin.

Giving a grunt of pain, Dalkin fell back against a pile of rubble, his coppery beard dripping a deeper red. Alonin stood his ground for a moment, uncertain as to what he should do. Dalkin put his hand to his bloody chin, glaring at Alonin, a look of pure, mindless hatred in his eyes. With an animal growl in his throat, the red-haired man heaved himself up. His left hand strayed a little behind him, raking up some of the sand covering the rubble. This he flung into Alonin's face as he started to charge forward.

Alonin gasped, blinded by the grit. Through watering eyes, he dimly saw the other man lunging at him. He skin prickling with abject terror, he desperately sank into a low crouch, bringing his blade up in both hands before him. Blurrily, he saw that the momentum of Dalkin's charge would carry him onto his blade, and at the last instant he attempted to divert it. As a result, instead of catching Dalkin in the stomach, it pierced him deeply below his right shoulder.

Dalkin gave a sharp inhalation of breath. With a stunned look, he sat back abruptly, sinking heavily to the ground. Alonin blinked and rubbed at his eyes. His vision clearing, he saw that the other man was just sitting there, grasping his shoulder, from which blood freely flowed. He wore an astonished expression, and his face was as white as bleached linen. His eyes fluttered closed. With a great sigh, he fell back flat against the ground.

Alonin dropped his dripping sword and crept to the other man's side. The red-haired man was unconscious, but his chest still heaved with breath. Feeling the shock of what he had done, Alonin murmured, "Oh, Dalkin— friend—I am sorry, sorry . . ."

The young lord lingered so for a long moment, then he roused himself, realizing that he had to find the Dylcaer, to nullify it. He leaned down over Dalkin and gingerly patted down the man's clothing, knowing that he would not have let the gem off his person. Alonin finally discovered the Dylcaer's square case beneath Dalkin's doublet and he removed it and slipped it inside his own garment, where his talisman would keep it inactive, he hoped.

Alonin returned his attention to Dalkin and tried to evaluate the extent of the man's injuries. The wounds on his wrist and chin were nothing, mere scratches, but the shoulder wound was another matter—it could very well prove fatal. Alonin peeled back the man's doublet and tore away the shirt beneath. He wrinkled his nose and clacked his tongue. The shoulder was a bloody mess, but Alonin suspected that it looked worse than it really was. He thought that Dalkin could survive it, if the bleeding could be stopped.

Alonin made a poultice of certain healing herbs from his saddle bags and applied it to the red-haired man's injuries. Then, with strips torn from an old shirt, he tightly bound the wounds.

The young lord felt a sudden wave of weakness sweep

over him. Remembering his own hurt, he separated the front of his doublet and saw a long gash across his ribs, slowly weeping blood. It looked to be superficial, but still it hurt like fire. Alonin ripped a few more strips from the ruined shirt and bandaged the gash. He sat back, then, keeping a careful watch on his companion.

The sun lowered, until it was an angry red eye in the horizon, sending a ruddy glow streaming hazily over the wastes. In this light, the bones of the ancient city showed pale crimson and purple, seeming almost beautiful in a mournful way.

At last, Dalkin stirred, giving a low moan. Alonin wet a rag and mopped the red-haired man's forehead. "Dalkin," he said softly, "are you awake? Can you hear me?"

Dalkin's eyes snapped suddenly open. When they fell upon Alonin they widened with surprise. The red-haired man rolled his head back and forth slightly, trying to take in his surroundings. Then he gave the pained moan of a man discovering that what he had thought a nightmare was in fact reality.

"O gods," he whispered. "I remember. I remember now."

"I know."

"I . . . I tried to kill you."

"And I would have killed you, once, had I had the chance," Alonin said. He told the other man of how the Dylcaer had wrought the evil between them, and of how he had defeated it.

But Dalkin did not seem to be listening—and when Alonin finished speaking, the red-haired man said, "I'm sorry, Alonin. I am sorry."

"There is no need, my friend. I told you."

"I'm . . . sorry." Dalkin closed his eyes once more, and the lines of his face eased. His breathing became heavy and regular.

Alonin stood for a moment over his friend, assuring himself that it was sleep and not death that had overtaken him. By this time, the sun had all but vanished below the horizon; an evening chill was stirring over the wastes. Alonin covered Dalkin with blankets, then wandered away in search of something with which to make a fire. But Klu was a dead land, and all he could find were some gnarled and thorny brambles, twisting among the ruins. Alonin got his hand axe and hacked at these for a time, but they proved extremely hard and fibrous, and the effort required to cut through them opened the wound in his side and started it throbbing. He finally had to return with only a paltry arm load.

The brambles, he found, burned indifferently well, yielding up some light but little heat. Alonin settled wearily beside the sputtering fire he had just built. The ache in his side had spread now to his arm. His long possession by the Dylcaer, his exhausting fight with Dalkin, the pain of his wound were all beginning to tell on him. He felt drained.

Looking over at Dalkin, he saw that the man's eyes were open and that they were fixed on him. "How are you doing?" Alonin asked.

"Fine," the other said in a flat voice.

"Do you need anything? I could bring you something to eat."

"No, I do not want anything."

Alonin was grateful for this answer. He doubted his ability to move at this moment. "Well," he said, his voice soft with exhaustion, "if you need anything, just call out."

Silence. Alonin could not think of anything else to say, and Dalkin did not seem in a mood for talk. Shivering, Alonin drew his cloak about himself. It was hard for him to keep his eyes open; after a while he did not try.

Morning on the wastes of Klu always seemed the same to Alonin. The sun—a burning white circle behind the glaring haze—rose slowly, exposing a bleak, tortured landscape of brown and gray. The vague formless terror of the night gave way to the ever-present oppression of the day. Always, the same eerie lifeless silence greeted him upon waking.

Alonin awoke stiff and aching. He lay observing the dreary spectacle of dawn for a long time before he could convince his abused body to move. It was a ravenous hunger that finally roused him. He had not eaten since the morning before, he realized.

Alonin arose and breakfasted on whatever came easiest to hand. After eating, he rummaged for a time through their bags, trying to determine how much food and water they had left. He was somewhat disturbed by what he found.

The sounds of his movements awakened Dalkin, and the red-haired man sat up with some difficulty, making a slight gasp of pain.

"Easy," said Alonin. "You don't want to start yourself bleeding again, do you?"

Dalkin winced and nodded, but remained in the sitting position.

"How are you feeling today? Could you eat something?"

"All right," Dalkin said.

Alonin went and got him some food and water—the latter he liberally laced with strong Dorian brandy. The red-haired man accepted both silently and began to eat, using only his left hand, for his right was made useless by his wound. His eyes stared blankly forward, looking on nothing.

Alonin sat down beside Dalkin. When the other man had finished his meal, the young lord said, "Tomorrow, if I can get you on my horse, do you think you can travel some? I know it's a little soon, but we've got to move quickly, or we'll never make it out of here. Our water is low, and we've only the one horse now."

"Go without me," Dalkin replied, speaking in a hollow voice. "Leave me here."

"What?"

"You heard me. You'll have a better chance without me."

"What are you saying? What's the matter with you?"

"Leave me."

"Listen to me," Alonin said quietly with an intent stare. "I certainly am not going to leave you here alone. If it is your wish to die in this place, then I will die with you. But I am not leaving without you."

There was silence as Dalkin considered this. There was something broken and tragic about his face. Finally he said, "Very well, then. I will be able to travel."

"Good. We leave tomorrow, then. Try and rest. I am going up on yon hill for a while, to see if I can find a way out of here. We cannot leave by the same way we came; our water will not last that long."

"All right," Dalkin said dully. He lay back down. His eyes stared upward, haunted.

Alonin left the camp and mounted the hill he had indicated to Dalkin, which was the highest ground in the vicinity. As he climbed the dusty mound, he worried over his friend's strange behavior. Something was obviously bothering the man, and Alonin assumed that it had to do with the events of the last several days. But this was foolishness! Dalkin could not hold himself responsible for what he had done while under the influence of the Dylcaer. Still, it could not be denied that something was troubling the redhaired man. Alonin could only hope that this rift in his friend's spirit would heal along with the wounds of his flesh.

Coming to the top of the hill, Alonin stood for a time scanning the great valley in all directions. Which way to go? In what direction lay their best chance of finding their way free of the wastes? The young lord could not decide. A wrong choice could well prove fatal, and this responsibility weighed heavy on him. He continued to search all about him, even as the sun climbed slowly toward noon, unable to come to a decision.

Suddenly he noticed something strange; a faint tingling could be felt coming from his talisman, almost too slight to notice. He found that if he moved in one direction the sensation would increase; moving the other way, it faded.

Alonin realized abruptly that the talisman was warning him of dangers lurking along certain of the routes; somehow he knew that this was so. But why had he never noticed this function before? Several explanations presented themselves to mind. Perhaps he had become more attuned to the talisman over the time he had borne it, or perhaps his struggle with the Dylcaer had in some way strengthened the powers of his mind. Or perhaps, simply, he had just never been receptive to such warnings before. Perhaps all of these, or none of them. Whichever, he was inclined to heed the warnings of his talisman.

Alonin slowly turned himself toward all the ways that could possibly lead them from the wastes before their water ran out, until he finally determined the direction in which he sensed the least danger, which happened to be almost due north, toward a range of sharp, blue-misted mountains.

The young lord checked this against his map and found that it would be as short and direct a route as any. Very well, then—north it would be.

Alonin returned to camp, redressed Dalkin's wounds, and devised a sling for him. Seeming stronger now, the red-haired man sat up and positioned his back against a huge stone block. But still he refused to return Alonin's attempts at conversation, and his manner remained apathetic and withdrawn.

Alonin stood this for as long as he could, but as the evening shadows grew, he could no longer hold his tongue. "Dalkin," he said finally, "what's the matter with you? All is well, all is well. Yet you act as if—I don't know—as if some great shame or guilt has been placed on you."

Dalkin did not answer immediately, and when he did, what he said surprised Alonin. "I tried to betray you," he said.

Alonin frowned. "I don't see why you must insist on taking that responsibility for yourself. I told you before—you had no choice but do what you did. You were driven—"

"No," Dalkin said emphatically, a bitter, pained expression pulling at his mouth. "I would like to believe that. I would. But I know that it simply isn't so."

"What are you talking about?"

"It just wasn't all the Dylcaer's doing, what I did, that's all. It . . . it may have pushed me forward, but it was I who acted." Pausing, he seemed to be wrestling with the words required to make clear what he was trying to express. "I wanted the Dylcaer. *I* wanted it. I wanted something for myself. A life . . . a place . . . a position. Something. I thought that the Dylcaer could gain those for me."

He fell silent, rubbed his eyes wearily. Then he said, "Can you understand?"

Alonin nodded slowly. Indeed, he understood, now. It came to him at that moment that the Dylcaer could not create its evil in a vacuum; rather, it depended on those dark urges that lurk in any man—his ambition, pride, anger, wants, and needs—bending them to its own purposes. He recalled how old Loness of the *Kirith-ber-Weirlon* had told him to beware of what he wanted. At the time he had not understood; later, he had thought that he did, but didn't. Now it was clear that it was against the Dylcaer she warned him.

Both he and Dalkin had been seduced through their own deepest selves. Their actions had grown from seeds long present, which the Dylcaer had only to bring into twisted flower. Small wonder, then, that Dalkin now mistrusted himself, for he had been forced to consider his own darker nature, and how he might be ruled by it. Alonin had been spared this suspicion of self, because he had been able to throw off the influence of the Dylcaer at the end, though only through the power of his talisman.

Alonin wondered what he might say that would reassure his friend. But words alone seemed inadequate in the situation. He reached out and lightly touched Dalkin's leg. "Are you surprised that your desires can be turned to evil uses?" he asked. "You shouldn't be. I know mine can. Such might be said of anyone. It doesn't make you any less trustworthy or true, nor does it lower my estimation of you. Do not be deceived into thinking that you would have acted in the manner that you did without the inducements of the Dylcaer; you would not have."

"Are you so sure?"

"Yes. Yes, I am." Alonin drew a long breath, staring into the dark sky. He said, "You would do well to consider this: all men may be brought to evil by what they hold most important, although few are ever made to realize this. For you, however, this truth will henceforth be inescapable, and will ever be a burden. Yet, as with all knowledge, it may also be a source of strength. Face it, use it, and it will make you far greater than any of those who remain in happy ignorance."

Even as he spoke, Alonin felt the truth of his words; so, apparently, did Dalkin. He listened with increasing concentration—and his eyes, which previously had been so empty and bleak, took to them a smoldering fire. "Yes," he breathed, softly. "Yes . . ."

"Rest, sleep, my friend; you will need all of your strength for tomorrow."

"Yes."

The sun had not yet risen above the needle-sharp peaks in the east, though the light had already grown bright and relentless, when Alonin put Dalkin on the horse, took the reins in hand, and started leading the way across the tortured barrens.

Dalkin clung bravely to the saddle in spite of obvious pain. At times, he would waver and look for a moment as if he would faint, and his face would go white and drawn. Alonin would brace himself to catch his friend if he should start to fall, but somehow the red-haired man maintained consciousness, and the two continued.

They went slowly that first day, and that night they camped in a shallow basin bordered by long, jagged teeth of pitted stone. They ate and drank sparingly; afterward, in a voice soft and breathless, Dalkin complained over the tastelessness of their provisions, a faint, wry smile curling his lips. Alonin breathed with relief at this, for he knew then his friend would be all right, if he could only survive his wound and the journey out of Klu.

Both men were very tired from the day's trek, so they settled down early for sleep. But before Alonin could drop off, he was disturbed by the clattering noise of a falling stone at the far perimeter of the camp. He sat up quickly and caught sight of a pair of eyes, red from the reflected glow of the thorn fire at the center of camp, regarding him from the shadows. In the dim light, the possessor of those eyes could be seen only as a hunched and twisted outline, but even so, Alonin was able to tell that it was not human, whatever it was. His talisman began to throb faintly, and he reached out stealthily for a fist-sized rock and threw it at the strange thing lurking outside the firelight. The eyes disappeared before the rock could reach them, though, and it struck only empty earth.

Alonin got his sword and cautiously searched the borders of camp, but found nothing. Returning to where he had made his bed, he threw some fresh fuel on the fire and tried, vainly, to divest himself of the lingering fear he felt.

He did not sleep well that night; and, starting with the next morning, he began to consult his talisman more often as he chose their trail, particularly when it came time to select a campsite. He did not mention to Dalkin what he had seen—and he never saw it again, nor indeed any other living creature while he remained in Klu.

The days wore on. The water, which had been rationed

with increasing strictness, finally gave out. It became more and more difficult for Alonin to keep himself going. His dry tongue seemed an alien thing in his mouth, bloated and reptilian.

Alonin felt himself more dead than alive by the time he reached the foothills of the mountains. His thirst had grown into a terrible, constant, burning thing. His heart thudded dully in his breast in exhaustion. Mile after weary, painful mile he plodded on.

Following a dry watercourse, the two men ascended the foothills. Over the blue spires of the mountains, heavy gray clouds hung. Alonin smelled moisture in the air, which promised the possibility of rain. He turned to Dalkin, who rode behind him on the horse. "Rain, do you think?"

Dalkin took in a wheezy breath. "I don't know. Could be. I hope so."

The day lengthened. A brilliant flash of lightning suddenly arced down over the mountaintops. It flared again, and then again. Thunder boomed among the peaks like the ravings of an angry god.

Leading the horse behind him, Alonin slowly scrabbled his way up the granite-strewn slope, tearing his garments and his flesh on the thorny shrubs that were the mountain's only covering. Finally, he could go no farther. His strength was used up, gone. He slid to earth and mopped his forehead with his sleeve, gasping for breath.

Wetness stung his cheek. He squinted up dully at the darkening sky. He felt his pulse quicken.

Rain!

Only an airy drizzle fell at first—but then, suddenly, the clouds opened up and loosed a driving shower.

Alonin picked himself up and stood on a rocky crest, letting the rain sweep over him, washing him clean of the filth of Klu. Dalkin managed to slip down from his mount and join the young lord there. The two men stood there for a long time, attending the storm with a trancelike devotion. Suddenly, Alonin heard a quickening roar coming from up the slope. Peering through water-beaded lashes, he was startled to see a mighty flood rushing down the mountainside, following the old watercourse. Within instants, a wall of water crashed by him and continued thundering down to the valley below, filling the old riverbed as it went.

Dalkin grinned in a way that recalled the man Alonin had known long ago. Nodding his dripping head to the newly made river now roaring beside them, he asked, very seriously, "You wanted water, did you say?" And then he threw back his head and laughed, and his laugh was beautiful to hear, clear and bright, full of youth and strength and vitality.

Alonin gave him a look of rueful amusement. Then he too laughed. He could not stop himself, for suddenly he realized the extent of their accomplishment—against all odds, they had defeated the Dylcaer and won free of Klu, leaving all of their shadows behind them.

15

THE inn of the Green Crow had changed little in all the long months that Alonin had been on the road. Perhaps it was a little more weathered, and perhaps the lush blue-green forest of Caladon had grown more thickly about it, but in all other respects it was the same.

The innkeeper met Alonin and Dalkin at the door—and he was the same innkeeper that Alonin remembered, still fat. He greeted the two men effusively, leading them to a table. Strangely, he seemed to recall the young lord's previous visit, for he made loud exclamations of how glad he was that Alonin had returned, even though the young man had been there only the once briefly, months before, and had not even introduced himself.

After bringing the two men their food and drink, the innkeeper left them alone, perhaps sensing that they had private words to speak. Yet the two remained silent for a long time after he left them, dawdling over their meal.

Finally, with forced enthusiasm, Dalkin slapped the table and said, "So. The day is here. The day of reckoning, as it were."

"Yes," Alonin said in a solemn, measured voice. "It is here."

"I don't suppose you'd change your mind and let me face Thudredid with you."

"No, I can't. This is a thing I must do alone. It is between the dragon and myself."

"I figured you'd say something like that. Well, nothing lost in trying, I say. I just hope that you know what you are doing. A dragon is a fearsome thing to have to fight alone."

"Such is how it must be, I am afraid." Pausing, Alonin slowly swept his gaze over all of the inn. His mouth set into a firm, hard line. He uttered a slight sigh. "Well, there's no more putting it off, I suppose. Time to see this thing through to the end."

He reached into his pouch and came out with a small doeskin bag, heavy with metal, which he dropped on the table in front of Dalkin. It made a weighty *clunk* as it came down on the thick oak of the tabletop. "What's left of my traveling expenses," he explained. "Hold it for me. If I don't come back, it will take you a long way."

"I don't want your money."

Alonin shrugged. "If I fail, I'd rather you have it than somebody else. You can think of me when you are spending it. Take it."

Dalkin reluctantly reached out and took up the bag. "Well, I am just holding it for you against your return, you understand."

"Certainly." Alonin got up, buckled on his sword belt, adjusted it. "Well, wish me luck."

"Luck." Dalkin rose and stood by awkwardly, his sober gaze dwelling long on the young lord. His mouth opened and closed slightly, as if he wanted to say something but could not find the words. Suddenly he went forward and embraced Alonin.

Feeling something tremble within him, Alonin returned the embrace. A stinging mist obscured his vision for a moment.

The two separated slowly, and Dalkin said with finality, "You will return."

"Of course."

Drawing himself up straight, Alonin started for the door. Then, abruptly, he heard a voice from behind him say, "Lord Caladon." He turned and saw that the voice had come from the innkeeper.

Taken by surprise, Alonin stared at the man. "How is it," he asked, "that you know who I am?"

Smiling with the pleasure of his own ingenuity, the innkeeper said, "I figured it out. Remember when you were here before and I thought that you reminded me of somebody. Well, after you left I got to thinking, and it came to me that you bore something of a resemblance to Gristan, the old lord. And then I remembered your sword and that ring you wear . . ."

Alonin held up his right hand and looked for a moment on the signet of Caladon which glittered dully on his finger. He smiled faintly. "Stupid of me."

"Lord, the people of Caladon have long carried a great resentment against the lords of this land. Yet you seem a decent man to me. I . . . I just wanted to wish you good luck."

"I—Thank you. Thank you very much." A solemn smile of appreciation twitched across Alonin's face, then he turned abruptly and fled outside. The two other men followed, and they stood watching him as he mounted his horse.

Looking back on the two men who stood bathed in the clear afternoon sunlight, he sketched a brief salute, his mouth set in a tense line. With a flick of the reins, then, he set off down the road.

The forest closed around Alonin, and the fragrance of pine enveloped him. The day was bright, cool, fresh, and the woods were lush with their spring growth. Were it not for that which was before him, he would have found the ride pleasant. As it was, however, he found any pleasure that he might have had overshadowed by grim thoughts.

The time had at last come. The months of hard journeying—and before that the years of grief and hatred and the dozens of years of striving and dying by the Lords of Caladon—all came to their climax this day. Yet Alonin felt no anticipation, no rush of fierce excitement, but only an urgent demand to finish what had been given to him to do.

Suddenly Alonin came within view of Castle Caladon. He pulled back on the reins and sat for a moment, gazing through a thin screen of cottonwoods at the ominous fortification. Stark and gray it stood, isolated from all the fresh growing things of the world; and not even the shimmering sunlight of that fine spring day could brighten or warm it.

Alonin spurred his horse forward, clattering down the old cobbled road. He halted at the base of the hill on which the castle stood and dismounted. From previous experience he knew that against the dragon a horse would be not only useless, but a liability.

With a hollow feeling in his stomach, he started to climb slowly up the hill. The mossy ruins of old Caladon Town rose on both sides of him. He passed them by without a thought.

Alonin came to the rotting oaken gates of the castle and he stood for a time looking up at the lofty stone towers, listening to the low keening of the wind. He felt none of his old hate and rage. He felt nothing; he felt empty. He was all purpose now, irresistibly forced along his preordained path. Drawing his sword, he hefted its deadly weight in his hand. His eyes moved across the fortification once more, then he called out: "Thudredid!"

A moment passed. Alonin squinted up the lichen-mottled walls rising dizzyingly over him. He cried, "It is Alonin, son of Gristan, Lord of Caladon, who summons you! I have returned, Thudredid. Come, dragon, face me!"

Alonin heard the dragon stir now, its scales rasping dryly against stone. Suddenly its voice rang out, reaching Alonin's ears with cold clarity. "I hear, O Man," it said. "Bide."

The ancient tower that was its lair trembled and rumbled, sending down a fine shower of mortar. Through a jagged hole that had once been a window, Thudredid's head suddenly appeared, then its wings and powerful shoulders, and last of all its sinuous lower body. A wisp of flame curled between its sharp jaws. The dragon flexed its wings, then beat the air with abrupt, rapid movements. Ponderously, it rose and began to circle over the castle.

Alonin tightened his grasp on his sword and held himself ready, in case the dragon should decide to make a dive at him, as it had done on their last meeting. But from this Thudredid refrained. It swung out and away from the castle, gradually gaining speed, and flew low over the forest, which rolled into the distance like a vast untroubled sea.

In spite of himself, Alonin could not help marveling. There was a savage magnificence in the dragon's flight, which spoke to him of the wild freedom of the wind, of the joy that must bring.

Thudredid spiraled back in toward the castle, its wings rising and falling with a grace that no man could ever know. Down it swept over the walls, hanging for an instant above the castle gates, before dropping slowly and taking hold of the wide stone arch above them. Folding back its wings, it stared down at Alonin.

Alonin forgot himself for a moment and met that gaze, and the swirling chaos living in those blazing yellow orbs threatened to sweep him away into a region that no man should ever be made to look upon. Gasping in a quick breath, Alonin dropped his eyes.

Thudredid said, "Well, Youngling, we meet again. Consider yourself fortunate—you are the first since Agwid to survive for a second encounter. Come, then, what would you have with me? Have you brought me my due? Or did you come to invite death with a challenge?—the which I may now answer, as you will discover to your regret, if this be your purpose."

Alonin frowned. "Tell me, Thudredid, what has changed since our last meeting that I am offered this choice? When we met before, you said that you would not contest with me unless I gained a son or returned to you that which was taken. I have no son."

Thudredid made a dry chuckle. "Not now, perhaps—but soon. Soon."

"What do you mean? I—" He stopped, his puzzlement turning suddenly to awed realization. Marda? It had to be—if Thudredid's words could be trusted. Alonin narrowed his eyes suspiciously at the dragon and said, "Is this the truth you speak?"

"It is not a matter about which I would lie, for it touches on me as well as you."

"This is glad news, then—though I might have wished for a different messenger. Still . . . I thank you."

Thudredid chuckled again, and the sound was like two great stone blocks grinding together. "Thank not me, for it may be that I must also bear you your death. You have not yet answered me. Have you brought to me that which is mine?"

Alonin stared long at the dragon, his gaze intent and piercing, like that of a proud young hawk. "Thudredid, I have," he said. Reaching into his doublet, he brought out the carved wooden box containing the Dylcaer. He opened it and extracted the gem. Suddenly he saw a small spark of blue fire flare in the heart of the dead black stone and he felt a power come over him, striking him instantly immobile. His talisman throbbed urgently, but still he could not move.

A voice whispered inside his head, a voice that reminded him for an instant of a place of darkness and cold fire. "You cannot," it said, arrogant and scornful. "You have not the strength to resist. You cannot."

Alonin felt a dull anger begin to smolder within him. Drawing strength from his talisman, he lashed back at the power that bound him. He exerted all of his will to force his arm to move. Slowly, trembling with effort, it drew back, stopped, then shot out from his body. The Dylacaer arced out and fell to earth a few yards away.

Alonin drew a long, shuddering breath as his muscles were abruptly released from that which bound them. He shivered, and his head snapped up to look at the dragon. "There," he said, "it's yours. Take it—and be quick about it."

From its lofty perch, Thudredid strained eagerly forward, its eyes gleaming covetously. Lifting up its dark wings, it leaped into the air and sailed downward, to land on the far side of the Dylcaer.

Alonin tightened his grip on the hilt of his sword. He watched the dragon hop in an ungainly fashion to the gem, surprised to see that this great lord of air and fire was so awkward on the ground. It would be a simple matter, he thought, to slay it before it could regain the sky.

Thudredid extended a claw over the Dylcaer, giving out a low hiss of what Alonin took to be pleasure.

Now! thought Alonin, *I can kill it now!* In his mind, he could see himself rushing forward to cleave that serpentine head from the dragon's body. But he did not move.

The creature closed its talons about the Dylcaer.

Alonin took his sword in both hands, the sword of his father and his father's father. Point held downward, he raised it high above him.

The dragon looked abruptly at Alonin, its head arching up on its long, sinuous neck.

With all of his might, Alonin plunged the sword down into the hard, rocky ground at his feet.

Thudredid's gaze continued to dwell on him, its head held with a vast, inhuman dignity. Suddenly, its powerful, sinewy tail tensed and lashed out. Moving too fast for the eye to follow, it came against a great black-speckled boulder, sweeping it effortlessly away. The boulder rolled ponderously end over end down the hill, until it finally crashed against a ruined wall, and so was stopped.

Alonin looked up and met the dragon's proud gaze. He recognized with respect the intent of Thudredid's demonstration. Clearly, if he had withheld when he might have dealt death, so had the dragon. And now, as their eyes met, it seemed as if an understanding passed wordlessly between them.

Man and dragon held their gazes steady for a long moment. Finally Thudredid broke the contact. Lifting up its huge black wings, it sprung into the air.

Higher and higher it rose, wheeling gracefully over Alonin. Swifter and swifter it flew, circling the castle once, twice, its wings cutting the wind at a breathtakingly steep angle. Then it made a wide, slow bank into the north.

Leaving his sword planted behind him, Alonin climbed to the top of a tall pillar of gnarled granite. He watched as Thudredid receded slowly into the distance, becoming a dark dot against the dense white clouds moving restlessly across the distant mountains of the north. When at last it disappeared, Alonin was left with a vague, inexplicable sense of loss.

Then, as he found himself staring into an empty sky, a great feeling of release swept over him. A tremendous burden seemed to loosen and fall from him, a burden that he had carried for so long that he had almost ceased to regard it as such. All of his life he had lived for this moment. Now it was over, done; he was at last free.

Yet with freedom came fear, a vague, whispering thing that taunted him now. Never in his life had he been without a goal, and now that he was, suddenly the future was dark, its features imperceivable. A vast void yawned wide before him.

Looking up at the bleak, ruined towers of Castle Caladon, Alonin felt his moment of uncertainty pass. The void healed. He realized that his task was not yet complete. Indeed, he had scarcely made a beginning.

His sense of continuity restored, he thought for a moment of all those people who waited for him—a good and loyal friend in a nearby inn, an old king in a castle surrounded by ancient stones that protected and sometimes gave dreams, and the one who dwelled in a vast far woods with a people who knew no castles or boundaries or kings.

The young lord thought finally of his father. Did he look down upon Alonin from the world of spirit? Was he made proud or ashamed of how his son had ended the ancient feud? These questions Alonin could not answer, not while he remained part of the substance of the world. Nor did he worry long over them, for he knew that he could have acted in no other way than he did.

Sounds came now to disturb Alonin from his musings— voices, hushed, but carrying thinly on the wind. Looking down the hill, the young man saw a crowd of people issuing from the woods. They proceeded with extreme caution, timorously scanning the sky as they went.

There was one who went before the rest, walking with considerably more confidence—and this one Alonin recognized as the old innkeeper from the Green Crow. The man was puffing steadily up the hill, weighed back by his years and his fat, yet apparently unafraid. As for the rest, they stayed well behind, eyes wary and searching.

Alonin thought: *They want to see if I am dead.* He wondered if they would be disappointed to find out that he was not. He smiled faintly. He would just have to see.

With that same small smile, Alonin climbed down from the rock, straightened his clothes. Then he started down the hill to meet his people.

16

THE morning clouds had finally broken when Alonin came up out of the woods and saw the old house and the oak grove before him, bathed in the pale, kind light of spring. As he rode up to the house, he considered how different it seemed to him now from when he had last seen it, under the weary sun of autumn.

He halted beside an oak fresh and green with its new growth and swung down out of the saddle. Standing there for a moment, he drank in the peace of the grove. He drew in an appreciative breath.

A door opened to the side of him. Hearing it, he turned and saw the old man in the gray robe who stood there in the doorway. "Mernon!"

"Lad!" the wizard cried. "Welcome! It is good to see you again. I was wondering when you would come to see me. I heard of your triumph; the news spread quickly."

"Triumph? I did not go against the dragon."

Smiling, Mernon nodded. "Well, come inside, come inside. I would hear of your journey—after you have rested and had something to drink."

"Thank you." Alonin followed Mernon into the cool dimness of the wizard's house. He looked around the room, well-satisfied with the comfortable simplicity he saw. "As a matter of fact," he said, "that is chiefly the reason why I came. I thought that I should tell you the story before I left."

"You are leaving Caladon?"

Alonin nodded, sinking into a deeply tufted chair. "Yes."

"For what reason? I find it odd that you should win that which four generations of your family have died for, then turn and walk away."

"I will be gone for only a little while, I trust. There is

something I must do, someone I must find—a woman of the *Kirith-ber-Weirlon*. She . . . bears my child . . . I think. I would bring her back to Caladon with me, if she would have it so." At this, Alonin's face softened and a gentle light shone through his eyes.

Mernon looked long and intently on the young lord. Then he said, "Yes, I see that you must do this thing. But what of Caladon while you are gone?"

"I believe that I have taken good care in this matter. I am leaving one to rule in my name, to protect the land and begin to restore it to its former state. It is a heavy burden I lay on this man, yet I feel that he is equal to it. He helped me on my quest, and I do not think that I would be here now without him. His name is Dalkin—a man common of birth, yet I think noble of spirit. It is in my mind to commit Caladon to his charge, should the time come that I am king in Yggrs."

Pausing, Alonin regarded the other man across the dusky room. In a tentative voice, he said, "Mernon, I know that I have no right to ask favors of you—you have done so much for me already—but if I could ask a boon, it would be that you look after Dalkin while I am away and help him if he needs help."

"I will while I can, lad. But the day draws near when I think that I, too, must leave. I have done what I came here to do. Thudredid is gone, the curse ended, and the Dylcaer guarded from use by evil men. Soon I must go."

"You will not be here when I return?"

"I do not know. My plans are not yet settled."

"I would be grateful if you decided to stay a little while longer yet. There will be difficult days ahead for this land, and many problems that must be faced. I had thought to look to your wisdom for some of the solutions."

"You must not look to my wisdom, nor to anyone else's. It is to yourself that you must look."

Alonin grinned. "I know. I try . . . but sometimes I think that I am but a fool, a hopeless fool."

Mernon laughed ruefully and shook his head. "Aren't we all!" he said. "Oh, my lad, aren't we all!"